The Next Civil War

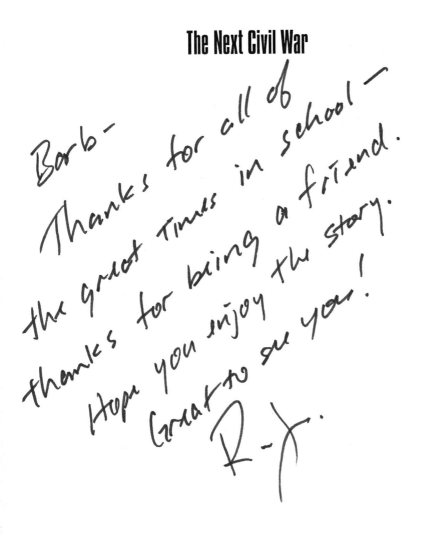

Barb —

Thanks for all of
the great times in school —
thanks for being a friend.
Hope you enjoy the story.
Great to see you!

R—J.

The Next Civil War

R G Arellano

Illustrations by Candice Tauger

ARCHWAY
PUBLISHING

Archway Publishing books may be ordered through booksellers or by contacting:

Archway Publishing
1663 Liberty Drive
Bloomington, IN 47403
www.archwaypublishing.com
1 (888) 242-5904

ISBN: 978-1-4808-2343-3 (sc)
ISBN: 978-1-4808-2344-0 (e)

Library of Congress Control Number: 2015916698

Print information available on the last page.

Archway Publishing rev. date: 10/23/2015

This book is dedicated to Kristy, for encouraging me to complete this work despite time and career challenges, and to Aunt Dianne, for telling me, "You should be a writer," in response to the letters I wrote to her before she lost her battle with cancer.

I love you both.

Acknowledgments

First and foremost, I'd like to thank my publisher, Archway Publishing, for taking a chance on me as a first-time author. Their support and coaching have been invaluable during what has proven to be a challenging, and sometimes confusing, process. I'd also like to thank the Archway Editorial Team for their insightful feedback and ideas about how to make this book even better.

I also received editing assistance early in the development process of this book from Monique Kamosi. Her insights, viewpoints, and feedback were amazing, helping me to take the first step toward being an author.

Thanks also to the United States Army. My time in the army, however brief, was instrumental in helping me to be more responsible in all aspects of my life. The discipline and work ethic that I learned while in the army have served me well over the years. Of course, my army experiences were the inspiration for this book.

I admire each of the friends I made while in the army, including, and especially, Reggie Ballard, Derrick Bryant, Caruthers "Chico" Echevarria, Paul Haines, Mike Lawson, Michael Hass, Z. Hester, Lawrence Martinez, Michael Suciu, Lee Tomlinson, David Veliz, and Bryan Yoakum. I also admire all the others from the Second Training Brigade, Tenth Battalion, Bravo Company, who graduated from basic training with me on 27 June 1986. Sergeant First Class Allen and Staff Sergeant Carr also played a role in my development, and were outstanding leaders as our drill sergeants.

My entire family has been very supportive, whether they realize it or not. Especially supportive was my wife, Kristy, who provided inspiration, acted as confidant, and proofread the early versions of the manuscript (which had to be very painful, I imagine). Also supporting me was my brother-in-law, LaRon Henderson. LaRon, who is African American, and I have enjoyed several thought-provoking discussions about race and religion over the years, many of which have helped to shape some of my views on both.

Last, thanks to everyone, in the past or present, who has served our country to preserve our freedom. Many have given the ultimate sacrifice during the course of their service, for which there is no possible way to thank them or their families. But know that many hearts and souls are with you.

God bless America.

Contents

Preface xi

CHAPTER 1   Enlistment. 1

CHAPTER 2   Conflict 15

CHAPTER 3   Planning. 29

CHAPTER 4   Understanding. 45

CHAPTER 5   Realization. 55

CHAPTER 6   Time for Change 65

CHAPTER 7   Is This War?. 81

CHAPTER 8   Out of Control. 97

CHAPTER 9   What about Love? 111

CHAPTER 10   A Failed Escape. 123

CHAPTER 11   A Big Mistake, and Union Forces 137

CHAPTER 12   Child's Play 149

CHAPTER 13   Love Sees No Color 161

CHAPTER 14   Does Color Really Matter? .173

CHAPTER 15   True Love Defends 187

CHAPTER 16   How Can You Tell Good from Bad? 201

CHAPTER 17   Where Do We Go from Here? 213

Epilogue. 225

Book Review Request 233

Preface

During my time in the US Army, I had the privilege of getting to know a great number of young men and women who came from a wide variety of backgrounds. Some of their stories fascinated me. Some of my army friends were raised in inner-city neighborhoods where they struggled to avoid gang life. Many were caught up in trouble back home, regardless of their desire to stay clean. Just like me, all of them were in the army so that they could get their life back on track, have a second chance, and possibly even go to college to start a second career later in life.

For most, they felt that they simply had run out of options and had no other choice than to join the military. I heard at least one story where a local judge offered to suspend sentencing if the young man chose to serve his country. Although I can't verify these stories myself, I do know for a fact that my own cousin was offered a similar option when he was arrested, thereafter deciding to become a marine.

For my cousin, it didn't turn out so well. He despised the structure and discipline that life as a marine demanded, and he was discharged after just one term. After returning home, he quickly fell right back into a life of uncertainty. In fact, to this day our family has no idea where my cousin is or whether he is even still alive.

My story was slightly different. I didn't have a criminal record. However, I could tell that I was on the wrong path. I couldn't keep a job, I had failed miserably in college (I was kicked out after only half of a semester), and I had no idea how to turn my life around. I saw an army billboard one day and drove straight to the recruiter's office.

I thrived in the army. I responded well to the discipline and structure.

For me, the army presented an opportunity to excel—as long as I played by their rules, accepted the lifestyle, and dedicated myself to becoming a better person. While I was in the service, I saw others around me choose to either embrace the life or reject it. Either way, the army treated everyone the same, regardless of race, as far as I could tell.

I think that I, for a variety of reasons, was accepted by all racial groups while in the army. Not necessarily all individuals of each race became friends of mine, but some of my best friends were African American or Hispanic. At the time, I saw this fact as an opportunity to bring each of these groups closer together, and I did my best to do so. I tried to bridge the gap between backgrounds and preconceived notions so that we could all get along well—not just superficially, but also in a way that led us to truly trust and respect each other.

The United States military branches demand this behavior of its soldiers anyway, expecting all of us to work together as one unified force. In practice, and in view of our leadership, we soldiers were indeed unified. However, there was always an underlying segregation of certain individuals, whether they kept themselves apart because of reasons of race, education level, or simply background. In many cases, people of the same race kept their distance from one another.

Let me pause to say that in no way would I ever claim to be an expert on race relations in the United States, or anywhere else in the world for that matter. Likewise, I could never possibly understand what it's like to be an African American in today's world. However, I've always been able to relate to people regardless of their color, religion, status in life, or background, which has opened my eyes to many different ways of life and allowed me to get to know some wonderful people—truly get to *know* them, and establish lifelong friendships that otherwise I would never have had.

However, regardless of my efforts and the efforts of others like me to bring the races together while in the army, there were some soldiers who simply couldn't break away from their lifelong prejudices. Because I could relate to just about everyone, there were times when a white soldier would confide in me, disclosing that he had racist feelings toward African Americans or Hispanics. I also had a few African American friends who would make racial slurs toward whites, voice their thoughts on black unity, and talk about their desire to separate themselves from whites. Honestly, I've never understood either side's position. And I still don't understand why more people can't put thoughts like these behind them and learn to think for themselves as they mature.

Some years later, after leaving the army, I read an article indicating that new minority enrollment in the army had exceeded Caucasian enrollment for the first time. I can't remember what year it was or the source, but it was then that the idea for this book came to me.

One of my goals for this writing is to offer the reader a sense of the diversity that our armed forces offer to enlistees, and to create a picture of how I and my fellow soldiers interacted with each other while in the army, based on my own personal experiences. This book might also offer a perspective on how, and why, men and women of all backgrounds find their way to the military, illuminating the variety of reasons for their choice. I hope that the early chapters in this book offer a few examples of this.

Another goal is to help the reader see that we are all good, or bad, relative to our beliefs, but that our skin color doesn't necessarily have anything to do with that. In other words, just because you're white doesn't mean that you are racist toward African Americans. Likewise, if you're Hispanic or African American, it wouldn't be right to assume that you have animosity toward Caucasians.

During my younger years in the army, and throughout my life in international business, I have witnessed racism and bigotry in Caucasians, African Americans, Hispanics—even in people from China and India. Based on my personal experiences, I am disheartened to admit that racism is very much alive and well in all parts of the world and certainly here in the United States.

As you read *The Next Civil War*, I hope that your mind will open to many possibilities, but especially to those pertaining to the common good of humankind. I also hope that you will look at our fighting men and women differently, with even more respect than you have in the past, and appreciate where they may have come from—or, in some cases, what they are running away from.

The point I hope to make is that not all people of any given race or ethnicity are prone to hate or racism. At the same time, no one should be judged by his or her skin color or ethnicity. Rather, a person should be judged by his or her actions. In my opinion, we're all God's people, and it is high time that we started to act like it.

CHAPTER 1
Enlistment

Los Angeles, California (South Central)

Daemon could hear the last two bullets whir past his head as the sound of screeching tires faded off into the distance.

"Michael. Michael! Where you at, dog?"

"Over by the hoops, Dae. Yo, we clear?"

"I think so—let's get the hell outta here!"

Michael, surprisingly calm under the circumstances and very aware of his surroundings, moved through the park gracefully. He and Daemon instinctually searched for good-quality cover in case their attackers were to suddenly return. "Daemon! Dae! Yo, let's split, bro! Meet at T-Rock's crib in fifteen! Straight?"

"Straight up!" Daemon turned his attention to finding a place to hide for the next ten minutes, just to make sure he wasn't still being hunted. That would leave him with plenty of time to carefully make his way to T-Rock's house.

Anthony (Tony) Rockson, known as T-Rock to his friends, was only fourteen when his mother passed away. After he found a creative way to cash the social security checks that came in the mail every month, he simply took over the house his family had lived in for two generations. Although very young at the time, he managed the situation so well that no one even took notice. Luckily for him, the social security checks continued to come.

As T-Rock got older and gang life became more inevitable, he converted the family house into a gang headquarters of sorts. His became the place where decisions about strategy were made, where members could hide out for short periods of time, where weapons and other supplies were kept, and, of course, where all the best parties happened.

T-Rock was sitting at his kitchen table, leisurely playing cards with a few others, when Daemon tapped on the back door. Without hesitation, T-Rock and his friends pulled out their weapons. The room became silent.

"Who is it?"

"It's Michael. Let me in, bro."

T-Rock stood quickly, shoved his pistol back into the back of his pants, and walked toward the door. The room was once again filled with the activity and energy of a spirited card game by the time Michael walked in. He was immediately followed by Daemon, who had just caught up to his best friend.

"Wazzup, fellas?" Michael said with a lopsided grin as he sat down at the card table. Sweat still dripping from his forehead, he used his left hand to wipe it clean. "Let me jump in here and show y'all how it's done. Deal me in, and get ready to give all your hard-earned money to ol' Michael. Know what I'm sayin'?"

Michael was always the fun-loving one of the bunch and by far the most handsome; he had a perfect set of teeth and a smile that instantly disarmed even the most hardened of people. He was able to project his emotions through his facial expressions, which were subtle but exaggerated enough to manipulate the outcome of nearly any conversation. As he settled into his preferred reality of spending time with his friends in a safe environment, the sweat caused by being hunted for the last fifteen minutes continued to trickle down his forehead, so he wiped his brow one more time.

Daemon and T-Rock made their way out of the kitchen and into the main room at the front of the house. The décor hadn't changed in years, which created the feeling of stepping back in time. Heavy drapes hung at each end of a large window centered on the street-facing wall.

The house, located in a neighborhood of small homes so close to each other that neighbors could literally shake hands by reaching out their windows, had been built at the end of a *T* intersection. This was good for T-Rock and his gang, as it allowed them to see approaching vehicles with plenty of advance notice.

"We didn't do nothin' to make the Martinez gang fire on us like that!" Daemon shook his head in disbelief. "We saw 'em comin', but we didn't think we was in trouble 'til the shots started flyin'."

"Damn, Dae, why the hell you think they tryin' to bang us like that? We've been good with those muthas for a long time now." T-Rock turned to the window and directed his gaze down the street as he rubbed his chin and tried to sort the confusion present in his mind.

Daemon simply nodded in agreement as the reality of being on someone else's hit list began to sink in. "I don't know, man. They've been staying out of our territory and we ain't been squeezin' in on their business. Maybe they just made a mistake, know what I'm sayin'?"

"I don't know, Dae. You know they don't make mistakes, just like we don't. They probably just decided to expand, bro, and we're right in their way."

"So what we gonna do, T-Rock?"

"I got some ideas. All this shit probably ain't worth it no more, though—know what I'm sayin'? Might be a good time to get out."

Daemon's eyebrows furrowed in mild confusion as a faint glow began to appear on T-Rock's face. It grew brighter as the living room windows filtered what was clearly a pair of oncoming headlights making their way straight down the road leading to their house.

"Get *down!*" Daemon lowered his shoulder and tackled T-Rock, bringing him to the floor and out of harm's way.

Everyone else in the house fell to the floor without a second thought as automatic gunfire echoed through the air and bullets began to fill the front room. Small pieces of debris ricocheted off the furniture. Daemon moved to a position that allowed him to see T-Rock's face, upon which he saw an emotion there that he hadn't seen before: fear.

The moment became surreal for him as he flashed back to memories of the neighborhood when he and his friends were much younger. Long before the perils of gang life, back when everything around him seemed to bask in the sunlight, life was very beautiful and so serene. Back then, even with trouble all around them, Daemon had always felt secure, never threatened or fearful. They had been so innocent and young, full of hope and the promise of a better life and—

"*Oh, shit!*" T-Rock's shouting abruptly shattered Daemon's daydream and brought his attention to a pipe bomb smoldering on the living room carpet. They both jumped to their feet and dove out of the holes that were windows only minutes before.

Everyone else, including those who were still playing cards in the kitchen at the back of the house, had escaped through the back door the instant the gunfire started. Of the other gang members, only Michael had a heart big enough to care about his friends and ignore the risk of injury, so he worked his way around to the front of the house, staying low and finding cover along the way. When he was finally reunited with T-Rock and Daemon, both were a little more frantic after having to jump out of the room that had taken the full brunt of the assault.

The explosion was akin to the sound of an Independence Day celebration: not very loud, but followed by the crackling noise that smaller embers make as they fizzle out into the night. Although the sound itself was not frightening, the explosion was definitely effective. T-Rock stood up and looked back to see his living room engulfed in flames.

Exasperated, T-Rock also felt something new. For the first time in his life, he was ready just to give up. All he could do was let out a sigh; he knew that any attempt to put out the fire would be in vain. The fire department never responded quickly in his neighborhood, and he was past the point of anger or revenge.

At that moment, Michael and Daemon appeared from the darkness. Michael had his shirt off and was holding it against a small flesh wound on his abdomen. The two walked toward T-Rock.

"I think you're right." Daemon spoke softly to his two lifelong friends. "Might be a good time to get out of this business. Problem is, how we gonna make it happen?"

"I know how." T-Rock placed his hand on Daemon's shoulder and gazed at Michael. "We just gotta hide 'til morning."

The next morning revealed a typical Los Angeles sunrise struggling to fight past the morning's blanket of smog. A few scarce rays found their way to the ground, creating a glare that pierced the eastern-facing windows of the army office. This made it difficult for the recruiter to see the faces of the three young men walking through the door.

He squinted to see their tattered silhouettes. "Can I help you, gentlemen?"

T-Rock looked at Daemon, then at Michael, and replied, "Yo, we came to join the army today. Don't care how you do it, but just get us in—and get us in now."

Omaha, Nebraska

"Thanks for the ride, Jennie!"

Seventeen-year-old Heather hopped out of the car with her usual smile and bounce in her step. As had been the case every other day, a warm feeling of security came over her as she entered the home she had lived in all her life. It was a charming little ranch-style house in a neighborhood with mature trees and a long list of memories, including all the years spent with a neighborhood full of the friends she had known for a lifetime.

From what Heather could tell, she was a typical high school senior. What she couldn't have known is how different her upbringing really had been. She lived in a world where blacks, whites, and Hispanics all meshed together to form one unified community.

Heather, who was blonde haired, blue eyed, and fair skinned, came from a family of German descent and her family still held on to their heritage in many traditional ways. Her best friend, Jennie, was black, but the girls had never allowed their difference in race to be an issue. In fact they had been such good friends for so long that their difference in skin color had never even occurred to them.

Both Heather and Jennie, two of the most popular girls in school, were very attractive by any measure. They shared a common interest in everything and inseparable since the first grade, they had developed the type of friendship that was a true sisterhood.

Heather's house was cluttered with her mother's collections of everything from small ceramic figurines to Beanie Babies. The furniture and décor was from a time long past but was clean and well kept. Family photos were everywhere; they lined the tops of bookshelves and were crowded on the TV stand. There were mismatched frames of all shapes and sizes arranged in collages on nearly every wall. It was like walking through a museum of history. Together, though, the photographs told a story of a happy, loving family that any first-time visitor could easily decipher.

Heather stood in the entryway and waved good-bye to Jennie one more time before she turned and started down the narrow hallway toward her room.

"Hi, honey. How was school today?" Her father was a typical gray-haired, slightly overweight, middle-class man. His only distinguishing characteristics were his ever-present smile and easygoing attitude. He greeted everybody with open arms.

"Oh, hi, Daddy! What are you doing home?"

"Well, since graduation is only a few months away, your mother and I thought we should sit down and talk about your options for college. So I thought it would be nice to come home a little bit early today. Have you got a few minutes?"

"Of course, Daddy. But don't worry, I think that Jennie and I have it all figured out."

"Oh yeah?" he replied with a proud smile and a bit of a chuckle in his voice. "Well, we'll just have to see about that. Your mother and I will wait for you in the kitchen."

He turned away quickly to hide the shame that he felt. Don Wilson was the type of person who tried to do everything right. He and his high school sweetheart, Paula, had married right after their high school graduation and had begun to raise a family almost immediately. He had burned the candle at both ends by working two jobs throughout college to buy groceries and hopefully, to pay for tuition.

It had all seemed so simple. The furniture store that he owned would put him in control of his family's future, or so he thought. Owning his own business was something that he had always dreamed of, but at the time he went into business for himself, he couldn't have imagined how difficult it would actually be. His only true goal in life was to provide his children with the type of opportunity that he felt he never had: a college degree without student loans or having to work two jobs.

As he continued to invest all of his extra earnings back into his struggling business, he would tell his beautiful wife not to worry about their personal savings and investments. Don knew in his heart that they would be able to start saving next month, next quarter, next year—as soon as sales were just a little bit better.

Now, faced with the reality of what he must tell his daughter, it seemed as though the years had all run together ... and tomorrow had become today. His eldest was ready for college and he hadn't saved a dime to help her pay for it. Where did all the years go? What could he possibly say to Heather to make things right? The stress of Don's disappointment in himself was clearly visible, but only when no one was watching.

"Okay, Daddy, I'm ready," Heather said cheerfully as she pulled out a chair at the dining room table and sat down to face her parents. She wasn't a child anymore. She knew that her father was stressed about paying for college, and she knew that he felt bad for not being able to help. But she also knew that she had a solution, one that her parents would not have considered. It was a solution that caused her to feel a level of excitement that was almost too much to bear.

"Honey, your mom and I can't begin to tell you how proud we are of you and all the things you have accomplished—"

"Yes, Heather." Paula interjected, as she rarely did. "Honor roll, volleyball, speech, and debate. You have worked so hard."

"Your mother's right. And again, now that graduation is only a few months away—"

"Daddy. Mom. Don't worry about it." Unable to hold back the news, Heather retained the smile on her face. "I know that it's not easy to pay for college. A lot of my friends can't afford to go to college right away, either."

"Don't talk like that, honey. Your mother and I have been thinking." Don glanced at Paula for reinforcement of their decision. "And we are pretty sure we can qualify for a student loan. Now, it won't be enough for a state university, but it could certainly be enough for the local college." In his heart he knew that more debt was not a good solution—even if they *could* qualify—but it was the only solution he could come up with. Like many middle-class Americans, Don had an income that was too high to qualify him for financial assistance but too low to realistically pay for his daughter's education.

"Mom, Dad, I said don't worry about it. I've got great news! Are you ready?" She could hardly sit still. "Jennie and I talked to an army recruiter last week. She said that we both qualify for full scholarships at Georgia Tech if we join the ROTC. Isn't that just awesome!? She even said that Jennie and I would be assigned to the same base after college! Won't that be cool?"

Don and Paula looked at each other in disbelief. Heather had always been thoughtful, appreciative, and easygoing, but to be so understanding and willing to make such a sacrifice at this early stage in her life was totally unexpected.

"Are you sure this is what you want to do?" Don tried to hide his relief, knowing now that he was off the hook. "Georgia Tech certainly is a better institution than we could have hoped for, but—"

"Daddy, of course I'm sure! Jennie and I plan to sign up by the end of the month. Four years of school, then we're off to being military officers and traveling the world!"

The middle-aged man who only moments before had felt his dreams beginning to fade simply smiled, crossed his arms, and leaned back in his chair.

Maybe next year we can start saving for retirement, he thought to himself, always hoping for a brighter future.

New Orleans, Louisiana

"All rise. The Second District Court in the state of Louisiana will now come to order. The Honorable William J. Carmichael presiding."

"Thank you. You may be seated. Bailiff, what have we got first?"

"Yes, sir, Your Honor. The court would like to begin with the state versus Julius Jackson. The charge is one count of misdemeanor assault."

"Mr. Jackson, please come forward." Judge Carmichael sounded as uninterested as usual in his docket. He moaned slightly as he reached forward to take the file handed to him by the bailiff. "Do you have representation today, son?"

"Yeah."

"I'm sorry, did you just respond to me with a 'yeah'?" The heavyset judge peered over his reading glasses and scowled at the young defendant. "When you address me in my courtroom, you will do so by saying 'Yes, sir' or 'Yes, Your Honor.' Do you understand?"

"Uh, yes, sir."

"Better. Now let me take a look at what we've got here. It appears that you've been charged with one count of assault. Is that right?"

"Yes, sir."

"Counsel, maybe you should speak for your client so that he doesn't risk the chance of screwing up again. It's only 8:05 in the morning and I still happen to be in a pretty good mood, which could work in his favor."

"Yes, sir, Your Honor." The young, state-appointed attorney rifled through his briefcase rather nervously and stammered for what to say next. "My client here, ah, Mr. Jackson, is charged with assault, and he would like to enter a plea of no contest."

"Very good, counsel." Judge Carmichael was known for wanting to help young offenders whenever possible, although his tough exterior did not indicate such. "Now let's see. Mr. Jackson has quite a file here. Mostly minor stuff, misdemeanor assault, petty theft, disturbing the peace, public exposure," he said while peering again over his glasses at the defendant, "and now you are pleading no contest again? Do you fully understand the implications of that plea, Mr. Jackson?"

"Yes, sir."

"I see." He paused. His leather chair let out a squeak as he leaned back. "Given the length of your rap sheet, I have no choice but to hand down a pretty stiff sentence this time. I think it's time you're taught a lesson. How old are you, son—sixteen, seventeen?"

"Eighteen, sir."

"Eighteen. That's good. Have you completed high school?"

"Yes, sir—well, I have my GED, sir."

Judge Carmichael tried to hide a small grin as he recognized his opportunity to actually help reform another young man as opposed to sending him down a path that almost certainly guaranteed further destruction. "Today might just be your lucky day. I'll tell you what I'm prepared to do. Because I'm such a nice guy, and because I am still in such a great mood—given that it's only 8:10 in the morning now—I'll give you a choice of sentences. How does that sound, Mr. Jackson?"

"Good, I *think*, sir?"

"You think right, son—this is good! Here are your options: either six months in county jail, immediately followed by two years of supervised probation, or a four-year enlistment in the United States Army."

The courtroom immediately buzzed with the sound of whispering voices. The judge's offer had people talking; although some knew that Judge Carmichael was the type who wanted to make a difference, it was rare that he actually had the opportunity to do so. Others simply didn't realize that military service was even a possibility for minor offenders. Either way, offering Julius the option to join the army came as a total surprise to most people in the courtroom.

"Now before you decide, remember that the first option has no fringe benefits, no pay, and no promise of a future. The second option, on the other hand, well, it pays pretty well—will even pay for you to go to college if you want to—it offers a good future, and hell, it's even kind of fun once in a while. I know because I've been there. So there you have it. What'll it be, son?"

The leather chair let out another squeak of pain as the large judge settled back, crossed his arms, and gazed over the top of his reading glasses once again. He waited for a response.

Not knowing what he should do, and certainly surprised by the offer, young Julius Jackson looked over his right shoulder to the last row of seats in the courtroom. There, sitting all alone, was a woman dressed in her Sunday best. The wrinkles in her face, caused by a lifetime of sorrow and fear, made her look much older than she really was. The tears in her eyes slowly made their way down her cheeks. It was clear that life had not been easy for her.

Julius remembered playing in the front yard while his mother was looking on from the front porch of their house; she looked so young and beautiful back then, before all of the struggles he had put her through. They never had money for elaborate toys, but he had always found a way to have fun, even if just playing in a pile of leaves. He could almost feel the heat of the warm sun on the back of his neck as he thought back to that more simple time.

He turned his attention back to the judge and to the reality at hand. Two of his brothers were already in prison for more serious offenses, and a stray bullet from a drive-by shooting had killed his younger sister less than three months ago. Young Julius Jackson, for the first time in his life, came to the realization of how hard it had been for his mother to raise six children by herself in the heart of the ghetto. He looked at his mother again—the sadness, the disappointment. She deserved much more than this. It warmed his heart to think that he could be the first in his family to make Mom proud.

Julius could feel the anger and tension begin to escape from his mind and body. He wanted nothing more than to repay his mother for her enduring love and support, and he was grateful for an opportunity that seemed like a simple way to change both of their lives.

The sound of Judge Carmichael clearing his throat brought Julius's mind back to the courtroom and the decision he had to make. He vowed to himself that he would be the first in his family to make a difference. He wanted to be the first to make the right decision and, at the same time, make his mother proud for a change. With a decisive look of determination on his face, he turned to the gray-haired judge, who was growing impatient, and said in a strong voice, "I'd like to join the army, Your Honor."

"That's a good choice, son, a good choice." The judge clamored for a rubber stamp located on the far corner of his desk and slammed it down onto the file in front of him. The thud echoed through the courtroom, startling the few people who weren't aware of what was going on around them. He smiled at the young man standing before him, gave a reassuring nod, and peered over his reading glasses. "Good luck, son."

Young Julius Jackson, firmly holding onto his paperwork and the opportunity of a new life, felt taller and suddenly more confident as he gave one more glance to the back of the courtroom. His mother wiped away a tear and smiled proudly. Somehow, she looked slightly younger again …

Washington, DC

It was the type of day that rarely shows itself in the East: warm, sunny, dry, and almost no wind to contend with. Still, the noise from the wind, caused by having the convertible top down, made it difficult to hear the radio, so Rob Lancaster slipped his thumb across the remote sensor on his steering wheel and turned off the music. Having just graduated with honors from Princeton, he knew that the only real challenge left for him was to follow in his father's footsteps by joining the law firm that his grandfather had started over fifty years ago.

He continued east on Interstate 68 and looked in his rearview mirror to confirm that the town he had just passed was Cumberland, Maryland. As he focused his attention back to the road in front of him, he was able to see the next highway sign: "Washington, DC, 100 miles." The smile on his face always seemed to fade at this point of the trip, because he knew that he was now less than two hours away from home.

If he caved in to the pressure from his father and applied his new law degree at the family law firm, he would be the third generation of the Lancaster family to live in the nation's capital city. Problem was, Rob wasn't sure that that's what he wanted to do. Sure, his father's firm was recognized as one of the best in the country—if not the world—and he could probably become a partner within his first ten years. Of course, the comfort of his convertible BMW, and knowing that money would never be a problem, were pretty good perks, too.

His entire family—his father, grandfather, uncles—had all made their names as top lawyers at Lancaster, Kennedy & Forbes in Washington, DC. But what challenge could there possibly be for Rob in working for his family?

Rob always knew that something else was calling him, but he couldn't read the signs. Everywhere he went in America's most influential city, people who knew his father had granted Rob special favors or made exceptions for him. Even at Princeton, he couldn't escape the reach of his family name and its reputation. His professors had always granted him extra time to turn in a project if he needed it, and provided him with staff tutors just prior to exams—at no charge, of course.

He had no interest in leveraging his family's name anymore; he was better than that—or at least he hoped so. With the radio off, he decided to give himself about thirty miles to come up with a solution. Certainly there must be a place where he could earn his stripes without the influence of his family. All he needed was a place where he could be more anonymous. Anonymity; that was it! That's the answer he was looking for. But where could he possibly escape the reach of his family name?

Rob squinted to avoid the glare of his brightly polished hood. The midday sun was beating down, so he reached across the seat for his sunglasses. As he slipped them on, he noticed a billboard he had seen a thousand times before but had never paid attention to: The United States Army. Be All You Can Be. Talk about anonymity! What better place to prove yourself as an individual than in the army?

He figured his education would get him started on the corporate side of the army. He didn't know all the details, but a friend had told him that a college degree meant that he could enlist as an officer. His starting rank wouldn't matter; he wanted to *earn* his promotions anyway. *Perfect,* he thought.

The army would be a place where Rob Lancaster would be measured purely by his own strengths and weaknesses—untainted by his family's successes or by his father's connections. Surely no one in the army would have heard of his father's law practice or of the family name. Even if someone did recognize the name, Rob could deny it. No one would be the wiser and he could truly be anonymous—free for the first time to build his own reputation and be his own man.

The more he considered the entire situation, the more he realized that this is what he was meant to do: join the army. Besides, if he didn't like it, he would always have a position waiting for him back at the firm.

With newfound enthusiasm, he quickly tapped the remote control, turned the radio back on, and tuned it to his favorite classic rock station. The speakers crackled as Rob turned the volume higher and higher in order to overcome the noise from the wind.

The band Boston was playing over the air waves and the guitar solo from their song *Don't Look Back* blared through the speakers. *Ironic,* he thought as he considered the name of the song being played, *don't look back. That's perfect for me.*

He smiled, content with his decision and eager to uncover the opportunities that lay ahead of him.

Now the only obstacle left was for Rob to come up with a way to tell his father. Actually, the more he thought about it, the more he thought that telling his father might just be the toughest battle he'd ever have to face—in the army or otherwise.

CHAPTER 2
Conflict

Eight Years Later

Morning reveille was met with a hazy thickness in the air. The spring flowers around Fort Benning gave a sense of something less commanding than a military base. The forecast called for rain later in the day, which was always a welcome respite to the spring heat. Staff Sergeant Rockson had been stationed here for six years, after his initial two years of training, and this was every bit the kind of day that he had grown to love and appreciate.

From time to time, Rockson would think back to when he and his friends Daemon and Michael had enlisted together. The trouble that they had left behind in South Central seemed so far away from them now—almost as if it were only a dream, a terrible dream from which they had finally awakened. He still didn't understand exactly how it had happened. None of them had finished high school before the day they arrived at the recruiter's office, but somehow they were all enlisted that very day and were shipped off to boot camp shortly thereafter.

All he could do was assume that the recruiter had somehow forged documents or records that allowed them to join without restrictions. It didn't matter now; the last eight years had been very good to them, and their troubled past seemed to have been erased. When they committed to another term last fall, extending their current enlistment by another four years, the army all but guaranteed that they would continue to be stationed together.

Because of this, the three of them were now determined to serve at least until early retirement, which would be twenty years total, meaning they would have to give only another eight years beyond their current commitment.

If the next twelve years passed as quickly as had the eight they had already served, then army retirement was definitely the way to go. They had heard all of the success stories—those who had served before them and had met the twenty-year-minimum retirement age then went on to have a successful second career.

The three friends worked at the motor pool at Fort Benning. It was located on the far end of base, which was out of the way from the normal hustle and bustle of activity that took place on the military base daily. To them, this was perfect. They preferred to fly under the radar at this point in their lives. In fact, there was still a certain fear in each one of them that they might be found out, that their ugly past might still catch up with them. Their juvenile criminal records, their forged records to get into the army without a high school diploma or its equivalent, their gang-related past—something, *something* had to be uncovered at some point, or at least they thought.

For this reason they mostly kept to themselves. They didn't want to make the mistake of mentioning part of their past to someone they didn't really know or trust. The risk was too great. The military doesn't take this type of thing lightly. If discovered, they knew that the punishment handed down by the army would be more severe than anything they might have faced in the civilian world.

Each of them had been tempted, for sure. There were plenty of young ladies who caught their eye, and plenty of opportunity when they would go to a local bar in nearby Augusta, Georgia. A man in uniform was considered a good catch by many a young woman, and the three friends from South Central were handsome, to be sure. Because of these opportunities, they weren't afraid to date women, which they did from time to time, but the thought of a long-term relationship seemed risky.

It was muggy at the motor pool that day. Michael and Daemon were hard at work replacing the transmission on an ailing Humvee. Rockson took a quick break to lean against the workbench and sip a soda. The humidity dripped from his forehead and trickled down his back. "Wish they'd give us air-conditioning," he mumbled to himself, knowing that no one would care to hear him say it out loud anyway. Partly due to his maturity, Rockson had been promoted one more time than his two friends had. Anthony Rockson was a staff sergeant, while both Daemon Johnson and Michael Masters had reached the rank of sergeant. This is why Rockson could sit back and relax a bit more than the other two.

He respected Daemon and Michael too much to take advantage of his rank, though. He jumped right in and helped more often than most higher-ranking soldiers did. Still, being able to obtain the rank of sergeant, like Johnson and Masters had, was pretty good career progress as well—especially for a couple of soldiers who had come in at the lowest rank of private, like they had. Using a system of *E* for "enlisted" followed a numeral after a hyphen is how the military keeps track of pay grades. "E-1" refers to the lowest pay grade of a private. A private could be elevated to a pay grade of E-2 and be referred to as a PV2. The rank of private first class, or PFC, is next, at a level of E-3, followed by the rank of specialist, which has an E-4 pay grade.

The rank of sergeant comes with a pay grade of E-5. Whereas this isn't necessarily a big jump up in pay, the rank of sergeant carries with it a certain level of respect and a sense of accomplishment. A promotion to staff sergeant is where the pay begins to catch up with the title, so to speak. The soldiers who receive this promotion are also recognized as those who have made the decision to remain in the army for longer than just one or two terms. Once again, more respect accompanies this rank.

Rockson's daydream continuing, his thoughts turned back to that fateful day eight years ago when he and his friends enlisted. Their recruiter had promised that they would stay together throughout their military careers, and somehow he'd made sure they had. Their background and lack of schooling nearly guaranteed them a life in infantry, so they applied for positions as field mechanics after boot camp. As it turned out, that was probably the best decision they could have made. Each of them had become very skilled at repairing vehicles and machinery. In fact, almost everyone on the base considered them to be the best at the job.

Their plan for the future was simple: Rockson, Daemon, and Michael were going to remain in the army for twelve more years until they were eligible for the army's minimum retirement, and then they would move back to California. There, they would become partners in a full-service auto repair center that they would own, using their pensions to help them through the early years while building their reputation locally. By that time, they would be only thirty-eight years old. With their abilities, they could easily build a very profitable business in just a few years.

Each of the three men had developed a specialty that complemented the others'. Daemon Johnson had studied hard to learn everything mechanical—drivetrains, gear ratios, suspension alignment, and engineering—even the more basic elements of a vehicle, such as the braking system. Daemon was an expert on all things mechanical, no doubt.

Michael Masters had become the expert in auto body, and his abilities were nothing short of phenomenal. Michael could align body panels more quickly and easily than the others because his mind worked in such a logical way. He could naturally understand the relationship between the body panels and the frame underneath, which is something that escapes most who work in the field. He could also weld, shape metal, and repair panels to the point that they were as smooth as glass. This, combined with his natural ability to lay a perfect coat of paint, made his expertise untouchable.

Rockson had focused on the advanced aspects of electronics and modern automotive computer systems. This is a critical skill when looking to the complexity of modern-day vehicles and their operation. Everything is controlled by a central computer, and the margin for error is very slim. Every aspect of engine tuning is dependent upon the accuracy of electronic sensors and how they provide information to the central computer.

There was no doubt about it—the three former gangbangers from South Central had turned out all right. With their combined knowledge and varying skill sets, there was no doubt that they would be very successful shop owners. Sure, there were the usual issues and occasional hardships that they had to face in their army careers, but overall they were far better off and their futures were solid.

The other addition to their lives was their faith in God. After boot camp and their initial training, life slowed down a little bit for the three of them. This allowed them more time to reflect on their checkered pasts and think toward the future. When considering the type of men they *wanted* to become, religion, and a faith in God, seemed like a good way to turn around their personal lives. The development of their professional lives seemed simple, as they each had natural talents and nearly unlimited opportunity to train in the army.

Over the years it was their faith that truly turned them around, however. As they became more focused on the teachings in the Bible, and as they vowed to live by the word of God, every aspect of their lives seemed to fall into place more easily. Of course, each of them had departed from a Christian way of life from time to time—no one is perfect—but they were always there for each other, helping each other back to their feet and back on the right track to a truly successful life.

Rockson was brought out of his daydream by the sound of three vehicles approaching the motor pool at a high rate of speed, faster than they should have been traveling. A light cloud of dust followed the outdated jeeps into the driveway and drifted into the shop as the vehicles screeched to a halt right in front of the main service bay.

Rockson set his soda down on the workbench and slowly walked toward the lead vehicle, squinting through the dust and into the sun to see if he knew the soldiers who had just arrived. Daemon, meanwhile, pulled himself out from under the Humvee and wiped sweat from his face with the same greasy rag he had been using for the repair, which left a streak of grease on his forehead. Both men knew that the jeeps could mean trouble, based on the way they had approached.

Michael had his iPod cranked up pretty loud but could tell something was going on, so he tugged on the cord to quickly release the tiny speakers from his ears. He looked at Rockson and Daemon, who were making their way out of the shop, their focus squarely on the arriving vehicles. This confirmed his thoughts, so he also made his way to the end of the garage bay and then leaned against the garage door's guide rail.

A tall, blonde-haired, blue-eyed sergeant hopped out of one of the jeeps just as Rockson walked out into the sunlight. "Shouldn't you be workin' a little harder than that, boy?"

Rockson's instincts were spot-on—this was going to be trouble. He'd learned a thing or two since his teenage gang years, so he knew better than to react impulsively. Instead, he patiently responded, "I think you'd better take another look at my collar and start over with a different tone in your voice. What do you need, Sergeant?"

If there was one thing that Rockson liked about military life as opposed to the civilian world, it was the concept of rank. No matter the circumstances, the person with superior rank commanded respect and got to call the shots, while the junior-ranking soldier had to abide by the superior's decisions, at least in theory. And in this case, Rockson outranked the cocky Sergeant.

The young man peered over his aviator-style sunglasses and looked directly at the insignia on Rockson's collar, dramatically implying that he hadn't noticed it before. "Yeah, right, *sir.*" The sarcasm rolled off his voice. Sergeant Peterson's name tag finally came into full view so that Rockson could see whom he was dealing with. Peterson looked over his shoulder to his two partners, who were just beginning to get out of their vehicles.

"Don't call me 'sir'—I work for a living." Rockson deadpanned the response that enlisted soldiers have been using since the army began, implying that officers don't *really* work as hard as the enlisted soldiers. He used the phrase in the hopes of bringing some levity to the situation. "And be careful, Sergeant, you're bordering on being disrespectful here." Rockson's smile was now completely gone.

"Look, *sir.* Just change the brakes on this jeep and give it the standard service. These orders are direct from General Street, so I suspect that you'll have it done first thing in the morning, ain't that right, boy?" By this time, Peterson had placed both hands on his hips and stood facing Rockson directly, his feet a shoulders' width apart. He twisted his upper body back toward his buddies, who were now making their way closer to the two men, and winked, almost as if he were giving them a signal of some sort. He, with a clearly visible wad of chewing tobacco bulging from his lower lip, then paused to spit before turning back to Rockson.

"You're out of line, Sergeant, but I'll choose to give you the benefit of the doubt. However, I'm going to suggest, one more time, that you change your tone with me and hand over those papers." Lowering his voice and speaking through clenched teeth, Rockson was trying hard not to let his frustration get the better of him. He had had enough.

But for the time being, he was able to keep both his anger and his fighting instinct under control. Rockson's long-term goals with his friends were far more important than the arrogance of some punk kid. Remembering this allowed him to put things back in perspective and helped him to calm down.

Daemon and Michael had been listening to what was going on. Michael finally came into view while wiping his hands on a shop towel, escaping from the stifling heat of the garage. As he walked toward Rockson and the other men, he glanced back at Daemon, who was still leaning against the rail just inside the shop.

"Look, boy. I don't give a damn what the hell your rank is," Peterson said, slowly making his way even closer to Rockson. The men now stood toe to toe, humidity building on their faces, their eyes squinting in the sunlight. He leaned forward and spoke softly into Rockson's right ear so that no one else could hear. "Just fix the damn jeep and do as you're told. Understand me, nigger?"

Despite doing everything in his power to stay calm, Rockson, finding this comment of Peterson's to be too much, lost his cool. He grabbed Sergeant Peterson's uniform and took him to the ground with the lightning-quick dexterity of an experienced fighter and with the confidence of a man who had seen combat before.

Sergeant Peterson was flat on his back; Rockson had his left knee on the ground beside his adversary and his right foot planted between Peterson's legs. Rockson was still clutching the handful of uniform that he had used to throw the junior officer to the ground. "You white mutha—"

"Whoa, whoa." Michael's cool, collected voice could be heard as he trotted over to the scuffle. He wanted to keep calm under the circumstances. Once he was right behind Rockson, he gripped the back of his friend's uniform to pry the two antagonists apart. Rockson reluctantly rose back to his feet, Michael still holding onto the back of his uniform and hoping to prevent the situation from getting any worse. "T-Rock, let's just get the papers from Sergeant Peterson here and fix the general's jeep," Michael said with a smile.

"T-Rock?! What the hell kind of jungle-bunny name is that?" Sergeant Peterson scrambled to get off the ground and dust himself off. He was obviously looking for trouble now. Both embarrassed and pissed off, he was trying anything he could think of to entice Rockson into a fight—but why?

Rockson sidestepped his friend with surprising agility for a man his size, broke free from Michael's grasp, and then charged at Peterson again. But Michael moved just as quickly and prevented Rockson from throwing Peterson to the ground for a second time. The last thing they needed was trouble with the military authorities.

"What's that? Was that some weak-ass attempt to take me down, T-Rock?!" Sergeant Peterson would not let it go. His sly smile was as offensive as his words. He spat chewing-tobacco juice one more time.

"Look, Sergeant," Michael said, stepping between them and trying to defuse the situation one more time with his ever-present smile, "since Staff Sergeant Rockson here outranks you, let's just forget the whole thing happened so that you don't get into trouble—sound good?"

"That all sounds so sweet, boy, but I think you 'T-Rocks'—or whatever the hell you want to call yourselves—should just do as you're told." He lowered his voice to a level that was just above a whisper. "Now hop to it, eh, nigger?"

Michael's smile vanished instantly. He squared to face Peterson toe to toe, nose to nose, and stared him down, allowing his anger to build, waiting for the right time to attack.

Taking in every little nuance of the situation, Daemon, pipe wrench in hand, was instinctively positioning himself by walking away from the guide rail and positioning himself to take out the two soldiers who had accompanied Sergeant Peterson, if needed. As it turned out, the lessons that Daemon and his buddies had learned back in South Central would prove to be invaluable in the days and weeks to come.

Peterson just chuckled and took one step backward. He turned to his two friends and smiled with a nod, as if giving them a signal that now was the time. He then turned his attention back to Michael.

Sergeant Peterson started to slowly unbutton his outer uniform. Once it was free, he let it fall to the ground at his feet. "Are you sure you want a piece of me?" He raised the bottom of his undershirt to reveal the Confederate battle flag tattooed on his abdomen in full color.

Rockson finally snapped at the intentional reference to white supremacy. He leapt past Michael and, with the force of his entire body behind him, delivered a left jab to Peterson's chin. The two fell to the ground and began to wrestle violently as Daemon and Michael took off after the other two men.

Within seconds, the six men were heavily involved in a brawl—a brawl that the three from South Central were clearly winning.

As the fight continued, another soldier working in the shop finally noticed what was going on and ran into the attached offices to find his commander. "Captain Lancaster! Captain Lancaster!"

"What is it, Private?"

"Rockson started a fight with some guys outside. I don't think we can stop it. We need your help." Trying to catch his breath, the young man was clearly frightened and intimidated.

Captain Lancaster had never done very well in the more physical aspects of his army career—particularly hand-to-hand training. However, he had established himself as a strong administrator since his days back at Princeton, which was why the base commander had put him in control of the entire motor pool and mechanical repair operation.

When he joined the army eight years ago, he had come in as a second lieutenant, just like everyone else with a college degree. It didn't matter if you had a master's degree or advanced education—you were still destined to be a second lieutenant, or butter bar, as they were known from the single brass bar that signified their rank.

Lancaster's first two promotions had come quickly: first lieutenant after just two years, then captain two years after that. Since then, however, he was beginning to think that being in charge of the mechanical repair unit might be career limiting.

Oddly, he also hadn't been able to escape his family name like he had hoped, nor his family's ties to men of authority. In fact, he had just returned from lunch with General Charlie Street, who was a close friend of his father. Lancaster had been appalled when only an hour before he heard General Street snicker and say, "There sure is a lot of *color* in this mess hall," referring to the number of African Americans, of course.

Lancaster himself had never bought into the idea of racism—or bigotry of any kind, for that matter. He simply viewed people for who they were, or at least as best as he could determine them to be. But there was no way that he was going to confront General Street or question the intent of his comment in any way. Lancaster was far too timid for that.

He was also fairly naive when it came to being able to read people. During his army career, and even back when he was in college, there were many times when he had placed his trust in someone only to be burned by them or let down later. He struggled to recognize the difference between someone he could trust and someone who wanted to take advantage of him or his family name.

"Call the MPs! Call the MPs now!" Captain Lancaster barked at the private. He stood from his desk slowly, trying to stall a little bit so that he might avoid having to get physically involved himself before the military police arrived. He reluctantly started to make his way outside toward the scuffle out front, still hoping that somehow the MPs would get there before he did.

Captain Lancaster walked into the shop area, which was the only way to reach the front drive from his office, and was relieved to see that another officer had already intervened. This sudden, fateful turn of events caused Lancaster's confidence to rise above his fears. He bolted out of the garage and into the sunlight, acting like he was ready to take control of the situation, but the other officer had already separated the brawling men by this time.

At the same time, two military police officers pulled up in their jeep, blue light flashing and siren blaring. They jumped from their vehicle so deftly that it appeared as though the jeep hadn't even come to a complete stop before their feet touched the ground. These two men were clearly prepared to intervene in any situation, confident they would always be the victor.

Always aspiring to be in control in order to further his military career, Captain Lancaster was quick to blurt out orders—even without knowing the details surrounding the situation. "Detain these three men, officers!" He pointed to Staff Sergeant Rockson and to Daemon, and Michael, who were all now standing next to each other at attention, thanks to Colonel Ballard, the officer who had come to Lancaster's rescue.

Sergeant Peterson and the other two white men smiled with pleasure as the military police followed Captain Lancaster's orders without question and handcuffed the three black men. Before anyone could dispute his orders, the military police were leading Rockson and his friends to the back of the jeep for a ride to the detention center where they would be detained.

"Wait just a minute!" Colonel Ballard was curious as to how the captain could make a snap judgment after joining the fray so late. "What makes you think that these three men and not the others were the cause of the argument, Captain?"

"Yes, sir." Captain Lancaster snapped to attention and saluted as he noticed Colonel Ballard's superior rank for the first time.

"As you were." Ballard returned the salute and let the captain know that he could drop the formality. After showing respect for a higher-ranking officer, this was the phrase used to acknowledge the gesture and to allow everyone in the room to return to what they were doing.

"Well, sir, Private Stinson over there, along with a few others, saw the entire situation and came to my office with the details—which is why I called for the MPs in the first place. Clearly these three men started the altercation."

"I see." Colonel Ballard was not comfortable with the situation around him. Initially, he found it peculiar that everyone except for him and the three men in handcuffs was white and that everything seemed to moving so fast.

But then, as he looked into the eyes of Captain Lancaster, he realized that these men probably had no ulterior motive. He looked around the shop and made eye contact with the other soldiers involved, feeling once again that everyone was genuine in their assessment of the situation. Besides, he could get to the bottom of the situation later in the day if need be.

"Very well then, Captain. I expect to be included in your report, and I will look for it at the detention center later today."

"Yes, sir!" Captain Lancaster and the entire group snapped to attention once again.

"Carry on, men." The colonel returned the solute, got back into his car, and proceeded to his office.

Still, he had a suspicious feeling that he couldn't seem to shake. However, he trusted that the army would get to the truth—just as it always had—so he decided to fight his own suspicion by not giving it another thought. Over the years, he had developed a strong faith in the United States Army and its procedures.

The sun was not as bright now, as the predicted evening rain began to move in earlier than expected. Staff Sergeant Rockson, his arms held behind him in handcuffs, looked up at the sky searching for an answer from God. He and his two longtime friends rocked back and forth and bounced slightly with every little bump of the jeep they were riding in.

He turned his gaze down toward his boots. Throughout his entire life to this point—no matter how bad things seemed at times—he had never lost, nor questioned, his faith. But this time was different. After only a few years of living a normal life, he realized that it could all be taken away because of a fight that he didn't start—or even want to be a part of, for that matter.

There was a chance that this altercation could be enough cause for the army to take a harder look at his past and that of his two best friends. This one stupid event could easily derail everything they had worked for and destroy all of their dreams.

He looked back toward the overcast sky, hoping, once again, for a sign. A single tear rolled from his eye as he realized that there probably would not be a sign from above.

He looked to both Daemon and Michael. "T-Rock is back," he said to them softly, referring to the personality that he had left behind all those years ago.

Daemon glanced in Rockson's direction. As he also searched from within, looking for an answer, he knew Rockson meant that they might as well return to their old ways, and act more like gangbangers and less like responsible army men.

Given their upbringing, theirs was always a tenuous situation. Any one of them could easily slip back into his old mentality of fight-or-flight at any time. It seemed to be a constant challenge for each of them, but the success they had enjoyed since joining the army continued to pull them in the direction of being responsible young men.

Daemon wasn't quite as ready to give up and return to the old ways, though. And he was disappointed in the attitude of his lifelong friend. "It'll be all right, T-Rock. Hang in there, brother."

The jeep's small engine strained to get the men to the detention center. The sound of an underpowered engine and the steady back-and-forth rocking of an overloaded suspension was mind-numbing. An overwhelming feeling of disappointment came over Staff Sergeant Rockson as the reality of their suddenly uncertain future began to sink in.

CHAPTER 3
Planning

Colonel Ballard, upon pulling into the reserved parking stall that had his name on it, noticed that the sky was now almost entirely covered by clouds. "I'll be damned, the weatherman might have been right about this one. Looks like a little rain is coming," he mumbled to himself with a chuckle. Colonel Ballard was the type of person who didn't let the little things bother him, and that helped him to be a little more lighthearted than most. This was another reason why so many people quickly warmed up to him and enjoyed his company.

He sat in his car for a moment and debated whether he should bring his umbrella in with him. Music was still being played by his favorite radio station. It was the type of station that played a variety of songs from several decades. Ron had always been a fan of music—any genre, any decade, any artist; he loved music. More often than not, he found himself singing along to songs while driving his car.

This had become a little bit of a joke around base because many people had seen Colonel Ballard singing while driving, oblivious to the world around him.

He cracked half a smile and shook his head as he listened to "Waterfalls" by the group TLC, one of his all-time favorites. Like many of his generation, he had understood the meaning behind the lyrics the day the song was released; it was all about the risks people take when chasing intangible dreams with no thought of the consequences. He continued to sit in his car until the final verse, with which he sang along, was complete. After the song was over, he took a deep breath of relaxation and thought of the personal memories that the song had rekindled.

Deciding to leave his umbrella behind, he twisted the ignition to the off position and started to make his way toward the grandiose building that housed his office. His office was located in one of the original buildings that had been built in 1920 after Congress had appropriated funds to make Camp Benning a permanent military post.

This was another aspect of the military that Ron Ballard relished: the history behind the military, and how the actions of the various armed services had in turn shaped the history of the United States. He had been a history buff since he was a child, and after joining the military he made it a point to spend most of his free time studying the remarkable history of the United States' Armed Forces. Throughout the course of his career, he had been to military bases and installations all around the world, marveling at the architecture around him. In his mind, the local architecture could tell the story of the area around him, decade by decade and in vivid detail, no matter where in the world he was stationed at the time.

He trotted up the stairway and then made his way down the hall to the Central Briefing Room. Here, his staff worked together as a team to coordinate the many activities that fell under his purview. Being an active leader, he wanted to have full visibility at all times. This is where he started each day, his entire leadership team around him.

"A-ten-tion!" Major Henderson, the first to notice that Colonel Ballard had entered the room, quickly brought everyone to their feet out of respect, as military custom dictated.

"At ease, people. At ease."

Colonel Ballard, although very appreciative of the respect offered, never did seem too comfortable with the attention that his rank commanded. He saw himself as more of an everyday workingman and less the high-level executive that he really was. This was yet another reason that everyone liked and respected Colonel Ron Ballard.

"Okay, everyone, let's give Colonel Ballard a quick rundown of where we stand today," Major Henderson chimed in, "starting with you, Specialist Carter."

"Yes, sir." Specialist Carter turned to face the three computer screens that made an arc around him. Using them as a reference, he said, "I'm focused on the Kelley Hill area, as you know, and this week we have a request for a total of twelve armored vehicles for the Third Armored Brigade Combat Team, who will be performing training exercises over the weekend."

Fort Benning, like all United States military bases, is organized into cantonment areas, the term used to describe permanent residential sections within a military installation. Cantonment areas are used to keep members of a specific division close to each other by providing barracks and housing for both officers and enlisted soldiers. Fort Benning has four of these areas: Kelley Hill, Sand Hill, Main Post, and Harmony Church.

"I've also got a request to support both the Fifteenth Infantry and the Sixty-Ninth Armor Regiment in two weeks, details yet to be determined. Both the First Cavalry Regiment and the Tenth Field Artillery Regiment appear to be pretty quiet at this time." Specialist Carter paused for a moment, making sure that he wasn't forgetting something. "Sir, that's it for my team."

"Good job, Carter." Major Henderson directed his attention back to Colonel Ballard. "Do you have any questions for Specialist Carter, sir?"

"None. Let's continue with just one more briefing today, Major. Whom do you recommend?"

"Right. Let's move to the Harmony Hill area. They're the only other cantonment that has a high level of activity right now. Sergeant Rainey, please provide us with your update."

"Yes, sir. The 194th Armor Brigade is pretty quiet, but the 316th Cavalry Brigade just sent us a requisition for their training exercises early next month." The 316th Cavalry was home of the United States Army Armor School.

Sergeant Rainey continued. "They will reach phase three for their current class, so we'll need to provide the usual accompaniment of equipment for them."

"So we've got everything under control, right, team?" Colonel Ballard seemed impatient all of a sudden.

Major Henderson responded immediately. "Of course, sir. This team is the best in the United States Army. No doubt we've got our arms around this. We will let you know if we need more support."

"Excellent, thank you. Great job, guys. Keep up the good work. And let me know if you run into challenges so that I can break down walls for you, if needed."

"A-ten-shun!" Major Henderson brought the room back to attention out of respect for the most senior officer, who was about the leave the room.

Colonel Ballard saluted the group and turned toward the door. "Major Henderson, would you join me in my office for a moment, please?"

"Yes, sir." Major Reggie Henderson quickly followed Ballard into his roomy but modest office, where the latter sat at his desk. Reggie thought it odd that Colonel Ballard had bypassed his daily routine by cutting his daily debrief short the way he had. "What can I do for you, sir?"

"You can start by letting me know if there's anything else that might need my attention, Reggie."

Colonel Ballard and his staff were in control of all combat inventory for the base—weapons, munitions, specialized combat gear, hazmat equipment, and combat vehicles such as tanks and combat-ready Humvees. Anything and everything that would be needed for a combat situation was under their watchful eye. This meant that when a combat situation occurred, Colonel Ballard and his staff would be very busy and, more important, responsible for the combat-readiness of every soldier on base.

However, during peacetime operations, preparation was the primary focus of his unit. Making sure that each and every piece of equipment was maintained properly and was in good working condition required a lot of man-hours. In addition, his unit needed to ensure that the base inventory was at all times adequate to outfit every soldier. This could be quite a task when considering the large fluctuation of military personnel at any given time.

Still, Ballard's operation was put to the test whenever one of the battalions needed equipment for their readiness drills. The task of the men and women under Ballard's command was a very difficult one because they rarely, if ever, were given more than a few hours advance notice for these drills.

Yet during his time as leader of the organization, the team had always performed admirably. Any given Unit Commander requesting equipment and supplies marveled at Colonel Ballard's ability to produce equipment that was always in working order, one hundred percent accurate, and on time. His ability to accomplish this consistently highlighted Ballard's leadership skills, making them all the more impressive.

"Well, sir. Everything seems to be holding up just fine. In addition to what you heard a few minutes ago, the Seventy-Fifth Ranger Regiment might have a readiness drill scheduled for next month, but, if so, we seem more than ready to accommodate them." Major Henderson was puzzled; it was odd that Colonel Ballard questioned him about simple business issues.

"Good. That's good, Reggie."

Colonel Ballard finally got to the real issue on his mind that he needed to sort through. "Do you know those three boys over at the garage—I think one of them is named Rockson?"

"Sure I do. Those boys are inseparable—best of friends. I think that they joined together and have been lucky enough to stay together." Major Henderson had a better relationship with the boys than he was letting on. He simply wasn't one hundred percent sure of Colonel Ballard's intentions.

"Good kids, are they?"

"Well, yes—what I know of them, anyway. Why do you ask? Are they in some kind of trouble?" Henderson's concern for the boys was recognizable in the tone of his response.

"They might be, Reggie. They might be. I didn't catch the entire situation, but they were involved in a fight today. It looked pretty serious. The boys they got in a tangle with obviously received the lion's share of the beating." Ballard gazed out the office window. "Anyway, as I left the scene, MPs were taking them to the detention center—Rockson and his two friends—which is where they are now."

Major Henderson had a lot to consider before responding the way he wanted. Colonel Ballard was not yet a part of their underground organization, and for good reason. Based on his experience, Major Henderson knew that Ballard might not be a good candidate for membership. First of all, he seemed to buy in to the army's "public" culture a bit too much. Another reason for Henderson's hesitation was that Colonel Ballard had been raised too soft in an upper-middle-class environment.

Henderson himself hadn't lived such a protected life growing up. He came from a lower-middle-class family, but he was raised by his mother and grandmother in an inner-city neighborhood. He was given enough direction in life to avoid the big mistakes—gangs, drugs, and crime—but his upbringing was still a far cry from what Colonel Ballard had known.

Reggie's mother and grandmother were smart enough, and strong enough, to keep him and his younger sister away from the troubles of the inner-city area. They even managed to have Reggie bused to a better part of town, where he attended high school and was introduced to the game of football for the first time. He joined the team as a running back and quickly made a name for himself.

Reggie proved to be the type of football player, and person, to power through any challenge placed in front of him. He was a strong runner, able to lower his shoulder when approaching the line and drive an entire group of defenders several yards after being hit initially. His high school football coach more accurately referred to him as a fierce running back, also calling him one that was the consummate team player.

By his sophomore year in high school, Reggie was elected by his team to serve as team captain. Thereafter he established himself as the team leader. Since Reggie was able to naturally motivate those around him, the coaches and the team counted on him to help everyone remain focused when they were down and to keep them even more focused when they were in the lead.

He led his team to a state football championship in his senior year, and his playing ability caught the attention of several local colleges. Realistically not good enough to play at the highest level of football in college, Reggie had drawn the attention of several Division II schools. Ultimately, he accepted a football scholarship to play at Fort Valley State University in Fort Valley, Georgia—just a hundred miles south of his hometown of Atlanta.

He wasn't quite good enough to start for the team during his freshman year, which was a good thing because he had to work extremely hard just to get passing grades. Even though he attended a better school relative to the area in which he had been raised, the high school he had attended was far behind the rest of the country academically. So although he qualified for college, he was grossly unprepared for the academic aspects of university life.

Because he wasn't a starting player his first year, he was able to focus on his studies and grades. He worked with tutors to make sure he would build a foundation of learning that would propel him to graduation and to a successful career afterward. As his grades continued to climb, Reggie found that he enjoyed studying and learning about new things. He became a self-motivated student who quickly excelled at Fort Valley State.

By the time he was a sophomore, he had his grades and study regimen well under control. He also became the starting running back for the Wildcats. He learned to relish game days at Wildcat Stadium. Although the number of people in attendance on game day was generally less than the ten thousand seats available, the sound of the crowd cheering him on was a pure adrenaline rush.

Although Fort Valley State was located in the South and its enrollment was heavily weighted to African Americans, he still saw more than his share of racism while at college. In his mind, some of his professors and a few members of the staff were racist, although they did a pretty good job of disguising it. And business owners in the surrounding community seemed to show no love for blacks at all.

All of this caused Reggie to have a perspective on life that was different from Colonel Ballard's.

After graduating from college, Henderson decided that rather than apply his degree to the business world at large, he would join the army, based on his assumption that racism may not exist there. He was hopeful that the time-honored system of military rank would reward a man for his accomplishments and not be so much based on the color of one's skin or one's political acumen. He also knew that his degree would allow him to start as an officer, already at a rank that commanded respect and, more important, might give him an opportunity to apply his natural leadership and motivational skills.

Unfortunately, he quickly discovered that racism was alive and well in the United States Army. After a few years of watching white soldiers get promoted ahead of him and witnessing subtle acts of racism everywhere, he decided to do something about it. Problem was, he had no one to turn to at the time.

All of the top-level positions in the army seemed to be occupied by a white man or a nonsympathetic black man. Major Henderson decided to begin putting out feelers to the other black soldiers with whom he associated—both enlisted and officer ranks—and that was what led him to start the Black Heritage Army.

The Black Heritage Army was code-named "Ubuntu" when referred to in more public circles. This was an exclusive organization of black men and women. To qualify for membership, one had to be a member of the armed services first and foremost. It started as a support group and as more of an opportunity for black soldiers and their families to discuss issues of racism within the army. One of the aims was to help each other to work through painful or difficult personal problems.

In his 1999 book, *No Future without Forgiveness*, Archbishop Desmond Tutu described the essence of Ubuntu:

> A person with Ubuntu is open and available to others, affirming of others, does not feel threatened that others are able and good, based from a proper self-assurance that comes from knowing that he or she belongs in a greater whole and is diminished when others are humiliated or diminished, when others are tortured or oppressed.[1]

---

[1] Desmond Tutu, *No Future without Forgiveness* (New York: Doubleday, 1999).

This captured the spirit of the community that Major Henderson and four of his closest friends at Fort Benning had intended to build when they started the organization. Because of this, they became known as "the Founders," and *Ubuntu* became the term that Black Heritage Army soldiers used to greet each other, compliment each other, or just acknowledge a job well done.

The term also seemed like a natural way to define the long-term goals of the Black Heritage Army and what they eventually planned to accomplish. More important, *Ubuntu* was the type of term that wasn't readily recognizable to anyone, black or white, so it allowed the group to keep their efforts hidden from view, secret.

The Black Heritage Army quickly became a community, and an extensive underground organization with a solid infrastructure. And, right or wrong, it also grew into more of a forum to aggressively and vocally point out injustice. As more African Americans joined the organization, a much more vocal group began to dominate its leadership. It wasn't long before the Black Heritage Army became more of a vehicle to support an uprising and less a mere peer group.

Over the years, and as word of the organization spread, many requests for membership came from other branches of the armed services. The United States Air Force, Navy, Marines—even the United States Coast Guard—all started local chapters of the Black Heritage Army in their towns and on their military bases.

At the same time, the club evolved into a more proactive organization with clearly defined goals and a blueprint to achieve those goals. Regional chapter meetings began to focus more on action plans and less on sympathy for what had happened in the past. As local leaders took their ideas beyond regional chapters and presented them to the national leadership, it became apparent that their goals and thoughts about the future were similar.

By this time, the Black Heritage Army had spread throughout the American Southeast, and there was even talk among members about their own version of a "civil war"—or a time when they would take back what was rightfully theirs, by force if necessary.

A monthly national leadership conference was developed so that the group's plans could take on more structure. This also allowed them the opportunity to refine their message and gain support from the entire Black Heritage Army enlistment.

It didn't take long for word to spread. The Black Heritage Army quickly became a safe haven for nearly seventy five percent of the black military population in the Southeast, with smaller chapters in other parts of the United States and around the world.

Amazingly, the club was still entirely a secret. Very few, if any, white people even knew of its existence. Of course, since Major Henderson was its founding father, he had been christened as the leader of the Black Heritage Army at the national level. Ultimately, whatever he decided as their plan of action was carried out—no questions asked.

Major Henderson turned to look at Ballard, trying to decide if he could truly be trusted and attempting to determine whether this was the right time to let him know about their organization.

"Ron, you said that they might be in trouble. Do you mean more than just the fact that they were taken to the detention area?"

"Reggie, the bottom line is that it looked like a possible case of racism. Rockson and his friends are black, while everyone else involved was white, everyone. In fact, the white soldiers were immediately released. I don't know, it just didn't look right to me, I guess."

That was the opening Henderson was hoping for, so he proceeded with his usual line of questioning. "You sound as if you're not sure. You know that racism exists everywhere—even here in the army, right?"

"I don't know, Reggie. There have been a few times in my career when I have wondered, but I just don't think that it's as prevalent as some people might think."

"Right. Well, then, why do you question what you saw today?"

"Good question." Ballard swiveled his chair around to gaze out of his office window once again. The thunderclouds continued to roll in. "I'm not sure that I can put my finger on it. Something just didn't feel right about the whole situation."

"Ron, can you keep a secret? I mean, *really* keep a secret?"

"Of course, Reggie, you know you can trust me to keep our conversations just between us." Sensing that Reggie had something important to share, he spun his chair back around to face Henderson and leaned forward to listen, placing his elbows on the top of his desk. "What's wrong? Is there something that you need my help with?"

Major Henderson began to tell Ballard details of the Black Heritage Army. He talked about the purpose of the organization, its broad membership, the group's meeting practices, and their communication network. The only thing he left out was their strategic plan to create a society where African Americans were no longer a minority or at the receiving end of racism. He simply didn't feel that Ballard was ready for that kind of information.

If there was one thing Major Henderson had learned while recruiting members over the years, it was that some people needed to have small bits of information spoon-fed to them in portions. Otherwise, they simply couldn't comprehend the magnitude of what the Black Heritage Army had become. This would increase the risk of the secret being discovered.

Other recruits, those who were angry or frustrated about injustice— those were the easy conversations. That was the time when you could unload the entire history of the Black Heritage Army to a prospective member, step back while his or her adrenaline rose, and behold the prospect of membership becoming more and more invigorating to that individual.

"Oh, I don't know, Reggie." Colonel Ballard leaned back from his desk and looked straight into Major Henderson's eyes. "I really don't think that the Black Heritage Army is for me. It's not that I don't appreciate the struggle that our people have been through; it's just that I don't think that more segregation is the answer."

He paused as if giving it more consideration, then shook his head from side to side. "Thanks for letting me know about it, though. You can be assured that I won't share this with anyone—black or white."

It was clear that Colonel Ballard fell into the first group of potential recruits, those who were skeptical, so Henderson knew that he would have to tread lightly until the time was right. No matter. He had planted the seed—and for now, that's all he had hoped to accomplish.

"Very well, sir. I'd like to leave a little early just to check on Rockson, if that's all right." The major stood and saluted Colonel Ballard, waiting for his response.

"Of course, Reggie. Let me know if there is anything I can do to help." Ballard stood, returned the salute, and watched his friend of more than five years walk out the door.

* * *

Major Henderson hopped into his ten-year-old pickup truck and began to make his way to the detention center. It seemed that everything in the cab rattled with every bump in the road. He had to fight the steering wheel, moving it left to right, just to keep the truck moving straight ahead. The crack in the windshield had been partially blocking his view for months.

Based on what he had just heard from Colonel Ballard, this was definitely a case of racism, in his opinion. The thought of another meaningless act—especially if directed toward Rockson and his friends—was more than he could stand. His temper began to build. He turned the steering wheel slightly left and then right, keeping the truck on track, shifting the gear lever with authority.

Reggie's mind shifted to the ultimate goal of the Black Heritage Army. He contemplated whether now was the time to launch the takeover operation. His anger built. His frustration rose to a level that clouded his thought processes. *Is now the time? Are we ready enough to succeed? Will our members be ready to support the decision?*

The brakes squealed and Major Henderson's truck came to a stop in the officers' reserved parking stall. The detention center was a small structure featuring a more modern design than most buildings on post had. He jumped out of his truck, slammed the door behind him, and checked in with the security guard, who took him to the holding cell.

Rockson, Daemon, and Michael were sitting quietly in their combined cell when Major Henderson arrived. They quickly but silently stood and came to attention as they noticed the major walking down the dimly lit hallway to where they were being held. There was a somber feeling in the air.

"At ease, men." Major Henderson turned and nodded to the military police officer as a sign of dismissal. Then he watched as the MP exited the hallway and disappeared from view. The major looked around carefully to make sure that no one else was within range of the conversation he was about to have. Once he was sure no one would overhear, he asked his three friends, "What the hell happened this morning?"

All three men began venting their frustration almost in unison, getting louder and louder as they tried to talk over one another. Rockson, in particular, was still so agitated that every other word was an expletive—

"Damn it, soldiers! Shut your pieholes!" Major Henderson's tone demonstrated the side of his character that explained why he was the leader of the Black Heritage Army. He could be very firm when the situation called for it.

"Now we don't have much time to screw around here. In thirty seconds or less I want to know what the hell happened, and I want to hear it from just one of you. Rockson, you look like you need to sit down and cool off. Pull yourself together, man. Daemon, I want *you* to fill me in."

Major Henderson clenched his teeth with frustration and a hint of rage, his mind reeling with possibility, as Daemon began to describe the events leading up to their detainment. Reggie was especially angered by the fact that Sergeant Peterson and the other soldiers who had started the fight were part of General Charlie Street's inner circle. Street was their base commander.

There was an eerie silence that lasted for more than a few minutes after Daemon had explained the whole situation. Major Henderson was searching through his mind for the answers that he needed. The Black Heritage Army had been preparing and planning for years, but he didn't think that it would come to this—not this soon, at least. The more he pondered the situation before him, and the more he considered the readiness of their organization, the more he realized that this was the time to act.

The Black Heritage Army had secretly been planning for the day when they would take over the South—reclaim the land that their ancestors, wearing chains, had first landed on. They simply wanted to take back what they felt was rightfully theirs. After all, it was *their* people who had built this land. *They* were the ones who literally broke their backs and gave their lives to build the plantations and clear the land for farming in early America.

Their people were the ones who built the entire nation's economy by farming crops that generated millions of dollars for the landowners, created jobs, and put America on the global map. It was the hard work of the early African Americans that funded the war for independence from Great Britain. In fact, if not for them, the United States may not be a sovereign nation at all. These were a few of the basic tenets that made up the core of the Black Heritage Army.

Major Henderson slowly looked into the eyes of Michael, then Daemon, and finally stared at Staff Sergeant Rockson. "Tonight's the night that Operation Freedom Reign begins," he said softly. "I will call an emergency meeting of the Black Heritage Army right away. I'll be back here to get you out before midnight."

The three men looked at each other almost in a state of shock. "Operation Freedom Reign" was the code name given to the ultimate sacrifice that the Black Heritage Army could make. They had talked about this in their meetings for years now, but no one had ever truly considered that it might actually happen.

As Rockson pondered the situation, he began to feel that maybe this was the right thing to do—and the right time to do it. In fact, the more he considered the possibilities, the more he felt honored to be a part of history, a history that would shape the future of this country and of his people.

More important, once his sense of responsibility returned, the desire, ever present in the background, to return to a gang mentality left him once again. He could see things clearly once more, and he was more than just a little excited about the prospect of what they could accomplish.

Daemon and Michael looked on, partly in awe, partly in disbelief, as Staff Sergeant Rockson stood and then saluted Major Henderson with a brisk snap. "Yes, sir!"

Major Henderson took a deep breath, returned the salute, and walked away without a word. He continued out of the building with a sense of purpose that he had never before experienced. The excitement was almost overwhelming. The time had finally come, and he was at the center of it all.

African Americans everywhere would soon find the freedom that they had been dreaming of for generations. The Black Heritage Army was strong and well organized, and its members were dedicated to each other. The chances of succeeding with Operation Freedom Reign had never been better, and Major Henderson knew it.

This would be a night that no one would forget.

CHAPTER 4
Understanding

The late-afternoon thunderstorms were beginning to form as Colonel Ballard parked his car at the main headquarters building. He could smell the humidity and the prerain air moving into the area. There was something comforting about this type of day for Ron Ballard, as knowing that rain was moving in created a serene feeling and gave rise to thoughts of spending time inside with his kids while watching logs burn in the fireplace.

He jogged up the flight of stairs to the second floor and then made his way down the hall leading to General Street's office.

"Hi, Betty. Is the general available?"

"Just a minute, sir, while I check." General Street's administrative assistant responded smugly before standing up and moving from behind her desk ever so slowly. She paused just outside the general's office, then slipped through the narrow opening of the door.

Colonel Ballard could hear Betty whispering to the general, but he couldn't make out the details. Then suddenly the quiet was interrupted.

"Of course I'm available!" General Street's booming voice could be heard through his partially closed door as he spoke with a chuckle. "Especially when it's my old friend Ron Ballard! Get your ass in here, Colonel Ballard!"

Betty looked over her reading glasses at Colonel Ballard with a bit of a scowl as she exited the general's office and made room for him to enter. She pointed her nose in the air, closed the door, and strutted her way back to the metal desk where she had toiled away for several years, at every beck and call of her boss, General Street.

Colonel Ballard watched her close the door behind him. "How are you, sir?" he said calmly with a smile as he turned toward General Street and stepped farther into the large room.

It was a lavishly decorated space with cherrywood paneling, fine furniture that brought back thoughts of a very expensive southern plantation home, and a multitude of awards carefully framed in an attempt to create even more awe than each deserved. Military achievement medals and letters of commendation, also neatly framed, were carefully hung on the walls in the oversized space that General Street used as his office.

"Oh, drop the 'sir' crap, Ron. How the hell are ya, ol' buddy?"

"Fine, Charlie, just fine. How are you?"

"Same old crap, Ron. I've got a dipstick young West Point commander that thinks he knows everything about runnin' a frickin' military company based on a bunch of crap he read in an outdated war manual, a manual that was written over a century ago, mind you. And it doesn't help that a bunch of idiot instructors—who've never seen combat, mind you—have made him think that he's the next coming of good ol' General Eisenhower." Street shook his head in dismay and meandered toward a fully stocked bar located at the other end of the room.

"General Ike knew what the hell he was doin'. I wish we still had that old-school attitude in this man's army." He paused for a moment, looked at the wall in front of him, and shook his head back and forth ever so slightly, reminiscing of another point in time. "Anyway, what are ya drinkin' this afternoon, Ron?"

"Nothing for me, Charlie. Thanks anyway."

"Yeah … right. Same old Colonel Ron Ballard, always on the straight and narrow—'high and tight.' Never steps out of line, always right in step with what the top brass want out of him—a perfect soldier in every way." Street chuckled as he sarcastically teased his friend. "You haven't changed a bit since military school, you ol' son of a bitch."

"You know me, Charlie. I'm going to keep doing everything I can to catch up with you in rank." He pushed a sly smile in General Street's direction.

"You've had a couple of good promotions, Ron—and you know that everyone 'round here's got a lot of respect for ya, my friend."

"Well, my uniform has changed a little bit, I guess—the collars are a little heavier." This was another age-old army saying that referred to being promoted. It arose because a new rank insignia was figuratively heavier than the one previous when pinned on one's collar. The colonel reached up and pinched the insignia pinned to his own collar as he contemplated the fact that he and the general had graduated from the same class, at the same rank, nearly seventeen years ago.

General Street, who knew Colonel Ballard very well after all these years, understood the underlying message his friend had just laid out: that Ron was only a colonel, whereas Street had obtained the rank of general during the same amount of time. Street knew that decisions like rank and promotions went beyond pure performance measures, especially when being applied to the more senior officer ranks. Very early in his military career, he had managed to get accepted by the group of men who *really* held control of the army. He was now a part of their inner circle.

This was a private club of sorts, and one that had survived generations of soldiers and countless wars. This small group of white, elitist officers had managed to keep their organization so private that it was written off as a rumor any time it was brought up, which is the case to this very day.

Getting into the club was nearly impossible, as membership was normally reserved for the sons, nephews, or other relatives of previous members. The secrecy and mystique around this unnamed group would easily rival that of the Knights Templar of Freemason lore, even if only within military circles.

Although he had no family or other connection to this group, General Street had demonstrated his rigid ideal of how the army should be run and his white supremacist views, which is why he was eventually invited to join the club that even he had thought was only a fairy tale at the time. He realized that at some point he must have voiced one of his extremist opinions to just the right person, and at just the right time, in order to be invited in and accepted.

Exactly how his membership had come about didn't really matter. For him it was an honor to be a member. His membership created an air of confidence in him from knowing that he always had the power of this organization behind him to support his every decision. Just as important, and because he was now a member, he knew that his son would have the inside track to membership, and an elite position in the army as well, assuming that's what he wanted, of course. And the Street family would always have a certain level of protection, regardless of whether any of them ever joined the military themselves.

Without question, General Charlie Street had done well for himself and was clearly established as an up-and-comer. In fact, many members of the elite inner circle he belonged to thought that General Street was made of the perfect material for a career in politics. The group had been coaching him recently to prepare him for a higher level of authority, making every effort to ensure that he would be ready when the time came. More important to them and their cause, they were grooming him to support their elitist views and policies.

Not wanting to let on that racism very well could be behind the difference in rank between him and Colonel Ballard, General Street could only try to avoid the impending conversation by sheepishly changing the topic. "How are Katherine and the kids, Ron?"

"Fine, Charlie, just fine, thanks."

"Oh, all right, Ballard, something's botherin' ya—I can always tell by your short little deadpan answers. What the hell is it? Let's get it out in the open."

"You heard about the altercation that happened over at the motor pool today, General?"

"Yeah, I think so. If we're talking about the same thing, that's where a couple of the bad ones got outta line an' Captain Lancaster took care of 'em."

"A couple of the bad ones, Charlie? What the heck do you mean by that?"

"Oh, come on, Ron. You know damn well what I mean. You know, a coupla the boys that the damn judges sent us."

The general's slight southern drawl now became more pronounced as his own frustration began to build. "Bad kids. Rap sheet as long as your damn arm. Kids are in and outta trouble all the time, in front the judge so much they start to call him Daddy. Problem is, these damn youth detention centers and minimum-security prisons are too damn full to take all of 'em in. Lazy government court system sends 'em to you and me to take care of. 'Fix 'em,' they say. 'Straighten 'em out.' All that these kids do is come in here with no respect for authority. They screw everything up for the good ones."

Colonel Ballard paused for a minute to keep himself from losing his cool and confronting Street in the way that he truly wanted to. Always able to control his emotions, and having an uncanny ability to slow down and think clearly in any situation, he took in a deep breath and turned away from General Street just a little bit so that he could gather his thoughts.

He also had to remember that Charlie was not just a friend; he was the commanding officer, and someone whom Ron had to treat with the respect that his superior's rank commanded. It seemed to him that Charlie's comments bordered on racism, but that would be a very difficult topic to bring up under the circumstances, even if he considered Charlie Street to be a friend.

Finally, after a few seconds of contemplation, Colonel Ballard thought of a tactful way to bring up what he believed to be the real topic at hand. He looked back toward the general accusingly and found the courage to speak his mind. His voice cut through the tension that was starting to build in the room after what seemed like several minutes of silence.

"It just so *happens* that these 'bad ones' are black. Is that right, Charlie?"

General Street was now facing away from Ballard and staring at one of his many medals of commendation hanging on the wall. He slowly set his glass of seventeen-year-old scotch down on the bar stand as his anger began to build even more. Here he was, a general, listening to a comment like that from a lower-ranking officer, with an accusatory tone to it, no less. General Street had always had a soft spot in his heart for Colonel Ballard, even though the latter was a black man. He didn't know exactly why, but he did—and to his friends or in public, he hated to admit it.

He took a deep breath and forced himself to remember whom he was dealing with—an old friend who had helped him before when he had needed it the most. He intentionally reduced his anger to a more manageable level, which was one of frustration, frustration in what he believed to be a misunderstanding—more specifically, frustration at being misunderstood. At least that's what he wanted Colonel Ballard to think it was, just a simple misunderstanding.

"Ron, I think that you and I have been through too much for you to accuse me of being a racist." General Street was still looking away from his friend, still staring at the wall. It was hard for him to lie to Ron if looking into his eyes, and he knew that Colonel Ballard would see right through him if they made eye contact.

Colonel Ballard felt a streak of guilt pass over him as he ran left his hand over the back of his neck, which he often did when faced with a confusing situation. Although cool under fire, Ron Ballard was the type of man who regularly second-guessed his intuition. It was almost as though his mind had been trained to see things the way that others wanted him to see them. Many times, his intuition, his heart, his gut feelings, had been relegated to obscurity as his well-trained mind took over. Candidly, he preferred to listen to his internal voice of reason, if for no other reason than it helped avoid confrontation, which he was never a fan of.

But now he was confused. Surely his old friend of many years, good ol' Charlie Street, was not a racist. After all, Ron was black, and he and Charlie had been together from the start: military school, offi-cers' corps—they'd even been in combat together. Heck, it was Charlie who used to defend Ron when the others—whites who were openly racist—would try to demean and belittle him! At least it seemed that way at the time.

Besides, this man's army was not like it used to be when he first joined. The lines between black and white had all but been erased, hadn't they? Now a majority of the men and women in the armed forces were black, and he knew that for a fact. There was no racism anymore; there couldn't possibly be, could there?

But what had he seen earlier in the day? Again, Ron's well-trained mind overpowered his intuition and instinct, which caused him to rub the back of his neck in contemplation once more. He was trying to rationalize everything in his mind, attempting to convince himself—one more time—that everything was all right and that he was making more of the situation he had seen earlier in the day than it deserved.

"Charlie, I'm sorry." Colonel Ballard began with an apologetic tone as he let out a deep breath, once again giving in to his more logical side. "I guess I'm just a little disappointed, and maybe even confused, by what I saw this morning."

General Street grabbed his drink and turned around with a sheepish smile, knowing that he had just pulled a fast one on his old buddy. He walked around his desk to sit behind it one more time. "Whaddya mean, 'what you saw,' Ron? Tell me what the hell this is all about. Is the fight you saw botherin' ya? Shoot, these boys are fightin' all the time around here. You know that as much as anyone."

"This time wasn't like the others, Charlie. Earlier today I saw white against black—not just soldier fighting soldier—"

"And it has been taken care of, Ron!" General Street began to get agitated again. "Captain Lancaster had the boys that started this whole mess detained, from what I'm told, and I'm sure he'll have a detailed report for us to look at soon enough."

The general took another deep breath, finished his drink, and quickly stood up. Ice rattled in the empty glass as he used his hand to motion toward Ballard, wanting to put an end to their conversation. "Now shouldn't you be gettin' home to that beautiful wife of yours?"

Colonel Ballard felt the chair legs resist as they slid against the carpet while the chair moved back, allowing him to stand slowly. He smiled somewhat sheepishly and reached across the desk to shake the general's hand, knowing that he had just been dismissed. "Yeah, Charlie. I guess I should be."

As they made their way toward the door, Ballard stopped one more time and looked at his old friend Charlie with his usual sincere and comforting smile. "By the way, Charlie, how are Belle and the kids?"

"Just great! You know, we leave for our vacation tonight—two weeks on the water just off of the New England shore. In fact, it's just Belle and me this time. The kids are stayin' with the daughter of some friends of ours here on the base."

"That's great, Charlie. I hope you guys have a good time."

"Always do, Ron, always do. You know, I've always said that maybe I should have been a sailor."

"Right, Charlie." Ballard smiled. "That's just what your staff would need, an overly energetic general cooped up on a boat somewhere and stuck in the middle of the ocean!"

"Are you sayin' that I'm too high-strung to be trapped on a boat for too long?"

"Charlie, you're too high-strung to be stuck in any one place for too long!"

"Yeah, I suppose you're prob'ly right, my friend."

The men looked at each other for a moment, chuckling at the conversation.

"Take care of yourself while I'm gone, Ron—and when I get back, let's get Belle and Katherine together with us for a nice dinner out. It's been a while, and I think it would be great for us to have a little fun together."

"Sounds good, Charlie. Let's plan on that for certain."

"You got it, Ron." General Street placed his left hand on Colonel Ballard's right shoulder, gently turning him toward the door.

Colonel Ballard pulled the office door open and paused for a minute, not sure if he should turn around and force his original concern with General Street back into the conversation. He shook his head as he thought better of it. He stepped out of the office and back into the greeting room, where he winked and smiled at Betty as he left—trying to soften her up a little bit. But judging by the scowl on her face, which appeared to be permanent, it didn't work. He chuckled to himself, realizing that nothing could likely soften Betty's scowl. *Too bad,* he thought. *It's too bad that anyone should be that unhappy.*

He paused at the door of the building, lamenting the fact that he had forgotten his umbrella, and watched the rain steadily fall outside. He took a deep breath, threw open the door, and made a dash for his glossy black BMW, raindrops beading off the overwaxed paint in every direction.

He slipped into the car as quickly as he could and fired up the engine. The leather seat squeaked beneath him from the rainwater on his uniform as he got himself adjusted and turned on the wipers. He reached back to rub the back of his neck one more time as he thought about all that had just happened in General Street's office.

What exactly had he seen earlier? Was it racism? His intuition told him that Captain Lancaster had intentionally singled out the black soldiers for disciplinary action when it could have been the white soldiers that had started the whole scuffle. Or was it? Maybe he hadn't seen enough of what happened. Maybe General Street was right—it was simply a matter of a few bad kids having a little disagreement, regardless of race or color.

Ballard continued to wrestle with the conflict between his intuition and what he was being told to believe. *Maybe it wasn't black or white but was just another juvenile skirmish,* he thought to himself, trying to justify what he had seen earlier in the day and, thereby, somehow convince himself that there was nothing to worry about.

He didn't like dealing with issues like this, or anything that could be considered negative for that matter. It had always been his preference to live on the lighter side of life, to push negative thoughts or challenging situations to the back of his mind so that he could maintain a more carefree demeanor.

He turned on his lights, placed the gear selector in reverse, and carefully backed out of the parking stall. He took a deep breath and began to relax as he started to make his way through the beautiful old military base that he and his family had called home for so many years now. With rain steadily falling on his windshield, the wiper blades slowly tried to keep up in an almost mesmerizing rhythm.

Colonel Ballard stared across the perfectly manicured lawns and looked past the large, old oak trees standing in stately rows along the road. He admired the grandeur of the plantation-style buildings erected nearly one hundred years ago.

As he looked on, he noticed a small group of trainees laughing and teasing each other, trying to take cover from the rain. He remained stopped at the intersection longer than he needed to, squinting through the side window that was wet from the rain, which distorted his view outside. He continued to watch the soldiers, who were making no attempt to get out of the rain at this point. Soaking wet, they, or so it looked, thought it more fun to stay in the rain. They held their arms straight out to their sides as they spun in circles, their faces pointed straight into the air, trying to catch every raindrop.

Checking his rearview mirror to confirm that no one was behind him, he turned his attention back to the young soldiers, now dancing in the rain. His eyes started adjusting to the distorted view when he noticed that three of the soldiers were white and two of them were black. Each of them was clearly enjoying the others' company, getting along just fine and seemingly oblivious to race or color.

A wry smile appeared on Ballard's face. "The general's right," he mumbled to himself. "It was obviously just an isolated case of fighting, not racism."

Instantly, everything felt right in the world once again. Ron Ballard's well-trained mind had found a way to win out over his instinct and intuition one more time. Where some people might have continued to struggle with their emotions, he chose not to, because accepting the world in the way that others wanted him to meant that he was able to fall back into his preferred state of mind—casual, relaxed, and positive.

He turned the music up, settled back into the soft leather seat of his well-kept BMW, let his foot off of the brake pedal, and accelerated through the intersection. *"Let's Get It Started."* He mumbled to himself, referring to the song by the Black Eyed Peas now playing on the radio. "I love this song." Colonel Ron Ballard slowly sat back and began to relax as he made his way home, singing along with the music.

CHAPTER 5
Realization

The Ballard household was a busy one.

Young John Ballard was the spitting image of his father—handsome, articulate, and well liked by everyone. Although he was only in the fifth grade, his strength and athleticism were obvious; he seemed years ahead of the other kids in his class, and in every way. Also, like his father, John always seemed to have a smile on his face. He appeared as though nothing could negatively impact his strong sense of self. He was very confident, but not cocky or conceited in any way—just a genuine, likable, energetic boy.

Being mature beyond his years, he would often be observed encouraging other students when they needed it most, standing up for kids who couldn't always stand up for themselves, and just generally lifting the attitude of everyone around him. He was a natural-born leader.

His younger sister, Elizabeth, was as beautiful as her mother. Quiet, but deep thinking, young Elizabeth was admired by all of her school instructors as the one student capable of achieving great success, and by her peers as the one person they would most like to be around. Elizabeth had always looked up to her brother with respect, and to her father with the kind of admiration that bordered on idol worship.

She and her brother would often overhear the way that other adults would rave about their father—what a great person he was, one who was always willing to help others around him—which left both of them with the indelible impression that their dad could do no wrong.

Ron's wife, Katherine, never went back to work after the birth of their eldest, John. That was just over ten years ago. And although John and Elizabeth were at school for most of the day, Katherine kept her time occupied by volunteering at the various organizations that supported noncommissioned soldiers and their young families. Katherine had always enjoyed the camaraderie that living on a military base offered—the sense of community, caring, and giving to people in need.

She also knew that they were blessed to be on the commissioned, or officers', side of the army. Of course, an officer's pay was significantly better that that of a noncommissioned soldier, but more important to Katherine was the way in which the officer's lifestyle gave them the opportunity to help others in a very real way.

Because both Ron and Katherine had come from such humble beginnings, they would never lose sight of the challenges they once faced and would forever remember living paycheck to paycheck while Ron was in military school. Oftentimes there hadn't been enough money to pay the bills or even put food on the table, but Ron was dedicated to serving in the United States Army back then, just as he was now. More important, being a leader in the army was meaningful to Ron because it gave him the chance to have a positive impact on others. A natural coach and motivator, Ron had the ability to make others not only feel good about themselves but also want to achieve more.

He also had the extraordinary ability to guide others in such a way that they could see the benefit of working harder to improve their situation. Then, he would do everything in his power to help that individual succeed.

Very early in their relationship, Katherine embraced the same philosophy of helping others, which is why she was such an active part of the military community. She was especially focused on their local base, Fort Benning, where she helped many a young enlisted family who were new to the military to find comfort and a place to fit into the army way of life, which was a very different culture, and unique in many ways that civilians couldn't possibly understand.

Anyone could sense the excitement building in the Ballard household as the kids prepared for the daily arrival of their father, Colonel

Ron Ballard. Ron had started a fun game with John and Elizabeth a few years ago, when they were old enough to actively participate, and it was a ritual that had become the highlight of their day. This day would be no different.

Daddy walked through the front door with a smile. He gently hung his hat on the rack after he quietly set down his briefcase. Then the hunt would begin. As the warm smell of Katherine's dinner permeated the entire house, Ron would begin the task of trying to find little John and Elizabeth as part of their nightly game of hide-and-seek.

There was a time when the task was easy for Ron—the children would invariably hide in the same place when they were younger. Lately, the game had become something completely different and a bit more challenging.

He slowly crept through the house, opening closet doors quickly and peeking behind furniture. "Where are my little monsters?" Ron checked under the table in their formal dining room. "Honey!" he yelled into the kitchen, intentionally loud enough for John and Elizabeth to hear, "Didn't we have two children when I left for the office this morning?"

"Gosh, I think so, Ronnie. Maybe they have decided to leave the family." Katherine's voice from the kitchen could be heard.

"Or maybe they just simply disappeared." Ron stood tall once again and casually walked into the living room as he yelled into the kitchen. "Either way, they're out of our hair for good! Maybe now we can get on with our lives—"

"Daddy!" Almost in unison, two excited voices yelled as John and Elizabeth leapt from their hiding places, immediately falling for the new strategy that Ron had applied to their game.

"Daddy, you can't live without me and Johnny. Who would take care of you and Mommy?" As usual, young Elizabeth was thinking of someone other than herself.

"Of course your mom and I couldn't live without you—we would get way too much sleep and would have to deal with being in an overly good mood all the time." Ron looked into his daughter's eyes as the sarcasm rolled off of his voice. He collected a big hug from Elizabeth and then looked to his son, John.

"Hey, Dad, wazzup?" John raised his hand to give his father a high five.

"'Wazzup'? Who taught you to talk like that? Is that what I pay all that money to have them teach you in school?"

"Aw, Dad, everybody talks like me; that's just the way things are. Gee, it's not the 1990s anymore. You're just all outta touch, that's all!" John rolled his eyes at his father. He was starting to show more of an "I know more than you do" attitude toward both of his parents now that he was getting older, but it was always with a smile and always with respect.

Ron picked up Elizabeth and placed his hand on John's shoulder as he led the two children into the dining room. "Well, go wash your hands and start setting the table for your out-of-touch parents, won't you, John?"

"Can I help John tonight, Daddy?"

"I don't know, Elizabeth. Do you really think you're ready for the responsibility of handling the dishes?"

"Yes, Daddy, I am!"

"Then wash up and ask John what would be the best way for you to help him, okay?"

"Aw-right! John! John! Daddy says I get to help tonight!" Elizabeth's voice faded as she and John disappeared upstairs to wash their hands and get ready for dinner.

Colonel Ron Ballard made his way into the kitchen, stood behind his beautiful wife as she prepared dinner at the stove, and gently wrapped his arms around her waist. He carefully leaned forward and kissed her on the cheek as he held her close. "Just exactly how did you get to be so beautiful?"

"Same way you got to be so handsome." Katherine slowly laid down her cooking spoon and turned to face her husband. All the while his arms never left her waist. They gently kissed and fell into a warm embrace, then leaned back slightly so they could gaze at each other. They knew each other well enough, and at a much deeper level, than did most married couples, such that they could feel how the other was doing by simply looking into each other's eyes for a moment—almost reading the other's thoughts.

Their corresponding looks confirmed that each of them had had a pretty good day. Ron stole one more quick kiss. As he pulled away, he quickly grabbed the spoon off of the counter and began to poke at what was cooking. "What's for dinner tonight anyway? I hope it's good this time."

Katherine lightly slapped Ron on his upper back and retorted, "You're terrible! You should be lucky I cook for you at all with what you've put me through over all these years—cookin', cleanin', raisin' yo' babies. Boy, you better change your tone around here." As with any Ballard family member, Katherine, as she teased her husband in return, never allowed the smile to leave her face.

The sound of feet pounding their way down the stairs echoed in concert with the thunderstorm outside. John and Elizabeth rushed back into the dining room and began to lay out the silverware and dishes very carefully. They relished every chance to take on a task or a new responsibility, and they were always careful to do the best job they possibly could.

They wrapped up their assignment by coaching each other along the way—teamwork at its finest—and then took their seats at the table with Ron. Katherine brought in the meal. Every serving dish had that wonderful home-cooked smell, and the added visual of warm steam floating above.

Ron could faintly hear the cool rain falling against the house now as he looked on and smiled at his family, thinking of how comfortable, and how wonderful, their life had become. Even still, his mind slipped back to work for a moment: it seemed to him that his promotions were easier to come by years ago. He hadn't been considered for one in quite some time, whereas friends of his—friends like Charlie Street—continued to gain recognition and were rewarded as such.

"Okay, everyone, time to hold hands." Ron shook his head slightly to break his own negative thoughts.

The energy in the Ballard home mellowed for just a few minutes each night when Ron offered up the mealtime prayer. "Heavenly Father, please bless this meal we are about to receive. Thank you for the many blessings you have bestowed upon this family, and please help each of us find the courage to reach out and help those who are less fortunate than ourselves. Amen."

As usual, any calm that had belonged to the night air before dinner was immediately tossed aside as the Ballard family began their animated nightly ritual of talking about their day.

John was anxious to share his accomplishments on the baseball field that day. Katherine talked of her latest concerns regarding the lack of assistance available to the new recruits that she was mentoring. Elizabeth spoke of nothing other than her girlfriends and the latest issues regarding the boys in her class until, all at once, she remembered to ask a nagging question that she had struggled with for most of the day.

"Mommy, what does 'nigger' mean, exactly?"

Suddenly, all conversation came to a roaring halt and absolute silence fell over the dining room.

Young John's eyes grew big. He was old enough to know what that word meant and the negative way in which it was used. He also knew that posing a question like that would bring their usual, fun-filled evening dinner to an end. More important, he knew better than to say anything. His maturity let him know that this was a situation for the grown-ups—there was no way that he was going to chime in with his own opinions.

Katherine looked at her husband in disbelief, not knowing at all what to say or how to respond to their daughter. The ever-calm and stoic Ron Ballard sensed this, so he gave her a reassuring look and a gentle nod in response. He took a deep breath and carefully picked the words he would use to ease the tension in the room and to reassure his innocent little girl. "*Nigger* can mean a lot of different things, honey. Where did you hear that word?"

"Today at school," little Elizabeth responded with a light-hearted tone, reaffirming the idea that she didn't fully understand the word nor the way it had been used against her. "That's what Meagan called me when she didn't like what I was doing at recess today."

Katherine still dumbfounded, was beginning to become angry, but she was somehow able to participate in the conversation after hearing the last part of what Elizabeth had said. "What in the world were you doing that would cause her to call you that, Elizabeth—"

"That's not important now, Katherine." A mixture of anger and concern was beginning to build for both parents as Ron tried to bring more clarity the situation. "Elizabeth, *nigger* is a very, very bad word that is sometimes used as a bad name to call black people specifically. Now, it doesn't matter *at all* what you did to this girl Meagan on the playground today. She had—and absolutely no one else has—no right to call you a nigger, ever. *Ever.* Do you understand, sweetheart?"

"Yes, Daddy." Elizabeth's voice cracked since she didn't know how else to respond to her dad's stern response. She could tell that he was angry—an emotion her father rarely let show—and she was concerned that maybe he was mad at her.

"Good. Now, it's very important that we do whatever we can to make sure that this is resolved properly and that Meagan also learns to understand what that name means." Ron sensed Elizabeth's fear, so he gathered himself, smiled gently, and resumed the tone that his kids were more familiar with. "Can you tell me Meagan's last name? Or maybe who her daddy is?"

"*Daddy-y-y.*" Relieved that her dad wasn't mad at her, Elizabeth was able to giggle slightly in her response. "You *know* who Meagan is. Her name is Meagan Street. You know her daddy. He's your general friend, Mister Street."

Ron took another deep breath and leaned back in his chair, which creaked slightly. He slid his hands down the edges of the table, loosening his frustrated grip. The anger started to build rather slowly as he contemplated all that had just transpired and the underlying possibilities. Then he noticed that his family were still staring at him, looking for an answer or a suggestion for what to do next. With the exception of Elizabeth, they could see that this was a big issue. *Don't let them know what you're thinking,* Ron thought as he took one more deep breath in an attempt to control his thoughts and conceal his anger.

"It's all right," he finally said aloud in his ever-calming tone. "Everyone just get back to eating your dinner. We can deal with this later, okay? I think we've all had a pretty tough day, and we should take this time to enjoy what's left of it. Don't you think?" He smiled.

As everyone quietly went back to eating their dinner, Ron Ballard began to consider the enormity of the issue placed before him. General Charlie Street, a man whom Ron thought had been his friend all of these years—someone whom he believed saw him for *who* he was, not for *what* he was or the color of his skin—a racist? How could that be? Obviously if his child was predisposed to using a term like *nigger* at the tender age of eight, then she was only emulating what she saw at home, following the example set by her parents.

Certainly, an eight-year-old child would not have been influenced in this way by her peers, or could she have been? This was a military base, a place where the majority of the population was black. *We had gotten past the issue of racism here, hadn't we?* This just didn't seem right. Meagan Street must have gotten her views from her parents. Her father. Ron's best friend. But still, it just didn't make sense.

As he chewed his food and stared in silence across the dining room, Ron Ballard began to remember his childhood in the Deep South. He remembered living with his parents and grandparents in a beaten-up old shack of a house. Back then, he was LaRon Ballard—his given name. He had been named after an ancestor who had fought bravely to overcome slavery more than 150 years previous.

Flashing through Ron's mind now were vivid memories, but with anonymous characters, of white men beating black people; crosses burning in the neighbor's yard; and the night the church the Ballard family attended was burnt to the ground. The events seemed very clear, but the details, the names of the people involved, and the ultimate outcomes were all very faint. Was it possible that he was blocking the details of his childhood so that the events themselves would somehow seem less real?

His mind turned to the events of the morning when Rockson and his friends had been detained. Ron came across the altercation after it had started, but now, looking back on it, he was confident that he had witnessed an act of racism. He suddenly realized he had been made to believe that it was simply a disagreement initiated by black soldiers, but now he knew better. Damn, he should have been more firm with General Street when he had the chance.

His mind then turned back to his career and his promotions, or lack thereof. His career *had* to be impacted by his race and by racism in general. He and Charlie Street were about the same age, had attended the same schools and the same well-recognized military academy, and had fought together, side by side—hell, they even attended the same career coaching classes—yet Charlie Street was a general and Ron was only a colonel. Now it seemed undeniable that Ron Ballard had been passed over for promotion because of his race and only because of his race.

In an instant, it all became very clear, everything. For the first time—possibly the first time in his life—Ron Ballard knew what he had to do. Convincingly his instinct—his intuition—had won out over his logical mind once and for all. The training, the indoctrination, the brainwashing that his mind had endured over the years, was pushed to the back of his mind as everything all at once became very, very clear to him.

Ron—no, _LaRon_—Ballard knew exactly what he had to do, and he would begin first thing the following morning. It would start with his going back to using the name that his mother and father had given him. Years before, he had dropped the name LaRon and had started going by the more traditional name of Ron. At the time, he felt that it helped him to fit in better and that it made it easier for the other officers to accept him into their inner circle.

But now he could see just how wrong he was. Suddenly everything seemed much more clear; it was high time that he fought back, fought the mind-numbing way that white men and the white establishment had convinced him to believe that everyone in the army was on equal footing.

Right now, however, he was dead-set on getting the usual cheer and lightheartedness back into his family and household. Forcing his thoughts back to his beautiful family who sat around him, he pushed the negativity to the back of his mind once more.

"Hey, why is it so quiet in here? I want to get back to hearing about what happened with you guys today." Ron added his often-present smile to what he said, just to bring a sense of comfort and levity back into the room.

"Well, I was talking about the cool play I made at baseball practice today. It was awesome, Dad!" John could hardly hold back his excitement. "So the ball was hit right up the middle, but I ..."

The details of what John was saying began to fade into the background as Colonel LaRon Ballard brought his internal thoughts back to the issue at hand. There was so much that he wanted to do, so much he needed to say, so many regrets that he had now looking back on his past actions. He was so eager to take action that it would be hard for him to wait until morning, but he would have to.

First thing tomorrow, everything would be different for LaRon Ballard and his family—everything. He was going to make sure that his kids would both understand and appreciate the struggle that African Americans had been through. He would be tenacious in his approach and unwavering in his resolve to return to his roots and honor those who had gone before him.

This was no fleeting emotion. Colonel LaRon Ballard was ready to fight back, and he would start with finding Major Reggie Henderson so he could learn as much as possible about the Black Heritage Army.

CHAPTER 6
Time for Change

Colonel LaRon Ballard awoke that morning with a newfound sense of purpose. He lay in bed for a few moments and stared at the ceiling. He was trying to relive in his mind everything that had happened the day before, wondering whether the issues of racism that he had encountered were not as bad as he had originally thought. Maybe he had let his emotions get to him.

Unfortunately not; the issues were real.

The thoughts of all that had happened the previous day raced through LaRon's mind. He considered once again all of the missed promotions, each with a very convincing excuse offered at the time by his superior officer as to why others, such as Charlie Street, were moving up in rank while he himself was not. Each time that this had happened, he had convinced himself that none of it was due to race. He had allowed himself to believe that his superiors had held him back due to poor performance, or some similar reason— completely justifiable to him at the time.

LaRon grinned and shook his head slightly. Looking back on it, being overlooked for promotions while others around him continued to advance had been a Godsend. The situation had caused Colonel Ballard to work even harder on becoming the leader he wanted to be, and the type of leader he knew he was capable of being. He had studied more, exercised more often—he even attended classes on leadership through the University of Georgia's online MBA program.

What his superiors could not have known at the time is how their actions toward him had motivated LaRon to become a better soldier—and a better officer—than most in the US military. Colonel Ballard had worked hard to become a far more qualified general and leader than Charlie Street could ever dream of being. Ballard was well trained, educated, and prepared for the highest of leadership positions, and now he was both mentally and physically ready to be a great leader: if only presented with the right opportunity.

LaRon's mind went back to the reality of the situation around him, and how he had always allowed his conscious mind overcome his gut instinct and accept how the army had been treating him.

He saw things differently now, however. He thought back to the many, many times that he had experienced racism in his career but had brushed it off as paranoia or his imagination getting the better of him. He began to see the truth about many things for the first time—even the daughter of one of his best friends, Charlie Street, as it turned out, was using a racist term. This meant that Charlie had to be racist too, and LaRon had considered him to be one of his closest friends and confidantes up to this point.

He began to recall what Major Henderson had told him about the Black Heritage Army and their purpose. The more he considered their mission, the more he realized that he needed to become a member and contribute in any way possible. From this point forward, LaRon Ballard was going to embrace his roots; he was determined to stand up for his people, for what they believed in, and for their individuality. What he did not know was that the Black Heritage Army was more than just a political advocacy—but for now that didn't matter.

On this day, and possibly for the first time in his life, everything was crystal clear to Colonel LaRon Ballard. He jumped out of bed and quickly walked to the shower, energized and eager to start the day, ready to begin making changes in his life. He also felt a burning desire to positively impact the lives of other African Americans—and he was invigorated by the possibilities.

The steam from the shower started to fill the room. On any other day, LaRon would have taken his time and lingered under the hot water, using it to relax before setting out to take on the day's challenges. But this day was different. He raced through his shower, breaking with his normal routine. After that, he quickly shaved and made his way to the closet.

He had an extra bounce in his step today, motivated by the thought of a new beginning caused by his more accurate view of the world around him. The hangers screeched across the closet pole as he slid them from right to left, looking for the uniform that was sharpest. All of his uniforms were pressed, starched, and ready to impress, but this day was different.

He continued to rifle through the closet and finally found the one uniform that had the sharpest crease in the pants, the flattest collar, and the best contrast in camouflage colors. He placed it on the bed to wait for him while he grabbed his best pair of boots and polished them to an extra-bright shine.

Now fully dressed, Colonel Ballard stood in front of the mirror for a moment and admired himself. He felt ready to impress, so he gave his reflection an approving nod and walked out of the bedroom toward the kitchen. The first thing he noticed was that the usual hectic bustle of a weekday morning was nowhere to be found.

"Would you like a cup of coffee before you go, honey?"

"Sure," he said softly just before kissing Katherine for the first time that day. "What's going on? Where is everybody?"

"Oh, not to worry. The school called while you were in the shower and said that classes have been canceled today because of air-conditioning problems. They also asked that we all stay indoors and remain close to the phone because they might call if the school reopens. I told the kids that they could go back to bed."

"Air conditioner? Is it really supposed to be that hot today?"

"I don't know. I guess so."

"Well, I'll take this with me." LaRon reached for the lid to his travel mug. "I've got a lot to do, and I'm excited about it."

"Oh, really? Are you planning to let me in on your newfound excitement?"

"Later." LaRon grabbed his hat and briefcase before he made his way out the door. "I'll tell you all about it tonight."

The first thing that caught LaRon's attention as he walked outside was that it was sunny, bright, and warm. He took a deep, relaxing breath, his face pointing directly at the warm sun, and decided to lower the top on his convertible. At first, he didn't even pay attention to the eerie silence of his neighborhood, which was normally humming with the daily activities of an army base.

He backed into the street and began driving toward one of only two exits of the base housing development he lived in. As his eyes adjusted to the morning sun, he spotted a group of people in the road ahead, and a few military police vehicles with their emergency lights flashing.

Colonel Ballard approached the intersection slowly. He was waved to the side by a young military police officer. "Good morning, sir. May I ask where you are going?"

Colonel Ballard looked around and noticed that everyone leaving the neighborhood was systematically being pulled over and questioned.

"I am going to my office, young man. What is going on here?"

"Yes, sir. And where exactly is your office?"

Colonel Ballard thought it odd that the lower-ranking MP had just completely ignored his question and, no less, had the nerve to interrogate him about his destination. However, he patiently answered the question before scolding the young man. "I run the Equipment Issue Department. Just what exactly is this all about, Private?"

"Sir, you work with Major Henderson in equipment issue, is that right?" The young soldier immediately changed his tone and stood tall instead of leaning next to Colonel Ballard's car.

"At ease, son." Colonel Ballard had no idea what to think at this point. He stared at the young man quizzically. "Yes, that's right. Major Henderson and I have been working together and have been good friends for many years."

"Very good, sir! You may proceed, but please go directly to your office. Major Henderson has requested your presence there. He wanted me to tell you that this is an urgent matter."

The young man snapped to attention, waved his white glove motioning to allow Colonel Ballard to pass, and saluted LaRon's vehicle as it passed through the intersection.

LaRon pulled away slowly, trying to figure out just exactly what the hell was going on this morning. Everything seemed completely out of place, out of order, and different, but he couldn't quite put his finger on why. He glanced in his rearview mirror just in time to see the MPs pull a white officer out of his car, handcuff him, and place him in a jeep.

That's when it occurred to him—all of the MPs at the intersection were black! "No," he mumbled to himself and shook his head, "it's just a coincidence."

Still a little confused and sensing that the base was in a state of disarray, he sped up in an effort to get to his office as quickly as possible. He was anxious to find a place that was familiar to him, a place that would somehow let him know that this was just another typical morning at Fort Benning, Georgia. As important, he wanted to know what Major Henderson needed him for.

While he turned his car around the last corner before his destination, he was able to see his office in the distance and again noticed that something was strangely out of place. There were military combat vehicles—Humvees, personnel carriers, even tanks—everywhere. They surrounded his office building in a random fashion, and soldiers moved about everywhere.

That's when it hit him. The soldiers! Every single one of them was fully armed and in combat gear! The men at the intersection in his neighborhood, the men around his building, men walking throughout the base—all of them were armed!

His car came to a stop in the parking lot. Colonel Ballard was immediately surrounded by armed soldiers. His car door was pulled open quickly.

"Please step out of the vehicle with your hands in full view, sir." The young corporal had a very commanding tone and demeanor about him as he signaled to his men. "Thoroughly search the vehicle, and then park it inside."

"Is there some type of readiness drill going on or training exercise that I've not been made aware of?"

"What business do you have here?" As the other one had, this soldier completely ignored Colonel Ballard and replied with yet another question.

This caused LaRon to realize that this was no drill.

"I run this operation, Corporal." Colonel Ballard was growing impatient. "Just what the hell do—"

"All due respect, sir, but Major Henderson is our commanding officer now. He did tell us to look for you, though. Come with us, sir."

The corporal nodded to a soldier standing next to him, did an about-face, and began walking toward the building.

Colonel Ballard followed, but not without the gentle nudge of the other soldier, who was now behind him. The hand holding his weapon pressed into the small of the colonel's back.

As they made their way to Major Henderson's office, Colonel Ballard was both amazed and impressed with what he saw. A very well-disciplined, organized operation was under way. Everyone had a job to do and was very busy. The primary storage bay had been converted into a command center complete with the latest in technological and communications equipment. His quiet admiration of what was going on around him was interrupted.

"Sir!" The corporal came to attention and saluted Major Henderson, who was sitting at his desk. "Colonel Ballard, as you requested, sir!"

"Very good, Corporal. You're dismissed." Major Henderson also nodded to the accompanying soldier, who likewise stood at attention and saluted before doing an about-face and quickly stepping out of the room.

"What the hell is this all about, Reggie!?"

"Are you with us or against us, Colonel?" Major Henderson stood and made his way around the desk to get closer to the colonel.

"Excuse me?"

"I need to know if you are on our side or theirs!"

"Whose side, Reggie? Who are 'they,' and what is this all about?"

"Can't you see what has happened here, Ron—"

"That's *La*Ron, Reggie—and maybe you'd better enlighten me a little bit. Stop beating around the bush, and tell me what you have done." Colonel Ballard assumed control of the conversation out of frustration.

Major Henderson took a deep breath, walked behind the small conference table at the other end of his office, sat down, and leaned back in a chair. "Sit down for a minute, my friend."

Colonel Ballard took a deep breath to cool his emotions. Finally feeling comfortable enough to sit down as well, he dragged a nearby chair over and settled into it opposite Reggie, on the other side of the desk.

"LaRon, huh? I see that you may have rediscovered your roots, is that right?"

"Just get on with it, Reggie. It doesn't look like we have a lot of time to waste."

"It's the Black Heritage Army, Ron—I'm sorry, *La*Ron. Yesterday I wasn't sure if I should tell you the whole story. I wasn't sure if you were ready to deal with the reality of what our people have to face every day. In fact, I'm still not sure if you even consider yourself to be one of us."

Colonel Ballard still needed clarification. "By 'one of us,' you mean who, exactly?"

"I mean a black man, LaRon, and a proud member of the Black Heritage Army, someone who sees the racism around him for what it is, not for what the white man *wants* us to think it is. By saying 'one of us,' I mean someone who is willing to fight for our freedom—*real* freedom—not this lip-service world that they want us to believe in. I'm talking about the kind of freedom that our people deserve—the kind of freedom that we should have been given more than a hundred years ago."

"Reggie, we have freedom, don't we? I mean, sure, there is still racism in the world, but no one is standing over us telling us how to live our lives. You can buy a house, buy a car, and get a job just the same as anyone else, right?"

"That's not the point, LaRon. Don't you see that that's just not enough? Let's take your situation for example. You changed your name from LaRon to Ron just so that you would be more widely accepted in social circles."

Major Henderson was beginning to get agitated and had to reach deep down inside himself to communicate the beliefs that had been passed down to him by his father and by his father before him.

"Think about it, LaRon. They *do* tell us where to live, what kind of car to drive, and what kind of job we can have. It's simply more subtle now, and the problem is that they have fooled too many of us—including you! Look at yourself, man! Why are you still just a colonel and Charlie Street is a general? Why is it that you still don't feel comfortable on the officers' golf course or in the officers' club? Why do you still have to worry about what your children hear at school or how they are treated? Why isn't your wife invited to participate in organizations other than those involving black people or black children?"

Major Henderson had struck a nerve when he mentioned children. LaRon couldn't help but remember the feeling that had come over him last night at the dinner table, the mixed emotions of anger and fear, and the sorrow that filled his heart as he looked into the eyes of his little girl. She had faced just the first of many hard realities in life, which is exactly what LaRon himself had been thinking about since yesterday's events.

Reggie was right.

"I see your point, Reggie. In fact, my mission this morning was to come in here and talk to you more about the Black Heritage Army and how I might be able to get involved."

LaRon Ballard felt a huge burden leave him as he finally told someone else that he had experienced an epiphany of sorts and was no longer in the dark.

He continued speaking. "I still don't know what you are trying to accomplish here, though. What can we possibly do to effect a change on an entire nation? Furthermore, what's the answer to the issue of our freedom? What exactly do we want, and how do you expect to get it?"

"First of all, it's good to hear you talk this way, my friend. I've been worried about you for quite a long time."

Reggie Henderson didn't have to force the smile that came to his face. He knew full well that his organization needed a leader who was more capable than he was. Being a Founder, Reggie had learned a little bit about leadership as the Black Heritage Army grew in both size and strength, but he also knew his shortcomings.

To be successful in the long run, the Black Heritage Army needed a well-trained leader: a thoroughly trained leader that knows not only the tactical aspects of warfare, but someone who can also manage the complex political environment in the event of a conflict. They needed a more formally trained, polished leader than Reggie was capable of being, and for years he had thought that Colonel LaRon Ballard was just that man.

"Well, Reggie, to be honest, we had a pretty tough day at home yesterday. Turns out that Charlie Street's daughter called Elizabeth a nigger. After I heard that, something inside me just snapped. For the first time in a long time, I was able to see things more clearly."

LaRon stood now, impatient in his thought process. He needed to pace while talking. "Everything you just mentioned—the lack of promotions, the subtleties that have made me and Katherine feel uncomfortable, the fact that I never seem to get the level of respect from higher-ranking officers that I should—has invigorated me. I don't know exactly what to do next, but I know that I want to do something, *anything*, something that will make a change, make a difference—not just in my life but also in the lives of all those around me. You know how I am, Reggie. I want to help others by coaching them to success."

Ballard realized that he was beginning to ramble on a bit too much, so he paused for a moment and then returned to sit in the chair. "Sorry, my friend, but I'm genuinely excited about the possibilities."

"No problem! I get it, LaRon, believe me, I do! I have to say that I'm thrilled that you've reached this level of inspiration, because it ties in perfectly with I'm about to tell you. I think you'll be even more enthusiastic after you've heard what I'm about to share regarding the Black Heritage Army and what we have done here today.

"What I told you yesterday was only the beginning, the way the club got started. Since the time of our first meeting almost five years ago, the Black Heritage Army has evolved into much more than just a place for black people to meet and to discuss political issues. At one of the meetings, a small group pointed out that we have a significant amount of power, and force, right at our fingertips."

Reggie stood now and became more animated, gesturing with his hands at every opportunity to stress his points to LaRon.

"Don't you see? Collectively, we have access to nearly forty percent of the entire arsenal of the United States' armed forces! The southeastern states alone have over twenty-five military bases—army, air force, navy—hell, a full forty percent of the stateside fighting force can be found within a thousand miles of here!"

"Reggie, that's ridiculous," LaRon said, responding to this statement rather condescendingly. "Are you suggesting that the Black Heritage Army might take over the United States military?"

"That's exactly what I am saying! In fact, we—"

"Reggie, even if you could pull off something of that magnitude, what would you do with the power of the US military, go conquer a small part of Africa and return our people to their home?" Colonel Ballard was chuckling slightly at his own suggestion. The whole situation sounded so far-fetched to him that he actually began to see some humor in it.

"Don't you get it, LaRon?" Major Henderson leaned forward and placed his hands on the desk between them. He responded to Colonel Ballard sternly through clenched teeth. "That's *exactly* what we've done; in fact, it has already happened. The only difference is that we don't want to go take over some other country. We've already set the wheels in motion to take back part of *this* country, the southeastern United States."

LaRon could hardly believe what he was hearing. He swallowed hard, looked around him in a slight panic, and stood quickly. His first thought was of the safety of his own wife and kids. Then he considered the safety of everyone else involved—both white and black. He looked into Reggie's eyes with a combined look of concern, disbelief, and urgency. He turned and took one step toward the door before Reggie grabbed him by the arm.

"Damn it, LaRon, they're all right!" Reggie knew LaRon well enough to read his mind in this case. "Everyone's okay. It is not our intention to use force or to harm anyone unless we absolutely have to. Katherine and the kids especially—they're black, so they aren't even considered a threat to us. Unless someone were to lash out at one of our men with lethal force—and we both know that's not going to happen—everyone on base is perfectly safe. Just calm down and sit."

He motioned back to the chair in front of the desk, subtly directing LaRon to sit down again.

Colonel Ballard hesitated at first, but then his shoulders dropped slightly as the tension released. He then looked at Reggie with an approving grin and made his way back to the chair. He found that the entire scenario made him feel emancipated, free, energized, and more powerful. He sat down slowly before Reggie carefully strolled back to the other side of the desk and sat back down in his chair so that he could continue his debriefing.

"Effective at 0100 this morning, this military base was officially contained and placed under full quarantine. All communication lines, both inbound and outbound, have been cut, and only the people involved with our cause have been allowed to leave or reenter the base. We have effectively blocked or scrambled all cellular and radio transmissions other than those that we use to communicate with our own people at other military bases. Of course, we are also confiscating cell phones as we apprehend people who are not a part of our cause."

"Other military bases? Good God, Reggie, how were you able to pull this off?" Colonel Ballard could not believe what he was hearing. As more of the plan was unfolded to him, however, he became more and more a believer in the cause. He was excited at the prospect of what could be accomplished—if done right.

Something of a proud smile crossed the face of Major Henderson as he continued to relay all that the Black Heritage Army had accomplished in the last eight hours.

"Well, as you know, each of our military installations has always had the ability to scramble cell and radio communications in order to protect US assets in the event of war on our soil. The rest have been more of a challenge, but I'd like to think that we have a good plan in place.

"Remember yesterday, when I told you that this club has grown rather quickly? Well, I wasn't exaggerating. We have chapters at every base in the Southeast—Fort Gordon, Fort Campbell, Andrews Air Force Base—and they have been receiving our instructions on how to initiate and carry out the plan. This is something that we have been planning for nearly four years now. I would like to think that we have gotten it right, but it's hard to say at this point—it's just a little too early to tell."

"What do you mean, 'it's too early to tell'?"

"Well, each of the bases I have mentioned and every base in the

Southeast has been notified—some later than others, however. The only problem facing us now is the possibility of a communication leak before a base is completely secure."

Major Henderson stood and walked over to a sidewall of his office. He lowered a projection screen to reveal a detailed map of the southeastern United States. "You will see that the area we plan to overtake basically includes each of the states that were original Confederate states during the first American Civil War—with the exceptions of Texas, Arkansas, Louisiana, and Tennessee."

"The first American Civil War?"

"Right. We view this opportunity as the next American civil war."

Major Henderson quickly continued with his briefing.

"Now, we've been sending artificial communiqués to both the White House and the Pentagon, and we have also scheduled daily interbase communications to those bases that have not been fully secured yet so that they don't catch on to us too early in the operation."

Colonel Ballard was very impressed, almost awestruck, by the amount of work that Reggie and the Black Heritage Army had put into the operation. The sheer level of planning required was itself astonishing. He marveled at the way they had not only in put the entire mission plan together but also, more important, the way in which they had executed the plan.

Reggie extended his retractable pointer and tapped it on the map to bring Colonel Ballard's attention back to the issue at hand.

"Our plan initially was to spend most of last night and all of today securing the military bases and issuing equipment to our personnel in preparation for phase two. Unfortunately, we may not have the amount of time that we had hoped for. Again, not all of the other bases are fully secure at this time. And with normal daily activity beginning now, we may not have full lockdown in time."

"In time to keep news of the situation from leaking to the rest of the United States, you mean?"

"Exactly! If information were to leak prematurely, phase two would become much more difficult and could even result in hysteria and heavy casualties—which is exactly what we hope to avoid, if at all possible."

"I see." Colonel Ballard rubbed the back of his neck in his customary fashion as he deliberated for a moment.

"I need to know the specifics of phase two as it was originally crafted. Also, I'd like a detailed briefing as to our current status and mission-accomplish projections for the next two, eight, twenty-four, and forty-eight hours."

"I guess this means that you are going to join us?" Major Henderson had just witnessed precisely what he had hoped for—Colonel Ballard was taking charge. More importantly, he was doing it with authority.

Colonel Ballard walked around the desk so that he was right next to Reggie. He looked seriously and very intently into the eyes of his longtime friend. "That's exactly what this means, Reggie! That is, if you'll have me."

Reggie's smile was brighter than it had been for nearly three years. The excitement of the entire situation, and the potential that he saw for the future of his people now that they had the commitment of a more qualified leader, had just come over him. It was a great feeling.

"I'll ready the war room and gather all of the commanders, sir. We should be ready to give you a briefing in less than five minutes." He stood at attention and saluted Colonel Ballard.

"Very good, Major." LaRon returned the salute and started to leave Major Henderson's office.

Colonel Ballard paused at the doorway and looked back at Major Henderson. "This is exciting, Reggie."

"LaRon, it's great to have you on board, my friend."

The men looked at each other and smiled. After all these years, they were pretty good at reading each other's minds. "This is going to be a good day, Reggie. A very good day."

Reggie walked around the desk, sat in the chair behind it, and spun so that he could look outside at the morning sun. The entire base was brightly lit with warm sunshine.

For possibly the first time in his life, LaRon Ballard felt very content with himself. He could see things very clearly now, and he suddenly realized that this might be his calling. So much was running through his mind as he made his way to his office.

He had just made a snap decision to join the cause—and to join the leadership of the Black Heritage Army no less. He wasn't prone to quick decisions like this, so the fact that he hadn't taken the time to deliberate, review all of the possible outcomes in his mind, and confer with Katherine created a little bit of anxiety for him, but he was still very content with his decision.

He strode into his office with purpose, the sun shining brightly through the window, creating a glare in the entire room. LaRon briskly made his way around the desk. He stood between his desk and his chair, staring at the pile of papers on top of the former. His left hand tapped on the desktop as he turned himself toward the window that was now behind him.

He squinted to focus his vision farther out the sun-drenched window, took in a deep breath, and thought more about what he was feeling. This was a good anxiety—if there could be such a thing. His nervousness created a level of energy that he hadn't experienced in a long time. The fact that he had made a decision without all of the extra thought, time, and collaboration was liberating in so many ways!

He had actually acted on his gut feeling, and he did so with confidence and commitment. All at once he was happy. More important, he realized that all of his actions prior to this point in time had been influenced by what others expected of him.

This time, the decision was his. He was eager to share his newfound revelation with Katherine. Just the thought of her and the kids warmed his heart. He was certain that they would be proud of him. He basked in the feeling just briefly, however, for the seemingly insurmountable task that lay ahead suddenly rushed over him like a tidal wave.

Colonel LaRon Ballard turned slowly, tightened his uniform by pulling down on the bottom front corners of his outer shirt, and paused for a moment, staring at the doorway leading to the hallway. He had no idea what challenges lay ahead, no concept of what was waiting for him on the other side of that door, but *that* was a good thing.

He walked to the doorway, stopped, and took a deep breath to help build his confidence and focus his resolve. Then, he charged out the door with purpose, energized by the future that lay ahead of him.

He turned right and made his way to the war room, where his life would change forever. Little did he know that Colonel LaRon Henderson was about to take over as *the* leader of the Black Heritage Army. History was about to be made.

CHAPTER 7
Is This War?

"**A**-ten-*shun!*" Major Henderson brought the room to order as Colonel Ballard entered. Everyone stopped what they were doing. All that could be heard was the familiar hum of computers and electronics in the room, and the occasional distant-sounding voice crackling through a radio speaker.

Ballard didn't immediately set the room at ease for two reasons. First, he wanted to establish his leadership by waiting a few moments and glancing at each of the soldiers around him. Second, he wanted to soak in the magnitude of what the group was doing and what lay ahead of them.

He finally relented. "At ease, men. Major Henderson, go right ahead."

"Certainly, thank you, sir. Everyone I think that most, if not all, of you know Colonel Ballard. The great news is that he just recently decided to join our team after learning more about the Black Heritage Army!"

Everyone in the room applauded energetically with a few cheers in the background as well.

Major Henderson raised his hands to quiet the group and then continued. "Colonel Ballard will bring a lot of value to our organization and help ensure our success. He comes to us with an intense understanding of combat techniques, learned both while he was a student at West Point Academy, and while defending the United States in real life combat situations. More important for our cause however, Colonel Ballard is very

well networked at the highest levels of the US military. He is known
by top generals in all military branches, and well respected by national
political leaders. The colonel is a fine addition to the Black Heritage
Army, and we're glad to have him!"

"Thank you, Major." Ballard was taken back by the amount of praise
that his friend Reggie had placed on him. He quietly scanned the room
one more time. "We've got a lot of work to do everyone, so we'd better
get back to it! But before we do, allow me thank each and every one of
you one more time. Thank you."

Formalities over, Colonel Ballard turned his attention back to Major
Henderson. "What's our current status, Major?"

"Yes, sir. If you'd like to join me right over here at the main viewing
table?" Major Henderson turned and walked toward the large lighted
table in the center of the room. At more than five feet wide and ten feet
long, the electronic table was very impressive. Indeed, it was somewhat
mesmerizing just by itself.

Instantaneously, the room returned to its hectic state of energy and
tension. The soldiers didn't have the time to stop and watch their leaders
discuss strategy. Every one of the thirty-five to forty soldiers in the room
had a job to do, and not one of them had time to pause—not even for
a split second. Half of the soldiers in the room donned a headset and
sat in front of their computer station, each with four large computer
monitors placed side by side in an arch, blocking their view of anything
else happening around them.

Their attention hastily jumped from screen to screen while they
attempted to keep up with the enormous flow of information and data
that they had to process. It was their job to quickly and accurately forward mission details to the proper leaders, whether the latter were out
in the field or at one of the command centers.

At the same time, runners were scurrying around the room, handing messages to each other or transporting them between workstations
at a frantic pace. There was no hesitation in their actions—these men
and women were well-trained professionals who were dedicated to their
work. And this was no makeshift combat operations room.

Colonel Ballard's attention was brought back to Major Henderson, who launched into his debrief.

"Sir, from what we can tell, the leaders in Washington, DC, and at the Pentagon aren't yet aware of what we've done. As you can imagine, we have a few of our own on the inside up in Washington. They're helping us by suppressing information whenever they can. Many are in a position to intercept communications on our behalf and in the near term—that is, before they're identified as sympathizers with our cause.

"Our inside team of men and women are also providing us with much-needed intelligence right now, at least to the extent that they can without being too obvious. Anyway, for these reasons, in addition to our outstanding execution up to this point, it appears that no one in Washington knows what the hell is going on yet.

"If they are aware, they seem to have gone out of their way to keep the Black Heritage Army and our actions well hidden and out of public view. In the next twenty-four hours, and when we know for a fact that they are on to us, I wouldn't be surprised if they even went so far as to manipulate the press.

"Of course, this would help our strategy for a takeover. We'd like our initial actions to be more subtle, and we certainly want to give the appearance of business as usual for as long as we can.

"In fact, the national government will be unknowingly helping our cause if they continue to suppress details of what's going on. So far, our strategy seems to be working very well. And as long as leaders in Washington and the Pentagon help keep our activities under wraps—whether they are aware of our actions or not—we can expect fewer casualties than originally anticipated."

Reggie paused for a moment, contemplating the devastating effect that casualties would have on their cause. Loss of life is something that the Black Heritage Army had never wanted, but he knew that some casualties would be unavoidable.

"You're absolutely right, Henderson," Colonel Ballard responded, keeping his gaze on the electronic intelligence flashing on the table in front of him. "Fewer casualties would certainly mean more support for us and the Black Heritage Army, especially once the rest of the country finds out about our true goals and what we *really* hope to accomplish."

"That's going to be the key to our success, Colonel. We have got to communicate our intentions accurately and as soon as possible so that we can gain sympathy for the cause. Our surveys and research indicate that we should be able to garner nearly 80 percent support from African Americans around the country and up to 30 percent of whites.

"Assuming that our studies are correct, those two segments of the population would combine to give us a simple majority in most voting districts. In addition, we fully anticipate that a large percentage of blacks will ask to join the Black Heritage Army cause and possibly even move to our territory, bolstering our power base even more."

Major Henderson resumed his briefing. "Immediately following our takeover just after midnight last night, we sent Black Heritage Army troops to the borders of each state in the Ubuntu territory: Mississippi on the far western border, Alabama, Georgia, Florida, South Carolina, and North Carolina.

"Their specific orders are to move into position very quietly and calmly. If they're asked by anyone, they are to reply that they are simply taking part in a training exercise. We're pretty confident that most people would prefer to think that nothing is wrong anyway, so their natural inclination will be to accept that any high level of military activity they might witness is just an exercise.

"Anyway, early reports tell us that they've been successful for the most part, and that we've established a strong perimeter at all major roadway and access points both in and out of Ubuntu territory. Our only remaining areas of concern, as it relates to securing borders, are along the East Coast corridor—Interstate 85 and Interstate 95 specifically—and what we're referring to as the Gulfport area, which includes Interstates 55, 59, and 10, each of these carrying traffic between the southwest border of Mississippi and Louisiana.

"These are all areas of extremely high traffic on any given day, as you can imagine, so at this point we'll put our troops in position, but we'll remain extremely patient. Once all of this is made public, we can lock down those checkpoints as well, but doing so at this early stage would certainly expose our plan. There's simply no way we could keep an action like that quiet at this time.

"Speaking of our territory, we decided that of the original Confederate states that came together during the first American Civil War, Texas, Louisiana, Arkansas, and Tennessee are too far from the Black Heritage Army's central headquarters right here at Fort Benning, Georgia. Furthermore, the military bases in those states are few when compared to the amount of land each state covers, which would make them much more difficult to defend."

"I see your point, Major. Any good military leader could easily see that it would be nearly impossible to take over and defend such large landmasses as Texas and Arkansas. Also, as I recall, there aren't many military bases in those states, so we'd have to move our assets far too many miles to be effective in the short amount of time we have to deploy."

"Exactly right, Colonel. We also felt that Virginia, which was likewise an original Confederate state, is too close to Washington, DC. As you know, many of our national leaders, foreign diplomats, senior military officials, and retired personnel live in Virginia, so that would have been a huge challenge for us."

"Another great decision, Major. The challenges associated with being that close to the enemy would be too daunting a task for any military force—and the political risk of trying to take over an area that contained that many people in the intelligence community would never offset the amount of gain. Because many of those personnel are retired, as you say, the press would eat us alive for taking that territory. And because so many residents of Virginia are military consultants, we'd never know who we could trust."

"Thank you, sir. I agree completely. So now, rather than eleven states in the new confederacy, as was the case in 1861 during the first American Civil War, there are only six. Since there are a good number of military bases throughout the six states that we've chosen, and because all military branches are represented—army, navy, marines, coast guard, and air force—the area taken by our Black Heritage Army forces should be relatively easy to defend."

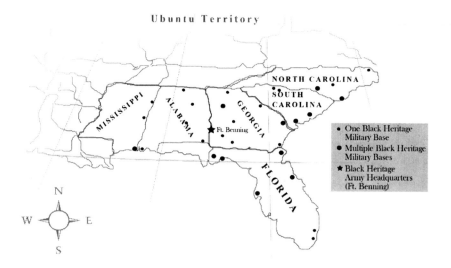

Ubuntu Territory

Major Henderson continued his briefing to Colonel Ballard for the remainder of the morning. It was both encouraging and refreshing for Reggie to get LaRon's input on many of the issues that, up to this point, he had to handle on his own. The men worked well together naturally, and together they discussed their challenges and developed strategies to ensure that the efforts of the Black Heritage Army would be successful.

Their biggest challenge at this early stage was the control of information and the difficulty of keeping their efforts out of the public eye until they were ready to announce their actions and start a campaign for their cause. This would be critical to the Black Heritage Army's ability to win over public opinion, maintain control of the information flow, and make sure that information released represented them in the most favorable light.

During this first day, however, the control of information appeared to be a little simpler than Major Henderson had anticipated. After much discussion, neither Henderson nor Ballard was quite sure why this was the case, but neither man wanted to question it, as luck seemed to be on their side so far.

Maybe the random nature of the day they chose for the takeover contributed to the ease with which they were able to control the flow of information. Their actions weren't tied to any particular date on the calendar or to any meaningful African American holiday. They also hadn't made lengthy plans or provided advance warning internally to the Black Heritage Army, which meant that there had been no time for an information leak or a change of heart by their own soldiers and staff.

It could also have been as simple as the busy and hectic nature of day-to-day life. Most civilians were so busy and distracted by their daily routine that they may not have noticed something as completely unexpected as a military takeover—even if it were to appear on the morning news shows.

No matter. As they moved toward the second half of the first day, the Black Heritage Army had executed their plan flawlessly. Even their plan to slowly increase the number of African Americans in their Ubuntu territory, and to decrease the number of people of other races, seemed to be working well.

The plan included having Black Heritage Army soldiers stop all people traveling by car in or out of each state in their territory, at which time they'd quiz them as to their intentions and the nature of their business. Because this movement was still underground, and because the leadership in Washington, DC, was apparently trying to keep the conflict quiet, civilians simply weren't aware of what was happening as they either entered or left one of the six states in Ubuntu territory.

The mission, as set forth originally by Major Henderson and his leadership, was to keep as many African Americans as possible in the six states they had chosen to take over. At the same time, their goal was to let as many whites or people of other races leave the territory without incident.

When African Americans tried to leave, they were pulled into private quarters set up as temporary outposts at each state line and were then told the story of the Black Heritage Army. Each soldier had a brief script that he had to adhere to, word for word. The script provided only the high-level details of the Black Heritage Army plan, the underlying reasons for the actions they had already taken, and their intentions going forward. Any African Americans were then encouraged to remain in the Ubuntu territory.

As it turned out, more than 90 percent would support the cause, choose to turn around, and return to their homes in the secured areas.

Whites, on the other hand, were allowed to leave without any further questioning, not knowing at the time that they may not be allowed to return. The entire mission of the Black Heritage Army, and even their existence, was kept from anyone who wasn't black. At each checkpoint, anyone who was not African American was convinced by the soldiers that the check stations were simply part of a standard readiness drill. Of course these civilians were then told that there was nothing to worry about, and were asked to move on.

The plan had been carried out so well that literally thousands of nonblacks had left the Ubuntu territory completely unaware of what was really going on. They had unknowingly just left their homes and belongings behind, essentially turning over their assets to the Black Heritage Army and anyone who would remain in the new territory. Little did they know at the time that they would likely never be able to return.

Airports, train stations, seaports, and bus terminals were initially treated in the same fashion, with small checkpoints set up at the main entrance and with Black Heritage Army soldiers applying the same policy as the interstate road system used. Although much more challenging, even these actions were working with no major setbacks. The Black Heritage Army soldiers who were used for this part of the mission were well trained, extremely intelligent, friendly, and very convincing when dealing with the public, leading no one to suspect something out of the ordinary.

Even with their good intentions, careful planning, and success thus far, both Henderson and Ballard knew that their plan couldn't be kept under cover forever. Suspicion quickly grew. As they neared the end of the first twenty-four hours of the operation, Colonel Ballard and his team could no longer control communication or pacify the suspicions of the people involved. Especially in this age of wireless communication and multiple electronic devices, people simply had too many options to use. They were able to notify family and friends that they had noticed something suspicious as they left state checkpoints.

But by the time suspicion began to take hold, the Black Heritage Army had a strong enough foothold to make their intentions public with little risk. If they were to make their actions public *before* the

United States government officially admitted to their own cover-up, then Colonel Ballard was convinced that their decision to go public first would create even more support for the Black Heritage Army and their cause—by people of any nationality or race.

Major Henderson's briefing was finally complete, so the men paused momentarily and looked around them at a room still buzzing with activity. It felt as though they were in slow motion and that the people around them were moving at a much higher rate of speed. It was surreal.

Colonel Ballard twisted his left arm so that he could see his watch face. The time was 1:27 p.m. "Major Henderson, I think that it's time to initiate our communication and information campaign. What do you think?"

Although still working hard and focused on the task at hand, everyone in the war room, including Colonel Ballard, was beginning to wilt from the constant stress of a long first day. But this is why he was such a natural leader. He knew that there was still a lot of work to be done, so he stood and gathered himself as he caught his second wind, after which time he confidently continued giving orders.

"I concur, Colonel. Let's beat the national government to the punch." Henderson turned away from the main viewing table and stepped toward one of the computerized work pods. "Lieutenant Sable, it's time to initiate our media campaign and make our official announcement."

"Yes, sir!" The lieutenant spun his chair to face the computer screens and reached for the headset lying on his desk. He secured it tightly over his ears to drown out the noise and chaotic activity behind him.

"Attention, all posts; attention, all posts. This is Lieutenant Sable at Command Center Alpha. Understand that Operation Freedom Reign is moving to phase two, and respond with your acknowledgement. I say again, Operation Freedom Reign is moving to phase two. Respond with your acknowledgment of this transmission. Over."

One by one, each military post and outpost responded in the affirmative. Lieutenant Sable listened intently and placed a check mark next to each location that was listed on the piece of paper in front of him. Major Henderson leaned over him in anticipation of the list's being completed. It took only three minutes.

Lieutenant Sable removed his headset and let it fall to the desktop. "I've got a one-hundred percent confirmation and acknowledgement from all locations, sir."

"Very good. Thank you, Lieutenant."

Major Henderson then made his way across the room to a different station. "Captain Engersol, it's time to initiate phase two: Communication and Media Management."

"Yes, sir!" The captain turned toward his station and got to work without hesitation.

"Very good. This is confirmed, Captain." Major Henderson raised his voice so that he could be heard, as he was already making his way back to the main viewing table to take his place next to Colonel Ballard.

"Excellent, Major, excellent," Ballard said to Henderson.

"Yes, sir, the wheels are in motion now. Our entire operation and the Black Heritage Army will be public within the hour."

"With that being the case, I think I'll head out for a while, Reggie. I'd like to get home and talk about all of this with Katherine. I'm sure you understand."

"Of course! It's been a trying day. Trust me, we've got it from here for the time being. We'll look forward to seeing you here again a little later, but for now, get home and spend some quality time with Katherine and the kids. Before you do, though, we've got a little something for you."

Major Henderson had been waiting for this moment all day, eager to show the ultimate display of gratitude to Colonel Ballard. He turned to face the room. With power in his voice, he yelled, "A-ten-*shun!*"

The room fell silent as the soldiers stood at attention and faced Major Henderson, who had Colonel Ballard standing at his side. All eyes were on Major Henderson as he continued.

"It has been a difficult, but an exciting and energizing, day for all of us. I would like to recognize each and every one of you for your efforts on this historic day, as you've been working tirelessly to help move the Black Heritage Army toward its goal of independence.

"Also, today we have witnessed the rise of a natural-born leader. This man has demonstrated strength and fortitude in the face of chaos, and a confident level of calm that has helped each of us through this challenging first day of operations. As is customary in a time of war, it is with great honor that I present Colonel LaRon Ballard with a field promotion." Ballard reached into his pocket and briskly spun to his left so that he now faced Colonel LaRon Ballard.

"Sir! On behalf of the Black Heritage Army, it is my distinct pleasure to promote you to the rank of general."

Carefully taking the back off of the single silver star that he had just taken from his pocket, he reached to pin the insignia onto Ballard's uniform. After pinning one star on each collar, he spun to face the room once again, snapped to attention, and raised his hand to full salute.

"Ladies and gentlemen, I present to you *General* LaRon Ballard, leader of the Black Heritage Army!"

The room erupted in applause and cheers.

General Ballard returned the salute and turned to his friend Reggie Henderson. Without saying a word, the two men looked at each other—confirming their friendship and showing gratitude to each other.

LaRon slowly scanned the troops in the room, making eye contact with each soldier before making his statement.

"Ladies and gentlemen, I want to thank you for a job well done today. While I appreciate the promotion and recognition for my efforts, it is you—not me—who are the reason, and will be the reason, for our success. I know that you're tired; we all are. I understand that all of this may seem confusing because of the sheer magnitude of what we are doing. We all feel that way. I also know that you're probably sensing a little bit of fear in your emotions, and that's okay.

"I want you to hold your heads high and continue with confidence. You are making history with every action you take, and we are going to change the course of this country—creating a better place for ourselves, our children, and our people."

He paused to scan the room one more time while the soldiers continued to wait patiently for direction.

"Now let's get back to it!"

The room instantaneously returned to the hectic state of near chaos that had been the standard for that day.

General Ballard was very surprised by the promotion. While he had fully committed himself to the cause, he hadn't expected to become its leader, at least not this soon. The emotions were almost overwhelming. He had a job to do however, and a lot of people were counting on him. The more he thought about it, LaRon agreed that he was the most qualified person to lead the Black Heritage Army—as long as he had Reggie at his side to educate him on everything that had led them to this point in time, and to retain the history and culture of the organization.

General Ballard wiped a tear of gratitude from his eye, nodded to his friend Reggie, turned, and made his way out of the room so that he could get home and share his excitement with Katherine.

Making his way across Fort Benning was much different than it had ever been. Armed soldiers were everywhere; military vehicles rushed from place to place. Anyone—military or civilian—would have noticed that something was awry. More important, Ballard just *felt* different.

He was concerned about Katherine and the kids. How much should he share with her? Would she understand and be supportive, or might she point out flaws in the decisions he had already made? Is it possible that he had made a mistake? Normally, he would have confided in his most trusted advisor, Katherine, and deliberated for hours before making an important decision such as this, especially one having such an impact on so many people.

The more he thought about it, the more he realized that he had no choice but to tell his wife every single detail. Since the communication campaign had just been launched, Katherine was going to be made aware anyway, along with everyone else around the world for that matter. She needed to hear about this from LaRon before she heard it from anyone else or worse: from some random media outlet.

He turned his car into the driveway and watched as the two armed security guards on either side of his front door took a step forward to ensure that it was General Ballard behind the wheel of the BMW. Word of his promotion had already spread throughout the entire ranks of the Black Heritage Army.

LaRon grabbed his briefcase, stepped out of the car, and headed straight toward the front door of his home. Both soldiers, weapons at their left side with the butt end on the ground and barrel pointing up, snapped to attention and saluted their new general.

General Ballard returned the salute, said, "At ease, men," and stepped inside.

"Where the hell have you been, and what is going on!?" Katherine was hysterical, her arms flailing demonstratively as her frustration and anxiety came to a boiling point.

"Not more than thirty minutes after you left, these soldiers charged in here and took away my cell phone! The damn regular phone lines aren't working, we don't have a television signal, and they will not let us leave the house!"

LaRon stood in front of her, both his hands at shoulder height, his palms open and facing her. "Please calm down, honey. Calm down." He moved toward her, put his arms around her, and held onto her tightly.

Katherine cried. Through the tears, she sobbed, "You son of a bitch. You should have called or gotten ahold of us somehow. We had no idea if you were even safe!"

LaRon held his beautiful wife even closer and began to stroke her hair slowly to help calm her. "You're absolutely right, honey, you're right. The day got away from me pretty quickly, but I have no excuse for not making sure that you were aware that I was okay."

He gently grabbed her shoulders and pushed her just far enough away to look directly into her eyes. "I love you, and I can assure you that you and the kids have been safe this entire time. You'll understand, and this will make a lot more sense, once you hear about what's going on."

General Ballard then proceeded to share the events of the day, particularly the details about the Black Heritage Army, their cause, how he was recruited, and how sudden his decision was, sparked by the events of the previous day and especially the conversation his family had had at the dinner table the night before.

He went on to talk about the actions of the day, the success they had had, and the challenges they would be facing. He also shared how everything seemed to be falling into place very smoothly. He used the term *luck* at least twice, shaking his head at times to outwardly show his own level of disbelief.

While their father was speaking, little John and Elizabeth made their way toward the entryway. They were sitting side by side on the second-to-last tread of the stairway, listening in fascination to their dad as he continued to talk about the strategies the Black Heritage Army had employed, his excitement and energy ever increasing as he shared more and more details.

LaRon paused for moment, looked over Katherine's shoulder at the kids, and winked at them. They smiled in return, knowing now for certain, given his reassuring grin, that everything was going to be all right.

"Katherine, this is a moment in time that will forever be recorded in history, and we can be an instrumental part of it. For possibly the first time in my life, I feel liberated and rejuvenated! I'm so excited. My mind won't slow down long enough for me to relax for one minute—but in a good way!"

He stopped abruptly and took in a deep breath. "But with all of that said, I am nothing without your support and encouragement. I hope that you can also see the value in our cause. And, for heaven's sake, I hope you are able to support my decision."

"Are you sure, LaRon? Are you sure that this is the best thing for us, this family, our kids?"

"I'm as sure as I'll ever be, honey. I know that there will be many challenges ahead of us. And I have to be honest with you: the risks are considerable. If we aren't successful, and if the Black Heritage Army fails, I can assure you that I'll be in danger as their leader, but I truly believe it's worth the risk."

"Help me understand that, LaRon. Help me understand that it's worth the risk. You say that like it's no big deal or something."

"It is a big deal, Katherine, a *very* big deal. The reason I say that it's worth the risk is because I am incredibly confident in our ability to be successful. Reggie has managed to build one heck of an organization—I mean, they have been building for years, honey. With African Americans having a strong majority in each of the armed forces, we've got our territory well under control.

"Candidly, I can't imagine anyone who might be against our cause trying to fight us within our new territory. They know that they'd be significantly outnumbered and that the risk to their own life would be too great. We're already realizing so much success, mixed with a little bit of luck for sure, but the primary reason for our success lies within our organization, our plan, and our people."

"I guess I just didn't realize how much of an issue racism has been. I'm still trying to wrap my mind around the need for such a campaign, LaRon." Katherine said, her ever-present optimism still in place.

"I felt the same way less than twenty-four hours ago, sweetheart. But think about it: the Black Heritage Army makes up more than sixty percent of the military population, and there are other African Americans who haven't officially joined the cause yet. That many people couldn't possibly fabricate a level of racism great enough to start a war.

"No, the issues of racism and discrimination are very real. I think that we've been sheltered from a lot of it to some degree, but I also think that we've unknowingly ignored the signs and chosen to think that everything was all right in the world around us."

"At the risk of human life, though, LaRon?"

"I'm not going to mislead you, Katherine. It's certainly our goal—without question—that no one give their life for the cause, but it could happen. It could happen without a doubt." He paused to contemplate the gravity of his own words.

"I will say this, though: keep in mind that the Black Heritage Army is going to do this with or without us. In fact, they already have. The wheels are in motion and there is no turning back."

Katherine turned to look at her children, who were sitting in the stairway. "That's a good point. I'll give you that. What would we do if we decided not to join the cause?"

I don't know, Katherine. I don't know. I'm not even sure if that's an option. Honestly, Reggie and I didn't even talk about our policy toward blacks who don't want to be a part of the cause. I'm not sure if they're being allowed to leave quietly, or what is happening to them. You know, you bring up a great point. That's something that I'll get to the bottom of when I return to base this afternoon."

Katherine looked up at LaRon and smiled, admiring his natural leadership skills and the way he immediately turned their conversation into one about how he could make a difference by improving the Black Heritage Army's policies.

"Anyway, honey," he said after making a mental note of the next item on his to-do list, "we've got a real opportunity to be a part of history and help a massive number of people. I'm truly excited about this—no, *passionate* about this."

Her body relaxed as the tension of the day left her. "Of course, LaRon. Of course I support you. In fact, I've never been happier for you. We're in this together now, and I'm with you one hundred percent."

She looked over her shoulder at the kids once more, smiled at them, and then turned back to LaRon. "Tell us what we can do to help!"

CHAPTER 8
Out of Control

When the Pentagon and the leaders in Washington, DC, realized what had happened, it was simply too late. Their plan to try to keep the Black Heritage Army and its efforts under wraps had backfired.

The first day of the Black Heritage Army's plan to retake the Southern states was successful and nearly complete. All military bases within the territory had been locked down during that first day and were completely secured. Their plan to expand into civilian areas was implemented hours before any communication of their intentions was released, so this too met with a high degree of success.

At this point, some of the more rural areas hadn't been approached or secured yet, but only because these outlying geographies required a great deal of man power—man power the Black Heritage Army didn't quite have. This meant that with a few small exceptions, six of the original Confederate states were now geographically under the control of the Black Heritage Army, at least for the most part.

The Black Heritage Army's plan had worked beautifully, and they were confident that the few unsecured areas that were more rural would not pose a threat to their overall goal.

However, many of the major cities weren't completely secured, and most of the high population centers, cities like Atlanta, Miami, Charlotte, Jacksonville, and even Birmingham, proved much more difficult to overtake. These areas were another story altogether. The Black Heritage Army was content to leave densely populated cities alone for the time being, to make sure that they had firm control of their state borders. They decided to keep with the goal of a completely secure Ubuntu territory first.

Once the Black Heritage Army controlled all state borders and potential transportation routes, they had planned to give residents of the high-population areas a choice: either stay within the territory and support their cause or be allowed to leave peacefully and under their own power. If everything were to remain on schedule as it had thus far, the Black Heritage Army would make this announcement public late during the second day of operation.

During these early hours of Operation Freedom Reign, they also found that even though many Americans owned firearms, this group of people had no organization and no way to coordinate their efforts against the Black Heritage Army. Any people with firearms who might have been inclined to fight back knew that their efforts would be futile, especially when an entire regimen of fully equipped soldiers marched down the street with tanks and other military vehicles supporting them. It was obvious there was no way to fight back.

However, as General Ballard would soon find out, it's not easy to control the ethics and behavior of an entire army, especially when that army, like the one he commanded, was motivated by years of oppression and a feeling of despair. Knowing that their people had been discriminated against for more than a lifetime, more than a few of his soldiers were ready to release their frustration. They viewed this as the perfect opportunity to do so—without repercussion.

★ ★ ★

It was a typical small farm, lost out in the far reaches of Alabama. Near the town of Harvest, not far from McKee Road, was a small plot of land managed by the fourth generation of a family named Hoch. It was very small as far as farms go—only 160 acres, barely enough to scratch out a living. But that was fine; the Hochs didn't have high expectations. Plus, they were so detached from the outside world, they didn't really know what they were missing out on anyway.

Their farm was a good distance from the nearest town of any significance, which meant that the Hoch family rarely had an opportunity to associate with others in the community—exactly what Butch Hoch wanted. His kids were homeschooled, if you could call it that, and Butch was doing the best he could to teach the next generation of Hochs the extremist views that his daddy, and his daddy before him, had taught him.

They didn't have cell phones. Butch wouldn't allow that even if they could afford them. Cable or satellite television was entirely out of the question; he didn't want his kids or wife to have too much exposure to what he considered to be the extremist views of the outside world. If they discovered what they were missing out on, he'd lose all control—and he knew it. He himself didn't want to hear what the liberal media had to say anyway.

It was a long time ago when Butch Hoch broke off ties with his wife's extended family. They saw him for what he was: an undereducated, unmotivated, abusive husband and father. It didn't take long after their marriage for his wife's family to see the problems that lay ahead for their daughter, so they tried to get her away from Butch. It didn't work.

Like most women in an abusive relationship, Julie was far too fearful of Butch. She knew firsthand what he was capable of. Although she knew that her family only wanted the best for her and that she would probably be better off without her husband, she wasn't about to try to leave. That would only bring harm to her and her family. This she knew for a fact.

It wasn't long after they were married that they had had their first child, a boy. During her pregnancy, Julie thought that Butch might have changed, as he didn't beat her or even yell at her during that time. He wasn't necessarily supportive by any stretch of the imagination, but at least he wasn't focused on abusing her like he always had been.

Just when she thought that life might turn out all right after all, and shortly after their son, Kevin, was born, Butch returned to his old ways. What Julie didn't know was that his only goal was to have a few healthy kids, not for the nurturing reasons that most people would choose for having children, but rather because he wanted laborers and little minds that he could brainwash to his way of thinking. That's the only reason that he didn't beat her when she was with child.

No matter what the reason, it was rejuvenating to have a break from his physical and verbal onslaught of terror, so she got pregnant again. This time it was a little girl, Lisa. Their second child was also born healthy. And just like when her brother was born before her, Butch got right back to the abuse and beatings shortly after her birth.

As hard as Julie tried, it took her a few years to get pregnant again, but that was fine with her, as the reprieve from Butch's violence was worth the wait. As far as she was concerned, and if she could have her way, she'd rather be pregnant all the time. Just four months along now, she was starting to show—not by much, but by looking at her anyone could tell that she was with child. She had already gotten past the morning sickness stage, so life was good. Butch had backed off, and Julie was relishing every moment.

On this particular day at the Hoch farm, the humidity was thick enough to cut with a knife. The early morning sun looked caught in a haze as it tried to burn through the moist air. Ten-year-old Kevin Hoch was already up and working hard, just like his father had always expected of him. He was in the barn cleaning out the stalls, getting pushed around by the few skinny cows they had been trying to get milk out of for years. Of all the chores, he hated shoveling cow crap the most, by far.

"Git yer ass movin'!" His pa, Butch, yelled to him. "We ain't got all God damn day, you worthless, lazy ass! I gotta ton more shit fer y'all to git done t'day!"

Kevin dug in hard and dreamed of the day when he would be big enough to stand up to his dad and free himself, his mother, and his sister from Butch's wrath. But somehow he knew that day was a long way off. His dad was pretty tough.

As Butch drove their old, beat-up tractor around the corner, Kevin heard what he thought sounded like thunder. He ran out of the barn and looked to the sky, expecting to see an airplane. But he saw nothing more than the humid haze. As his eyes fell to the eastern horizon, he began to see the outline of what appeared to be an army, followed by a cloud of dust. It was difficult to see exactly what it was in the morning sun and humidity, which caused a wavy, mirage-like view of the thunder that was approaching, but he thought for sure that he could see military vehicles with a lot of people around them, walking straight toward the Hochs' house.

Kevin dropped his shovel and ran into the house to get his ma. He didn't give a damn about his dad, figuring that his dad could take care of himself, but he naturally felt the need to make sure his ma would be all right, just like he always had. While running to the back door, he knew that the vehicles and people were getting closer because the sound of what was coming got louder and louder.

As usual, his mother was working hard in the kitchen. She cringed when she heard the screen door slam behind Kevin, thinking that it might be Butch coming back inside the house.

"Ma!"

"What, Kevin? What is it?"

"I don't know—looks like the armed forces is comin' off the east fields!"

Julie leaned out the kitchen window and saw the parade of military trucks, tanks, and vehicles kicking up a monstrous cloud of dust as they got closer to the Hochs' tattered old farmhouse. Not knowing exactly what to do, she found that self-defense was the first thing to come into her mind.

"Kevin, I'll git your little sis—you go git yer damn paw!" she yelled to him. Then she grabbed the shotgun standing in the kitchen corner and pumped a shell into the chamber. "Run! Run now, Kevin, run!"

Kevin slammed through the door and ran around the corner of the house toward the barn just in time to see his pa walking out, also with a shotgun in hand. Kevin stopped dead in his tracks as the military group from Redstone Arsenal Army Base ground to a halt not more than twenty yards from where Butch was standing.

"What the hell'r y'all doin' on my goldarn property?" Butch stood defiantly in front of the lead Humvee. Tanks and other track vehicles were stopped close behind, fanned out in a semicircle around him.

A soldier in full combat attire hopped down from the Humvee, removed the goggles from his eyes, and rested them on the top of his helmet.

"Think you want to talk to me with that tone of voice, cracker? Looks to me like y'all oughta be talkin' to me with a little more respect." Julius Jackson gazed over his shoulder, letting his eyes point to the army behind him.

"Respect my butt, nigger. Get off my land!" Butch was as defiant, and as stupid, as he had always been.

"What did you just call me?" Sergeant Jackson arched his back, looked over his shoulder, and made a hand gesture to the tank driver on his right.

Young Kevin could feel the ground shake when, without hesitation, the tank driver slowly rolled the huge track vehicle forward and simultaneously rotated the turret in the direction of the Hochs' house. The entire scene was captivating to young Kevin Hoch. It was like he would have thought a war to be like, based on the outdated schoolbooks they had in the house. But to him this was better than the pictures he had stared at in that book, that was for sure. He wasn't afraid at all. For a reason he couldn't fully understand, he was surprisingly calm.

It seemed as though it had been a long time since a very young Julius Jackson stood in front of Judge Carmichael back in that Louisiana courtroom. For Julius, it was a memory that he had chosen to put out of his mind.

At the time, his sentence of leniency from Judge Carmichael seemed like a positive event and a new opportunity. However unlike other people new to the army, Julius had no friends to interact with, and no one to talk with or confide in, as he powered through the drudgery of boot camp and the subsequent transition to army life. He was still an angry kid at that stage in his life, so he hadn't made any effort to make friends either.

Without any direction to guide him to self-improvement, and with no adults that he respected enough to listen to, Julius fell in with the wrong crowd—just like he had back in Louisiana. Then, not a year after joining, he learned that his mother had died. She was the only reason that he *may* have wanted to turn his life around in the first place. But now that she was gone, what was the point?

The group of soldiers with whom he had fallen into favor was no different than the gang he had hung out with back at home. They were a rough group of guys who were detached from the rest of the army and the world in general. Marijuana was readily available to them, and they partied regularly with no fear of retribution. After all, what was the worst that could happen? They'd get sent back home?

For Julius, he felt as though he had found the perfect place to display his anger and exert force on others—and it was as if he had permission to do it! The army turned the other cheek on guys like him because they knew that at some point they would need people like Julius in combat: men with no conscience, with no regret—men who lived their lives without knowing what fear was.

The army also knew that people like Julius made for some of the best soldiers in a wartime environment, as they were not just willing to kill but were also eager to do so if given the chance. It was clear that the army wanted, and needed, soldiers like Julius. The real purpose of any army is to win wars after all. The type of hardened fighter that Julius could be described as was exactly the kind of person needed to staff a lethal fighting force.

Of course the traditional thought of the military was that there would be enough recruits of good conscience and good character to offset the ones like Julius Jackson. They assumed that the "good ones" could lead and control the "bad ones." Either way, Julius had nothing to fear as far as punishment was concerned.

Everyone standing on that hard, rain-starved patch of ground had been standing silent long enough for the dust to settle from the most recent tank movement. It appeared as though no one from either side could believe what they were seeing unfold before them.

Several of the other soldiers in this group some fifty strong looked at each other in a sort of dazed state of disbelief when the tank driver stopped the vehicle and locked onto his target. Sergeant Jackson was their leader, but this didn't mean that they had to agree with all of his actions and orders. All eyes were on Julius as he took two steps toward Butch and leaned in so that their noses almost touched.

"Now listen here, you white-trash, redneck son of a bitch. Take a good, hard look around you and at my men, then tell me what you see."

In a gut reaction of defiance and without saying a word, Butch jumped back from Sergeant Jackson and raised his shotgun, snapping his aim left and then right, not knowing where to point it or exactly what to do. He squinted in the morning sun as he looked over his gun barrel at the military group in front of him, trying to make sense of it all.

Now that the initial adrenaline rush was beginning to wear off, he was able to comprehend the magnitude of what was around him. Butch slowly lowered the shotgun and stared in amazement and disbelief. Every single soldier that he could see was black. There was not a single solitary white man in the bunch.

"What the hell is goin' on here?"

"It's real simple, whitey. We are here to take back what's rightfully ours—"

"I ain't got nothin' o' yours, damn it!"

The sergeant took a deep breath, arched his back, and looked around as if he were trying to find a bit of patience with this little man for whom he had absolutely zero respect. "You're standing on it, cracker."

"You ain't takin' my land, you som'bitch!"

Sergeant Jackson cracked a confident smile and slowly strode back toward Butch, coming nose to nose with him once again.

"You see, that's just it. You can't admit that this land—all of it—belongs to me and my brethren. By 'all of it,' I mean Florida, Georgia, the Carolinas, Tennessee—every one of them damn states that fought to keep slavery alive, and my people down, during the American Civil War.

"We—all of our ancestors," he said as he motioned toward the soldiers behind him, "are the ones who built this part of the United States. We dug the ground, planted the seed, picked the crops, worked in the factories, and built the homes and buildings. Hell, half the time we were even the ones who invented the machinery and equipment that made the job of building a country less difficult for you frickin' white folk.

"You see, ever since that little incident that you like to refer to as the American Civil War, my people have been planning and preparing for this day. This is the day that we—descendants of Africa—take the original southern states back from the union. We are here to lay claim to our country, and your little, piece-of-shit, dried-up farm, along with that white-trash shack and barn, is in our damn way!"

He signaled his tank gunner by raising his right hand and flicking his wrist without ever turning around.

Everything seemed to be moving in slow motion for young Kevin Hoch. The powder blast from the long barrel of the tank was surreal when, an instant later, an explosive shell completely destroyed the only home he had ever known.

Kevin shook his head to clear the dust as he tried to force his eyes to focus. His only concern was for his ma and little sis. He looked around in a panic until he saw them both; they had made their way close to the barn. While the blast had knocked them off their feet, they were both starting to stand up, pounding on themselves to hammer the dust from their clothes.

Butch raised his shotgun and pointed it directly at Julius. Just when he thought to squeeze the trigger and blast a hole in Sergeant Jackson's chest, his head was blown back, the result of a shell from an M1 rifle. His body went limp but remained upright for a split second. The shotgun fell from his body's grasp, and then Butch Hoch crumbled to the ground in a heap of dirty clothes, and dust.

From where he was lying, Kevin could see his pa's body. Not too far away from him, it was now covered in blood. Strangely, it actually gave him a sense of relief.

As Kevin sat up, he was able to look around the blast zone. He saw his ma and sis up walking now, making their way toward him. They were glassy-eyed and in a daze. *Like zombies,* he thought to himself.

Kevin got to his feet, dusted off his coveralls and walked toward his ma and sis, knowing that he would have to take care of them now. He looked at his pa's motionless body one more time and then shook his head.

Kevin turned to look up at Sergeant Jackson as he walked by. Julius paused for an instant to look back at the boy. The two made direct eye contact for the briefest amount of time. When they did, Kevin looked into Julius's eyes and saw nothing, nothing at all—no soul, it seemed, just a hollow shell of a man.

Sergeant Jackson whistled loudly with a simultaneous flick of his wrist, now extended above his head, and the entire regiment snapped into action. Tanks and vehicles, with some foot soldiers marching alongside, continued west and acted as if nothing had just happened.

* * *

It was midafternoon now, and General Ballard was finally content in every way. He and Katherine had just talked about his recent decisions in detail and she was supportive, very supportive in fact. She had embraced the concept and the actions of the Black Heritage Army so swiftly that LaRon could hardly believe it. This helped him begin to realize that recruiting new members, and earning their loyalty, may not be as difficult as he had originally thought.

By the time General Ballard returned to the headquarters building, he found that someone had already replaced the reserved parking sign located closest to the door. It now read, "Reserved: General Ballard." He shook his head in disbelief of how quickly the sign had been installed and of the fact that he was a general and the leader of the Black Heritage Army. This had all happened very fast.

"Sir! Sir!" He was greeted by a young private who ran from the entrance of the building and met him just as he was closing his car door.

"What is it, son?"

"Sir, Major Henderson needs to see you right away. It's urgent, sir. He made sure that I caught you immediately upon your return."

"Roger that, Private. I'm here now, so you can relax."

"Yes, sir. He's in his office. I'll take you there."

"No need for that, son. You're dismissed." General Ballard trotted up the stairs and down the hall to Ballard's office.

"What's going on, Reggie?" The door was ajar, so he had walked in without knocking.

"We've got a problem, General, a big one. I just received a communiqué from the field, and I have to say that I'm not pleased at all."

"Are we losing ground, Reggie?"

"No, it's not that at all. I'll get right to the point. It turns out that the field commander of one of our smaller units took it upon himself to destroy a family farm and kill its owner in the outskirts of Alabama."

"Holy shit." Ballard's left hand instinctively reached up to rub the back of his neck. "Damn it, Reggie, this is exactly what we don't need to have happen. What are the details?"

"Well, the small unit is led by Sergeant Julius Jackson, who was based right here in Benning for quite a few years but who recently moved up to Redstone Arsenal. Honestly, I don't know much about the man yet, but I think that Rockson and the others know him pretty well. I intend to get their take on the young man."

"I think that's a good start, Reggie, but I also think that we need to relieve Sergeant Jackson of his command immediately and get him back here to Benning for an interrogation."

"Great point, sir. You're absolutely right. We need to send a strong message to the troops that this behavior is simply not acceptable."

"You've got it. I'll let you do a little more research on his background, and then send me an update if you would. By the way, how did we hear about all of this?"

"Well, that's the good news. We've still got a majority of men and women who understand the overall goal and who want to go about reaching our goals in the right way. One of Sergeant Jackson's direct reports radioed in to headquarters while the unit mobilized to the next checkpoint.

"I can only imagine the risk that it placed this young lady in, but she made the decision to send us the communiqué regardless. Clearly she's the type of soldier we need in order to help balance our actions in the field."

"Right. Well, we've got to learn more about this, as I've said. It could be that they were confronted by the landowner and had to respond in self-defense. Either way, we need to get Jackson here, find out what happened, and then be prepared to spin this for the press." General Ballard's tone was clearly one of disappointment.

Major Henderson said, "Speaking of the press, here's some news that's potentially positive. This happened in an area that is so remote, no one else knows what has happened, and there were no witnesses other than our troops and members of the family that survived. I don't think that we'll have negative reporting on this situation. At least not anytime soon, that is."

"Just when we start to think like that, we'll lose control of our information-management campaign, Reggie."

"Yes, sir, I was just being optimistic—and maybe even a little bit hopeful, I guess. I'll get on this right away."

"Very good, Reggie. Thanks for coming straight to me on this and for moving so swiftly. I'll look forward to getting your feedback on the event itself while both of us ponder the larger issue of a few bad apples whose actions might be impossible for us to control."

"Right." Major Henderson shook his head in disbelief and disappointment. He felt personally responsible since he was the founder of the Black Heritage Army and had been its highest ranking leader not more than thirty-six hours ago. He thought he had done a better job of setting the tone and establishing the culture of their organization such that an event like this wouldn't happen.

"I think I can see what you're thinking, Reggie." General Ballard interrupted the Major's thought process. "I don't want you to take personal responsibility for this. No matter what we do, remember that we're always dealing with a bunch of individuals—people with their own thoughts, people who are willing to take their own actions in certain cases.

"We can't realistically expect ourselves to control each and every soldier and their actions."

"Thanks, LaRon. I just can't help feeling a bit guilty on this one."

"I get it, my friend, I get it. Listen, you've done an outstanding job with this organization, simply outstanding. When do you think was the last time in history that someone gathered such a massive number of people and motivated them to take control of their lives, all the while working together as a unified community?"

Major Henderson just sat and stared at his friend who was standing on the other side of his desk. A tear slowly dropped from his eye. All at once, his emotions came to the forefront. Feelings of pride, fear, and doubt all came to the surface. He couldn't hold them back for another minute.

"Keep that emotion focused on the future, Reggie. Take pride in what you've done, and remain focused on what is yet to be done. Follow me?"

"Of course I do. Thanks, LaRon. Up to this point, everything has been such a blur. We've been so busy with the details of our mission that I guess the magnitude of it all hasn't been fully absorbed by my conscious mind." Major Henderson now stood, wiping the single tear from his cheek.

"You know, I still wonder if I even made the right decision when I activated Operation Freedom Reign. I hope that I didn't let my emotions run away with me at the time and let them cloud what would otherwise be a sound decision."

"No second-guessing, Reggie, none. I won't allow it. Point is that here we are, right? Those decisions are behind us, and now we're going to be measured by the decisions we make going forward.

"You and I have an army to lead, and we're in a wartime situation. There's no way that we can control—or be responsible for—the actions of each individual under our command. There isn't a war in the history of the world where every foot soldier followed their orders to the letter and acted honorably one hundred percent of the time."

"Thanks again, LaRon. I appreciate your perspective. I really do, my friend." Reggie reached across the desk to shake LaRon's hand. "It's time to move on; we've got a war to win."

"Roger that! Let me know what you find out about Julius Jackson and the crap he pulled out in the field. We can talk strategy later tonight or tomorrow."

"Yes, sir." The men smiled at each other, and then General Ballard made his way out of the Major's office.

For General Ballard and the Black Heritage Army leadership, violence and bloodshed were to be avoided whenever possible. Events such as what had just happened at Butch Hoch's farm were not a part of their plan and would prove to be very uncommon as the conflict unfolded.

Most civilians caught in the Ubuntu territory who didn't agree with what the Black Heritage Army had planned simply gathered their belongings and left the region peacefully. Many of these people fled to Northern or Western states in order to stay with family members who did not live within the acquired territory. Some didn't have the luxury of staying with family or friends, so these had to deal with the additional expense of a hotel room while they were gone. But that didn't matter, as nearly everyone outside of the Black Heritage Army thought this would be a short-lived event in American history. They expected to return to their homes, and for everything to return to normal after just a few days.

Of course, this way of thinking was preferred by General Ballard and played perfectly into the Black Heritage Army's plan. Over the first few days, which soon bled into weeks, even more detractors would leave the territory that the Black Heritage Army had taken, while supporters and sympathizers would continue to pour into the territory from all over the United States.

Within just a few days, African Americans from all over the country were flooding into the Southern states wanting to join the fight if necessary. More important for them was the chance just to be a part of the Black Heritage Army family and the Ubuntu community. The US government's attempted cover-up accentuated this in the early hours of the operation, which created even more distrust, especially among African Americans.

In fact, the federal government's actions caused more than a few of those that were on the fence to decide to join the cause. Many of the African Americans who may have supported the federal government, or at least been sympathetic toward retaining the Union, were now firmly behind the Black Heritage Army.

People of many other races, including Hispanics, Asians, and Middle Easterners, also wanted to be a part of the movement. However, the Black Heritage Army wasn't necessarily open to the idea of letting others join their cause quite yet. In their view, racism against blacks had persisted for far too long and they couldn't trust anyone other than their own race. The entire operation was by African Americans, for African Americans, plain and simple. And for the time being, it had to stay that way.

The Ubuntu Six, as the six states making up the new Black Heritage Army territory were now called, were close to each other geographically, emotionally, and in spirit. This was why they decided to refer to their effort, and the territory of the six new confederate states, as Ubuntu— which was also in keeping with the code name they had used for years.

CHAPTER 9
What about Love?

Jennie and Heather completed college life together as ROTC students, just as planned. Georgia Tech University was a great place to be, and they enjoyed every minute of it. Even though they were committed to the army and had the added responsibilities demanded of a junior officer, they were also able to experience college life to its fullest.

Dormitory life, occasional weekend parties, football and basketball games, and all of the great friends they made—everything in college was picture-perfect. All the while, they worked hard to help each other keep their grades higher than average and also strengthened their bond of friendship. Anyone who met them knew right away that these two young women were inseparable.

Because the main campus that they attended was located right in the heart of midtown Atlanta, the two young women from little Omaha, Nebraska, were able to experience big-city life together for the first time. They became quick fans of the well-recognized Yellow Jacket football team and attended every game they could, especially if it was against an Atlantic Coast Conference rival. Heather and Jennie were dedicated fans, which earned them the opportunity to party with the team after games. Each of them had dated a football player—once or twice.

The Georgia Institute of Technology, as it is formally known, was a national leader in many of the engineering and technology disciplines, but both young women chose to pursue degrees in business administration. A business degree simply suited their personalities better than one in engineering. Plus, the skills they learned at Georgia Tech carried over very well to their being officers in the army.

The two young women spent most of their time in the west campus area. After their undergraduate stay in the Montag dormitory, they moved to the Crecine Apartments, which is where they completed their college careers. Both Jennie and Heather were athletic themselves; they were frequently found playing pickup volleyball games at the campus recreation center. It was a great way for them to meet new people and work off a little bit of the stress caused by being college students.

In 1959 the Georgia Tech student population voted overwhelmingly to endorse the integration of black students. Three years later, it would become the first school located in the Deep South to desegregate peacefully and without a court order. However, most people aren't aware of the university's important role in history, because the population of students while Jennie and Heather attended was sixty three percent white and fewer than seven percent African American. The remaining 30 percent consisted of people of other races from all over the world.

Being a clear minority at her school in the heart of Atlanta, Georgia, never occurred to Jennie. Like her best friend, she simply didn't think in terms of black and white. Plus, she had never encountered a racist act while in school, at least not that she was aware of.

After five years of college, the two friends were stationed together at Fort Benning—just as promised by their recruiter. The young officers were immediately caught up in the fray of army life, and they enjoyed every minute of it. One of the reasons that Heather and Jennie were such close friends was the fact that they were both able to live on the lighter side of life. Each was always positive in the way she approached the daily challenges faced by a female in the army. This was something that carried over from their days back in college. Even with the stress of their demanding schedules, rarely would either of them be caught without a beaming smile on her face.

College life had been great, but Heather and Jennie seemed to enjoy their first three years in the army even more. They were still rooming together, and their difference in race had never even occurred to them. Of course, their friendship had a history that went far deeper than their time together in the army or in college. They had been friends since the first grade and were fortunate to have lived in a neighborhood and community that didn't measure people by the color of their skin. Even though they knew it existed, racism was completely foreign to Heather and Jennie.

Although Jennie was African American, she was not aware of the Black Heritage Army and had never been invited into the organization. The Black Heritage Army knew that their best prospects for membership were African Americans who were frustrated with their situation, who felt that they had been slighted in some way, or who were generally supportive of separating the races, black from white. Jennie fell into none of these categories. She still had the type of personality that always seemed positive. Her attitude was on the lighter side, and she always gave the impression that she had not a care in the world. Because of this, when members of the Black Heritage Army met her, they soon realized that trying to recruit Jennie would be difficult, if not impossible.

Jennie was taking a shower, so she could have had no idea what was going on as a group of soldiers made their way up and down the halls of the army-subsidized apartment complex in which she and Heather lived. Judging by the noise being made, people who lived in the building would have been able to tell that something unusual, or possibly something very important, was going on. But at this point, no one could have known what the Black Heritage Army had done, nor could they have any idea of what the soldiers in their apartment building were up to as they combed the structure and inspected each apartment, going door to door.

Thinking that she might have heard something unusual, Heather used one hand to tug on the cord leading to the earbuds that were providing her with some of her favorite music. The small speakers fell from her ears and landed in her other hand.

"Jennie? Did you just hear that?" No response. At the moment, Heather didn't realize that Jennie was still in the shower. Then she heard another unusual sound. This time, unable to ignore that something uncommon was going on, she wanted to confirm that she wasn't just hearing things.

"Jennie! Are you hearing this?" Still no response.

She stood still to try to decipher the noises she was hearing. It sounded like banging and pounding; their apartment seemed to shake from the vibrations caused by combat boots stomping around hurriedly. Heather leaned toward the door to listen more intently, at which time she heard soldiers pounding on her neighbor's door. Moments later came the pounding on hers.

"Open the door, please!"

Heather pulled away from the door and hesitated; she was a little freaked out. She peered through the peephole, but she didn't recognize the face staring back at her.

"Who is it?"

"Just open the door, ma'am."

"First I need you to tell me your name, your rank, and what your business is." Heather was determined to hold her ground. Clearly this was a pretty unusual situation. She was smart enough not to take any chances.

"I'm Sergeant Michael Masters, and this is a routine check. Something has happened on base today." He paused to prevent himself from providing too much detail before confirming who was in the apartment. "We've been given orders to debrief everyone as quickly as possible, miss. Can you open the door, please?"

Convinced, Heather cracked the door open to see Michael's face. Their eyes met immediately. Michael was still as handsome as the day he'd enlisted. He carried his physically fit, six-foot-two frame very well. Heather, hoping to impress, smiled her best smile, pushed the door closed so that she could release the safety chain, reopened the door, and motioned for Michael to come in.

Michael knew that his mission was of high importance, but he couldn't help but smile back. He lost sight of the task at hand for just a moment when Heather smiled at him. She was beautiful. There they stood, staring at each other for what seemed like several minutes, when he finally broke the silence.

"Are you the only person here?" he asked as his mind snapped back to his orders and the task at hand.

"No. My girlfriend Jennie is still in the shower. What can I do for you, Sergeant?"

Michael paused and looked around the room, partly to assess the situation and partly because he really didn't know what to do next. At this point, Michael didn't know if the woman in the shower was white, like Heather, or black. He also didn't want to ask the question outright and cause Heather to be even more suspicious, so he decided to be patient until he could properly assess this location per the orders he was given.

"If it's okay with you, I'd prefer to wait until your roommate joins us. That way I can provide you both with an update of what's going on and carry out my orders properly. Do you mind?"

"No, I don't mind at all. Can I get you something to drink? We've got water, soda, juice. What would you like?"

"Nothing, thanks. I'm good."

He made his way further into their living room when a wall full of framed photos caught his attention. Feeling a bit uncomfortable in Heather's presence, awkward because she was attractive and he found himself wanting to impress her, he walked over to the grouping of memories that were carefully placed in full view of anyone who entered. "So what are these all about?"

"That's what Jennie and I call our life story together. That's her right there." Heather motioned toward the wall, brining Michael's attention back to the photos.

"That's your friend Jennie? She's the one that we're waiting for to get out of the shower?"

"Yep, that's her. Here." Heather moved closer to the wall and pointed out a specific picture. "This is the very first picture ever taken of the two of us together. Our first day of school in the first grade. That's the day we met, and we've been best friends ever since—more like sisters, really."

"Wow, and you've been able to stay together this entire time? I mean, by the looks of these pictures it appears that you both stayed in the same school, went to college together, and joined the army together. How did you manage that?"

"I'm not sure, to be honest. We just have this commitment to each other, and so far it's kept us together—with a little good luck being mixed in, of course." She smiled in her bubbly way. Just talking about her best friend made Heather giddy.

Michael adored the charm in her behavior and perceived it as flirtatious, which caught his attention even more. As he scanned the multitude of photos on the wall, Heather continued to tell him stories about each one. It was like a storybook being read to him as he looked on. His mind started to drift back to his best friends, Rockson and Daemon.

"You know what, Heather? This reminds me of my best friends. We've also known each other since grade school, and the three of us are still together—right here at Fort Benning."

"No way! That's awesome. Jennie and I grew up in Omaha, Nebraska. Where did you guys grow up?"

"Los Angeles." He was shy about his hometown and was so focused on making a good impression that he hoped Heather wouldn't ask more questions about his childhood. He didn't want her to know that he grew up in the 'hood, surrounded by gang life.

"Hey, what's going on out here?" Jennie, having just finished getting dressed, asked as she came out of the bedroom.

"Jennie, this is Michael. He's on some secret mission, from what I can tell," Heather said with a smile. She slapped Michael's arm playfully. "But he wouldn't tell me more until you got out here. So, here we are."

Jennie also admired Michael's presence at first, but she could tell that her best friend was already trying to get Michael's attention. Being the good friend that she was, Jennie tried to restrain her normally flirtatious demeanor for Heather's benefit.

Still a little on edge now that his mission came back to the forefront, Michael turned his attention to Jennie. "I need to talk to you, miss. Is there a place we can go that's private?"

"Talk to me in private? You don't even know me. Whatever you want to say, you can say in front of Heather, too."

"Miss, please." Michael wasn't expecting a situation like this, but he felt like he had no choice. He turned to look at Heather before turning back to Jennie.

"I think that you'll understand if I can just have five minutes with you. An event has occurred on base that has to do with race relations."

Both women could sense that Sergeant Masters was sincere, and they knew that in the army—especially in base housing—the risk of their being in any kind of danger was slim to none. Not only was everyone a part of the same fraternity of sorts, but also every soldier wanted to keep his or her position and rank. In the short time they had chatted with each other, Heather felt she had gotten to know Michael well enough to trust him, so she encouraged Jennie to talk with him privately.

"Don't worry about it, Jennie." Heather slowly moved toward the kitchen, keeping eye contact with, and a slight smile locked on, Michael the entire time. "I'll get out of the way so that you and Sergeant Masters can talk."

Michael and Jennie moved to a quiet corner of the living room so that he could share the story of the Black Heritage Army. He shared the high level aspects of their mission, their plans to separate from the union, and all of the details that he was allowed to disclose at this time.

All the while, Heather was in the kitchen, straining to hear what was being said. She was hopeful that Sergeant Masters was as interested in her as she was in him. Still having no idea that something serious was happening, she listened for any sign that Jennie was trying to set her up on a date with Michael, knowing that her best friend would help her out if she could.

But soon it became clear that Jennie and Michael weren't having a friendly conversation at all. In fact, it sounded more like arguing. Trying to keep their voices low, they were clearly having a disagreement. But about what? Heather leaned closer to the door, listening anxiously.

"So you're saying that it's just because she's white?" Jennie was clearly frustrated.

"Yes, but those are just my orders. You don't understand what's at risk here—besides, if she is left on her own, she could get hurt."

"Hurt? Heather and I have been friends for a lifetime—she is not a racist! And I'm sure there are a lot of white people that aren't racist. What's your big plan for that, Sergeant?"

"Sorry, but I don't make the rules. I only follow orders. You know that."

"Sorry is right. But since you follow orders, I'm ordering you to let Heather stay here in the apartment until I can talk to someone else about this!"

Because Jennie and Heather had completed college and were a part of ROTC, they were officers. An officer would always outrank an enlisted soldier, regardless of the enlisted person's rank. So even the lowest-ranking officer could give orders to the highest-ranking enlisted soldier, and technically the former would have to follow those orders. Jennie tried to exert her authority on Sergeant Masters, but it was in vain.

"I can't!" Michael's whispering had the obvious tone of anger and frustration. "My orders come directly from an officer that outranks you. You *know* how this works; I can't simply ignore my orders."

"Listen, Sergeant, I'm just trying to do what's right here. I can guarantee you that Heather is no risk. Let's just leave her here for a couple of hours. If I can't convince your boss, then she'll still be here, waiting for you to come back and get her."

Sergeant Masters turned and stared back at the wall that was filled with the lifetime of pictures telling the story of Jennie and Heather's friendship. Each one displayed the kind of smiles that he had only dreamed of as a kid: genuine, relaxed, completely innocent, and harmless.

"I guess that's fine." He let out a breath as he gave in to her request. "But I'll deny everything if word gets out."

"Heather?" Jennie's loud voice startled Heather.

Heather made her way back to the living room, still smiling. "Hey. What's up?"

"Heather, there's something going on right now. For your own safety I can't tell you what it is, but I really need you to trust me on this, okay?"

"What are you talking about?"

"Listen, please don't ask. Just trust me. I talked to Sergeant Masters, and he agreed to let you stay here instead of ... well, instead of having to go somewhere else."

"Jennie, what the *heck* are you *talking* about?"

"Heather, please stop asking!" Understanding the gravity of the situation, Jennie began to get emotional; her response caught Heather's attention. Something was wrong, and Heather knew it.

"Heather." Sergeant Masters turned to her, his deep, warm voice breaking in. "I'm going to need you to stay in your apartment for the time being, that's all. Please go get your cell phone and computer. I'll need to take those with me."

Heather's head snapped in Jennie's direction. "Jennie, what the hell is going on?"

"Heather, just trust me ... please." She placed both of her hands on Heather's shoulders, pleading with her. "Do like Sergeant Masters says. And whatever you do, don't answer the door or make any noise until I get back. Do you understand me?"

"Yes, but I need to know."

"You don't want to know anything right now—trust me. Just do like I'm saying. Stay quiet and out of view. We're going to mark the door from the outside so that no one else tries to bother you. I'll be back as soon as I can." Jennie was throwing her gear into a backpack now, sounding calmer than before but still clearly concerned.

"Jennie, please," Heather said as she looked at Jennie with pleading eyes. The situation was frightening to her, especially without her knowing any details of what was going on.

Jennie and Sergeant Masters were standing at the doorway now, ready to leave. Everything had happened so fast, Heather didn't quite know what else she could do.

Giving in, she left the room briefly and returned with her cell phone and computer in hand. She hesitated and then walked closer to Michael, handing them to him reluctantly.

"Thank you, Heather." Sergeant Masters knew he shouldn't, but he smiled at her. Even with everything going on around them right now, he simply couldn't resist her charm. His smile was full of his attraction for her, but both knew that this was not the time for it. Still, Heather smiled back sheepishly, with an almost guilty expression, and closed the door slowly behind the two as they left.

Michael's million-dollar smile and the feeling it caused inside

Heather couldn't be held back. "I can't wait to see you again," she whispered to herself as her back slid down against the door until she was sitting on the living room floor.

Heather let her emotions focus on the excitement caused by the prospect of new love. "Oh my goodness," she muttered, "he is beautiful." She closed her eyes for a moment, relaxing in the thought of a relationship with Michael Masters, but then it hit her.

She had no idea what was going on, but something didn't feel right. She could tell that something big had happened—or was about to happen—but what was it? She had no way to communicate with the outside world, and both Jennie and Michael were pretty adamant about her lying low until they returned.

Her feelings of love and solace were replaced with fear and anxiety. From her spot on the floor, she looked up and scanned the room. She suddenly felt very alone.

It was the initial plan of the Black Heritage Army to round up all the white people on base and secure them in a holding area. Even though cellular phone and Wi-Fi signals were electronically blocked, the plan was to take away the phones and computers of anyone that wasn't African American—anything to prevent them from contacting the outside world. The soldiers of the Black Heritage Army gradually gathered everyone on base that wasn't black and placed them in one manageable area. The strategy had been working well so far.

Most soldiers, black, white, or otherwise, answered their doors and invited the Black Heritage Army soldiers in without question; they had no reason to resist or even suspect that something was awry. And since their lines of communication were severed immediately, they had no way to warn others when they realized that this was not a drill and that something was completely wrong.

But by the time a person realized the truth, it was simply too late. Black Heritage Army soldiers moved swiftly from house to house, through apartment complexes and barracks, both on base and in surrounding areas. Their mission was carried out almost flawlessly.

The only immediate challenges were the soldiers and families who lived off base, in private housing. But in the end, even that proved to be not too much of a challenge. People outside the Black Heritage Army had no idea what was going on. In the usual daze of their daily routine when they reached the main gates to enter the base and report for work, they, just like the people at the state borders, were stopped, questioned, and dealt with individually.

The other, much larger challenge for the Black Heritage Army was the number of mixed-race households. Families who had a black and a white parent presented a situation that the soldiers weren't properly trained for. It was for this reason that each situation had been treated differently in the early days of Operation Freedom Reign.

Just like the situation with Heather and Jennie, a mixed-race household was difficult for a lower-ranking soldier to deal with on his or her own.

In this case, Jennie had convinced Sergeant Masters to make an exception for Heather. She explained the depth of their friendship and convinced him that Heather would support their cause. Although he went against orders, he was willing to take a chance, not just on account of what Jennie was saying, but also because he thought he had just experienced the impossible: love at first sight.

CHAPTER 10
A Failed Escape

Non-black individuals on military bases, as long as they were not married or had no children, were rounded up and placed in barracks. This was no easy task. Most of the bases within the Ubuntu territory were rather large, but at least each one was gated, with only two or three entrances surrounding the base perimeter. Their ability to restrict travel into or out of each base afforded the Black Heritage Army more time to have troops go door to door, looking for people of other races who might pose a threat to their operation.

On the other hand, married families, especially those with children, were allowed to remain in their homes or apartments. Each neighborhood would be guarded twenty-four hours a day, ensuring that no one would try to escape. The Black Heritage Army was of the opinion that families would not try to escape anyway, principally because they had children, which would make it nearly impossible for them to make their way to the base perimeter. More important, they would be putting their children at great risk. For this reason, the Black Heritage Army's strategy seemed bulletproof.

General Street's kids were quarantined in their house just like many other white families who had homes on base had been. Since Charlie Street and his wife had left for their vacation the night before, only their nanny, Kristy Jefferson, was home to take care of the kids.

The soldiers who secured the Street residence didn't think twice about its being the general's house. They were low-ranking enough that even though they noticed that the general was not home, they had nothing out of the ordinary to report. When they searched the home, the soldiers saw that the nanny was in charge. Judging from her appearance, they felt there was no way that she could possibly pose a threat or otherwise cause any trouble. So they moved on to the next house.

General Street's nanny could tell that something was wrong, without question. When the soldiers stopped by, they didn't share any details about what was going on, but their story about performing a routine check of high-ranking officers' homes didn't settle well with her. She was never known for being the brightest young lady in the room, but she was known for having a sharp intuition.

Kristy had agreed to watch the kids while the Streets were on vacation partly as a favor to her parents, who had known General Charlie Street for years. But when the opportunity came for her to make a little extra money by house-sitting and taking care of the Street kids as a temporary nanny, she jumped at the chance.

Just like Charlie Street and his wife, Kristy came from a well-to-do southern family. In fact, it was rumored that Kristy was a descendent of Thomas Jefferson—although this was never confirmed and was not a public claim of her family. Like other southern girls of her age and similar upbringing, she came across as the spoiled daughter of a wealthy plantation owner. In her case, this was an accurate assessment. Daddy made sure that his little girl got anything and everything that she wanted, whether she needed it or not.

At only five foot two, Kristy still caught everyone's attention. She was beautiful by any measure. Some might say "cute" before "beautiful," but she turned the head of many a gentleman she passed, regardless. Her personality was alluring; her charisma and energy combined to make her appealing in every way. Always with a smile and a carefree demeanor, she was the type of person whom nearly everyone found entrancing.

It seemed natural—and safe—for her to spend some time with Charlie Street and his family. Kristy's daddy saw this as a chance for her to mature a little bit. It would offer her new experiences. And with her being away from the familiarity of her overproviding family and self-centered friends, her daddy was hopeful that his daughter would develop into a person who had a much deeper appreciation of life than she had already.

Seeing as Kristy was still very young, only twenty-four years old, her daddy knew that one week at the Street house watching their kids wasn't going to change his daughter's level of maturity, but he thought it might be a good start. He was hopeful that her having the responsibility for someone other than herself, in this case Charlie's kids, would be good for her. Besides, Charlie was the general of one of the nation's most well-known military bases. What could possibly go wrong? If Kristy were to run into trouble that she couldn't handle on her own, the army would jump in immediately because of Charlie Street's rank, he thought.

But right now, with all of the confusion surrounding her and every means of communication taken away, Kristy was in over her head. She had no idea what to do, only that she had to somehow take care of the Street children and make sure they were safe. Without any form of communication, she had nowhere to turn for advice or guidance, and no way to alert the base chain of command that had been given to her before Charlie Street and his wife left.

There had to be someone else on base whom she could trust, someone who would also understand the importance of the children in her care, someone who would be willing to help her reunite General Street's children with their parents. But who, and how in the world would she find them? The soldier at the front door had made it clear that Kristy was not allowed to leave for any reason. Early in the day, Kristy tried everything she could to get through to the young man, but nothing seemed to work.

Still, she thought that she had to give it one more try. "Excuse me, mister soldier man?"

This being at least her fourth attempt to get past the assigned guard, he tried to ignore her altogether.

"Mister army man, can you hear me?"

"Look, miss, haven't you had enough for one day?"

"I only want to know what's going on so that I can help the children to be more relaxed. They're really getting scared by you guys and the idea that we can't leave."

"Miss, I've said this already more times than I care to: I can't tell you anything. I don't even know what's going on myself, not entirely, anyway. Would you please just go back inside and try to relax?"

"Come on, you can at least let me contact someone in the chain of command, can't you?"

He turned to look her in the eye. "Just go back inside. And don't try to come out here again, understand?"

Kristy could tell that her smile and charm simply weren't going to work on this guy. She gave him a dirty look bordering on a pout and then slammed the door behind her.

After a full day of fear, worry, and anxiety, Kristy was becoming restless. Her mind couldn't process what was happening around her. General Street's kids, able to sense this, were beginning to act more and more anxious. They were bouncing off the walls and not paying attention to anything that Kristy asked them to do. Their misbehavior added to the tension in the Street house.

Kristy went from optimism to tears, to a fake kind of happiness, which was an obvious ploy to make the children feel better—but they could see straight through her. The Street kids—Jacob, who was five, and his older sister, Meagan, who was eight—sat in the living room and watched as Kristy slowly began to lose control. Not knowing that there was reason for real concern, Meagan and Jacob found humor in Kristy's stress, which did nothing more than add to her frustration.

Because Kristy was immature herself, she felt that Meagan and Jacob were directing their humor at her personally, as if they were old enough to intentionally make fun of her in this situation or even capable enough to do so. This would have been a ridiculous thought for anyone who had been around children of that age or someone who had the typical maturity level of someone Kristy's age.

Kristy turned her attention to the living room window. Finally, the sun began to fade in the western sky. She knew that she wouldn't have to wait much longer to be alone with her thoughts, so she prepared a dinner for the kids and tried to settle them down for some early sleep. She gradually found a sense of purpose coming over her. Her mind grappled with the transition from fear and anxiety to the confidence and clear thinking that having a clear mission can create.

With her new found focus, she started to come up with a plan that included waking Meagan and Jacob in the middle of the night and trying to escape. She had lived in the area long enough to have a good sense of her surroundings at Fort Benning. She had a rough idea of the best pathway to get off base—or at least the shortest. If she could just get past the concentration of houses, barracks, and apartments, Kristy was confident that they would have the cover of the woods to aid their escape.

If the night sky was dark enough, she just might be able to get herself and the kids out of there and go to her parents' house. It wouldn't be easy, but she had to go for it. She also knew that she would need the kids to be as alert as possible for her plan to work properly, which is why she sent them to bed early.

At 12:30 a.m., she woke Meagan and Jacob. They had been sleeping soundly when she woke them, groggy and completely out of it, as any kids their age would be at that time of night. Still, Kristy knew that she had to get them alert enough to be focused if her plan was going to work.

"I don't want to get up now, Kristy," Little Meagan moaned, still half asleep.

"I know, sweetie, but we have to. Trust me on this."

"No! I'm going back to bed."

"You know, I'm taking you to see your mom and dad. Won't that be great?" Kristy leveraged a little white lie to motivate Meagan.

"Mommy and Daddy?"

"Yes. We just have to sneak over to where they are. It'll be fun."

Meagan found enough motivation to sit up, after which she started to gather her thoughts. Jacob on the other hand was no problem at all. He was up and moving right away, ready to take on the next adventure. He didn't have to be bribed to think midnight game would be fun.

Kristy encouraged them to get moving, offering candy and treats in some cases in an effort to pump them full of sugar, hoping this would get their blood flowing and make them a little more alert, perhaps.

At 1:15 a.m., the trio slipped out the back door as quietly as possible. Kristy had told the kids how serious a game this was, that they needed to be perfectly quiet, and that this was truly a life-or-death situation if they wanted to win the game. All of this sounded like fun to them and helped them focus the way they needed to. The game Kristy had fabricated seemed to be working out well.

Across the large backyard they ran. There was only a partial moon that night, but it seemed brighter than it had to be. Kristy led Meagan and Jacob toward the edge of the lawn, attempting to use the darkness offered by the shadows that the large trees provided, and there ran into a problem. The backyard was fenced in.

Not the simple chain-link kind that would be easy to jump over, this fence was the really tall wooden type used for privacy. She had no idea how she was going to get over it, let alone the two kids. *Damn,* she thought, *the moon is so fricking bright!* Problem number two.

"This is fun!" Jacob could hardly hold back his excitement about what they were doing, thinking it was just a game.

"Hush." Kristy was getting more nervous. "Is there a gate that we can get through?"

"Over there; it's in the corner." The boy pointed to the corner farthest away from them.

Kristy and the kids made their way to gate and carefully pushed it open so that they might escape the yard. Lucky for them, it didn't squeak.

Once on the other side of the fence, Kristy noticed that their challenge was increased. There was little to no cover for them to hide behind because they were still in the developed area of the base. In this area, the houses were larger and spread apart, with very little vegetation around them. They were going to have to make a run for it; there was no other option.

They stopped for a moment, crouching under the protection of a few shrubs that grew next to the fence. Kristy panned her vision left, then right, and then over the open field that they would have to sprint across in the moonlight. She didn't see anything. Once she signaled the kids to do so, they started to run.

Kristy instructed the kids to run in front of her so that she could see them clearly and, this way, make sure that they would be all right.

She was now encouraging them to keep running, her voice muted so as not to be heard by anyone else and her breath getting short because of her exertion.

Meagan and Jacob heard the sound of a three-round burst of rifle fire, but it hadn't registered with them consciously. They were familiar with the sound only because they were raised army and had spent their entire lives on military bases. They had even joined their father at the shooting range once or twice.

At their age, and thinking that they were all just playing a game, it didn't occur to them that the rifle shots were real or that they may have been intended for their nanny, running behind them. They continued to flee as fast as they could, Meagan giggling as she ran.

Kristy Jefferson didn't hear the shot that took her life.

"This is getting out of hand, yo! What did you shoot her for, man?!"

Meagan and Jacob heard the soldier's voice, so they turned to look behind them, but they kept running. They came to a stop when they saw two soldiers come out of the darkness and walk toward Kristy's body, which lay lifeless in the field.

"Damn it, Ray, what the hell were you thinking?!"

The second soldier didn't say a word.

"Go get those kids before they come back and see this. Go get 'em now!"

Meagan and Jacob had already gotten close enough to see Kristy lying on the ground in an awkward way. The moon cast an eerie beauty on Kristy's body and sharp facial features.

That would prove to be the final, lasting memory that young Jacob and Meagan would have of this fateful night.

* * *

The sudden ring of the telephone startled General Ballard. He instinctually reached for the phone, knocking over just about everything else on the nightstand before grasping it. He was lying in bed not really sleeping anyway; the day-to-day issues of running a war were beginning to take a toll on him. He picked up the receiver.

"What is it?"

"Sir!" The voice on the other end was obviously shaken with anxiety. "We have a problem with General Street's children. I have been told to request your presence at headquarters immediately."

"What is it? Are they all right?"

"Yes, sir—they seem to be fine. That's all I am allowed to say over the phone. Again, we request that you come to headquarters immediately."

"Understood. I'll get there right away."

* * *

He stood at the helm of his forty-five-foot Hunter sailboat, gazing into the sun. It was a perfect northeastern day on the ocean. General Street had always dreamed of being a sailor, but the army had gotten in his way. Still, he had bought the deck-salon-style cruiser a few years ago so that he could keep his dream alive.

He kept his sailboat at Bar Harbor at the south end of Frenchman Bay, which was an easy drive from Bangor, Maine, by taking Highway 1A, then connecting to Highway 3. The route took him right into the heart of the perfect little ocean town of Bar Harbor.

His Hunter sailboat was the perfect oceangoing vessel for him and his wife, Belle. It held enough freshwater and supplies for the two of them to remain out on the water for days at a time. It had a huge galley, a significant amount of storage space, and a large stateroom that made vacationing out on the ocean a very comfortable—and memorable—experience.

The kids weren't quite old enough to join the Streets at this point, at least not for long vacations. They would be far too cooped up in such a small space for any extended period of time. Besides, what's the point of a vacation if not for just the two of them to enjoy each other's company and rediscover each other?

This area, referred to as "down east Maine," was the ultimate sailing destination. There were hundreds of islands and what seemed to be thousands of miles of shoreline that had been left completely undisturbed.

This place brought General Street back to a time, maybe two or three hundred years ago, when America was at the very beginning of building its rich history. Being a history buff, the general discovered that this region made him think of when times were less complex and the area around him was yet undisturbed. Back to a time when men fought the ocean with their small boats, like the size of his, but with much more risk than he'd ever have to face.

Casually adrift now, General Street stared at the spruce trees peppering the unbelievable pink granite that made up the majority of the islands in the area. The only other boats he typically saw were owned by lobstermen, small groups of men working their tails off to scratch out a living off of fewer and fewer lobster. But that was what he respected about these men and their crews: their hard work and dedication.

He loved that he and Belle were always able to catch a glimpse of whales, puffins, ospreys, and the occasional bald eagle soaring high above and looking for its next meal. They also saw thousands of seals. This was the life he hoped to live on a full-time basis after his retirement from the army, but today he was simply enjoying some time off and letting it all soak in.

For Charlie Street, the best thing about these trips was the solitude, as he enjoyed being left alone for days on end. It was refreshing to be completely out of touch. There was no television, no radio, no news, none of his direct reports needing him to hold their hand—only a man and his thoughts. Oh, and his wife, Belle, of course.

"Honey, there's a message coming in on the VHF radio." Belle was underneath in the galley getting lunch ready.

He casually made his way below. "This is General Street. How can I help you?"

"Sir, this is Colonel Dade. There's been an emergency. Your presence is requested at the Pentagon."

"The Pentagon!? What's going on, Colonel?"

"Sir, it is apparent that several of our own armed forces have taken over military assets and are in the process of securing territory in the southeastern states."

"Taking over? What are we talking about here? How many states?

What locations, specifically?" All at once the ridiculousness of what he was hearing made him smile. "Hey, Thompson, is that you? Are you trying to pull some kinda joke on me, you ol' son of a bitch?"

"All due respect, sir, but this is no joke. My name is Colonel Dade, not Thompson, and I can assure you that the situation is very real."

"Damn. Okay then, tell me what the hell is going on. I want details."

"Again with due respect, sir, but this really isn't the time to talk about the particulars. The commander in chief has asked for your presence immediately. What I can tell you is that the opposing forces are being led by Colonel Ron Ballard."

"Ballard? That son of a bitch!" The thought of that alone made Street's blood boil. "I'm east of Frenchman Bay, Colonel. It will take me some time to dock and get to Bangor, but I'll get moving as fast as I can."

"Understood, sir. We will have a bird at the airport awaiting your arrival, and I'll make everyone aware of your estimated arrival time."

"Very good, Colonel. Hey, if you said Ballard is in charge, then does that mean Fort Benning is under seizure?"

"I'm afraid so, sir."

"We left our kids behind. Do you know if they are safe or if anything has happened to them?"

"Unfortunately, sir, our intelligence indicates that they may have been taken captive, but—"

"Captive!?" His anger now turning to rage, he was just about to rattle off his usual litany of expletives, but he noticed Belle standing there, looking at him. She appeared to be in shock. Not wanting to upset her more than she already had been, he bit his tongue and simply replied, "I'm on my way!"

Belle stood silently, frozen in the fear because she'd heard only one side of the conversation and didn't know whether her kids were safe. Her voice began to crack with emotion. "Charlie? What's going on?"

"That fricking Ballard has stolen military assets and is trying to take over some of the Southern states." General Street's face was red hot with anger.

"Oh my God!"

"Don't worry, Belle, as soon as we get back to shore I'll take care of this! Nobody's going to hurt my kids or destroy my country—especially no good-for-nothin', half-cocked nigger like Ballard!"

"Charlie! What do you mean by 'destroy my country'? Please tell me what's going on!"

"I can't Belle, I just can't. Like I said, don't worry. Let's just get our shit together and get the hell outta here."

Belle, overcome with emotion, nearly fell to the floor, but the galley countertop caught her elbow. Charlie stepped over to her and kept her from falling any farther. Then he held her for a moment.

"Come on, Belle. I need you to be strong right now. We both need to be. Trust me, the kids are fine. We've just got to get back to Washington and put an end to all of this nonsense."

Belle looked up and peered into Charlie's eyes. He had a history of holding information from her, and she knew it. She didn't necessarily know what he was hiding from her this time, but she was smart enough to know that something about Charlie wasn't completely authentic. She had always thought he led some kind of double life, but there was no way to prove it.

Right now, none of that was important. She had only wanted to look into his eyes long enough to see if he was lying to her. She could tell that he wasn't.

"Okay, Charlie, let's get going. What do we need to do?"

"The sails are already down, so I'll pull the anchor and then fire up the diesel engine. We'll use that to get us back to Bar Harbor more quickly and without having to man the sails, we can get things packed up more easily." He darted out of the galley to get topside, eager to get going as soon as possible.

Belle understood what was needed from her, so the fact that her husband had left abruptly without providing further instruction didn't faze her. Starting to round up all unsecured items, she was almost in a daze as she tried to comprehend everything she had just heard. But she still wondered more about what she *hadn't* heard.

* * *

The local sheriff was at Bar Harbor. The emergency lights of his cruiser were flashing as he waited for General Street to dock his boat. A couple of men in police uniforms scurried down to the dock, ready to help secure the vessel. One of them said to Charlie, "We'll stay behind and make sure she's all buttoned up, sir. We're both familiar with boating and the area, so you can be rest assured that she'll still be in one piece next time you come to take her out."

"Very good, men—thank you!"

Charlie and Belle made their way from the dock up to the parking area as quickly as possible. The sheriff reached out his arm with respect. "Nice to meet you, sir, although I wish it were under better circumstances."

"Let's get going, Sheriff. There's a lot of work to be done." Charlie said this after shaking the sheriff's outstretched hand.

The drive to Bangor took far less time than it normally did since they were traveling in a squad car. The siren was blaring, so they were able to make it through lights and intersections without stopping. Traffic continued to make way for them all the way to the airport. The patrol car raced right through the fencing that bordered the airport and then took General Street directly to the helicopter used for high-level army brass. Its engines were already running.

Street yelled to the sheriff so that he could be heard over the propeller and turbine engines. "I want you to take Belle to the best hotel in town. Make sure that she's taken care of, will ya?"

"Of course, sir, I'm happy to do it! I just hope you guys can fix this mess!"

"Well, thanks for the lift, Sheriff. And don't you worry, we'll get white America back!"

The roar of the large propeller, combined with the side-mounted turboshaft engines, echoed around the small airport as the helicopter lifted off and pointed its nose toward the Pentagon. Inside, several military commanders began to brief General Street on a few more details, but they had strict orders to wait and let their leaders at the Pentagon describe the exact events of the day with him.

They told him about the Black Heritage Army and of how its leaders had built their organization right under his nose, using Fort Benning as their headquarters. The commanders talked about the many missteps that had been taken in Washington during the course of events thus far and mentioned that they were now looking to him for guidance because he was a close friend of the person still known to them as Colonel Ballard.

All of what had transpired was completely unexpected, of course. And unlike with other enemies of the United States, this time they had absolutely no knowledge of the enemy. There were no historical tendencies for them to reference and no previous political action that might help guide their strategy—nothing to base their decisions on. This conflict would prove to be the federal government's biggest challenge of all.

Their only chance for success would be to leverage any and all knowledge they could gain about the *individuals* they were up against. By doing that, the government's national military leaders felt that they might be able to anticipate Black Heritage Army actions and predict their next steps. If they could anticipate the enemy, they could quite possibly be able to win the fight.

However, the president preferred that the majority of General Street's debriefing happen at the Pentagon so that he could brainstorm and strategize with the other military leaders as a team. He felt that the planning session would be more productive if Street was hearing some the details for the first time. And with everyone else gathered in the room, they would have the same perspective.

Charlie Street was so angry, he could hardly pay attention to what the other officers were telling him anyway.

CHAPTER 11
A Big Mistake, and Union Forces

It was pitch-dark while General Ballard made his way back to head-quarters. Many possibilities raced through his mind. He had gotten the phone call about an hour ago requesting that he get to the office right away to meet with Major Henderson. The only detail he had was that the Street children were safe. *That's good,* he thought to himself. He glanced at the clock on the dashboard; the time was 4:13. It was too damn early to start the day, but it had to be done.

Even at this early hour the base was well lit and the entire area was visible to the naked eye. This was a combat situation, so all available lights were being utilized. This gave the entire base a sort of eerie feel, like something he recalled from an Alfred Hitchcock movie. He parked his vehicle and then dashed upstairs to find out what was going on.

"General Ballard thank you for coming in so early, sir." Major Henderson was there waiting for him along with several others soldiers, so the major had decided to speak more formally to his superior officer.

"Of course, Major. Clearly this is a very important situation, so let's get right to the point."

"Yes, sir." Major Henderson stood to pace the room. Everyone else was seated around the large oval table, which was perfectly centered in the conference room that resembled something more fitting for a cor-porate board room. High back leather chairs surrounded the table, and there was a large flat screen monitor at one end of the room. Fluorescent lights reflected images off of the windows surrounding them so that they could see themselves when looking in that direction. It made the room seem much larger than it was.

"At approximately zero two hundred this morning, just over two hours ago now, a couple of our guards noticed movement in the neighborhood adjacent to General Street's home. I'm not sure if you're familiar with the area, but there's very little light in that vicinity. The men were operating under moonlight only. I'm not making excuses for them, but we need to understand that their ability to make visual assessment was impaired.

"Our soldiers spotted three people crouching down and running across an open area while trying not to make any noise. Naturally their movements were very suspicious. One of our guards caught the movement out of the corner of his eye and reacted without properly assessing the situation first." Major Henderson paused; he found it difficult to go on.

"Major?" General Ballard stood. The wheels of his chair squeaked from the friction of rolling against the carpet when he used his legs to push it away.

"Sir, the soldier fired at the three subjects in question."

"You've got to be kidding me! What the hell was he thinking?"

"We'll get to that when we question the men and learn more details. Candidly, we haven't taken the time to do that yet."

"Understood, Major—so get to the point."

"Sir, a young lady by the name of Kristy Jefferson, General Street's nanny, was shot and killed."

The room remained completely silent. Everyone in attendance, other than General Ballard, was already aware of what had happened, but none dared make a comment until the general spoke.

This being a very important situation given that it involved Charlie Street's kids, Major Henderson made sure that he had plenty of witnesses in the room. He had invited mid- and upper-level officers from several different disciplines to join he and General Ballard for the discussion and debriefing. He also knew that they needed to document every spoken word and provide a transcript to the leaders in Washington, DC, so he had arranged for an assistant to be present to transcribe.

Once again, General Ballard's hand instinctively reached for the back of his neck, which he rubbed while contemplating what he had just heard. LaRon looked up to notice that everyone was staring at him, waiting for direction. He gathered himself and sat back down calmly, ready to display the level of leadership that he knew he was capable of.

"Well, for starters, let's make sure that the kids are in good care— first and foremost. Has anyone spoken to the kids?"

"I have, sir. Captain Olivier at your service." Her tone was confident, which impressed the general. "The kids seem fine at this point. I can tell that they didn't see the event itself happen, although they may have seen the young lady's body. That said, I've spoken with them in detail, and they're fine emotionally."

Major Henderson interjected. "Captain Olivier is our chief psychology officer and leads our counseling department, general."

"Very good, thanks for that, Major. And where are the kids now?"

Captain Olivier continued. "The Street kids are back in their home, safe, and sound asleep. We have a couple of soldiers there, but I do recommend that we handpick someone to watch the children for the next few days."

"Very good, Captain, this is understood. Major Henderson, that'll be your job. Find someone responsible—and with common sense, for God's sake—to take care of these kids."

"Right away, sir."

"As for the soldiers, especially the idiot that fired his weapon, where do we stand with them?"

"I'll take that one, sir. I'm Colonel Bates with the military police. We have them in holding right now, allowing them to sit quietly in different rooms for the time being. Obviously we'll make this our number one priority and interrogate them in the next hour or so. I'll have a full report, along with a recommendation for punishment, for you later this morning. I can guarantee you that, sir."

"Excellent. Are there any other witnesses, or has this situation gone beyond the people in this room?"

"No, sir," Major Henderson said, jumping back in, "we've made sure of that. We were benefited by the time of day; of course, very few people were moving around at that time of the morning. We also made every effort to clean the situation very expeditiously. The bottom line is that we're very confident we've kept all events under wraps."

"Very good. We absolutely cannot have knowledge of these events leave this room, understood?"

"Yes, sir," all those who were present said in unison.

"Last—and this is extremely important—I want each of you to commit to me that we will make every effort to ensure that this doesn't happen again. We have got to let our entire force know that these actions are simply not acceptable and that punitive action will be taken, whether it was an honest mistake or not.

"I understand that everyone is under a great deal of stress and that this country hasn't seen an event the likes of this since the last Civil War, but we have got to get ourselves under control. Is *this* understood?" General Ballard was visibly angry.

"Yes, sir," all replied, again in unison. The group stood, came to attention, and saluted General Ballard.

He, still angry, allowed them to remain at attention and full salute while he scanned the room with his eyes. He turned and stormed out of the conference room without returning their salute.

* * *

General Street arrived on the helipad on the roof of the Pentagon and was immediately greeted by a group of officers. They had confused looks of doubt combined with fear on their faces.

These boys really need me, Street thought as he strode toward the top of the stairwell, as cocky as ever.

"Which war room are we going to?" he barked at his escorts. "And I want the details of what's going on around here—now!"

"Sir, the vice president might be able to join you in the bunker later today. The president is not available right now, but he will be joining us soon. That's all I can tell you for the time being, except that the secretary of defense is currently in charge of our efforts and has asked for you personally."

They were walking with such a sense of urgency that one of the soldier escorts was having trouble keeping up and was skipping from time to time in order to keep pace. Street thought it odd that the secretary of defense would ask for him, as he had only met him once. That was at a function a few years ago, but the two hadn't developed any type of relationship. In fact, they hadn't even spoken to each other since that night.

Street and his escorts turned abruptly and then entered the large strategy room referred to as "the bunker."

"General Street! Great to see you, sir, although I wish it were under better circumstances." Secretary of Defense Robert Stranahan was a red-blooded American by any measure. Part warrior, part politician, Stranahan was a man who had both worked and clawed his way up the ladder. Whether in combat during his early career or in political circles more recently, he took no prisoners and crushed anyone who got in his way.

In fact, Stranahan enjoyed his position because it gave him the freedom to bully his way through life. Corporate America couldn't have handled his methods, and he knew it. Purely political circles would wilt in his presence—and he knew that too. Stranahan was the type of badass that General Street looked up to.

Street had the same personality as Stranahan and a similar way of dealing with people; he just did a better job of covering it up. Street knew how to make others in the room *think* that he really cared about them, even when he didn't. He had an uncanny way of making people feel good about themselves when they left the room, but actually Street was manipulating outcomes to his advantage, just like Stranahan.

Both men enjoyed having power and using it to their advantage; both slept just fine at night, never giving thought to the trail of emotional distress they left in their wake.

"Mr. Secretary. The pleasure's all mine." Street reached out to shake hands, but Stranahan ignored the gesture, acting as though they had too much work to do, and looked toward the electronic maps lining the wall from floor to ceiling.

The Pentagon war room was bigger than most basketball arenas. It was lined with wall-to-wall computer screens, and it had several rows of computer terminals with more than seventy staffers pounding away at keyboards. The staffers were organized in pods, or small islands, all across the main floor.

Runners were hustling from pod to pod, relaying information by hard copy in some cases, but mostly sharing information with each other by talking about their findings. Nearly everyone had a headset on, and the room emitted the steady hum created when more than seventy voices are all talking at the same time and are backed by the audible vibration of as many computer processors.

Stranahan was always one to make sure that he firmly established the pecking order. In this case, he did so with his actions by ignoring General Street's offer of a handshake and by putting him in his place through the orders he gave.

"Street, you're here for one reason and one reason only. You know the son of a bitch that started this damn uprising, so you're the one that's going to help us eliminate the asshole and help bring order back to the United States."

"All due respect, sir, but what are you talking about? I mean, I think I understand what my role is in this situation, and I have a general idea of what's going at Benning, but when you say 'eliminate' Ballard...?"

"I think you know what I'm talking about. I don't give a damn what the top brass, or even the president for that matter, *thinks* we should do to resolve this. You and I are going to take care of this in our own way."

"Wait a minute, Stranahan. Just because he's taken over a few assets at Fort Benning, I don't think—"

"Sorry, General! I just realized that you have only been partially briefed and I'm the one who was supposed to give you all of the ugly details. Actually, that damn Ron Ballard has taken over more than just Fort Benning; hell, they've got control of six of our previously united states!

"That son of a bitch has somehow managed to secure each and every military installation within those states. Air Force, marines, army, navy—hell, even the coast guard! According to what one of our insiders is reporting, they've got some organization called the Black Heritage Army, which is why they are so well organized."

Street, shocked to learn the details, was dumbfounded by what he was hearing. "How in the hell did he manage to pull this off?"

"Apparently, he and several others had been planning this for years. We may never know how they managed to keep their organization underground for so long, but that doesn't matter now. What does matter is that they've succeeded so far. Our intelligence has also intercepted something that Ballard and his boys are referring to as 'Operation Freedom Reign,' which seems to be the code name they've been using for the operation.

"Honestly, General, we screwed up. Initially, we thought it best to keep the whole thing under wraps, as we had assumed it was just a small, isolated event. We had no idea of the scope of their operation.

"As important, if not more so, is that you screwed up." Stranahan reveled in one more opportunity to put General Street in his place. "These guys came up with the idea for the Black Heritage Army and built the massive organization right under your nose, using Fort Benning as their central headquarters.

"If we didn't need your help so much, I'd probably recommend that we string you up for being such a poor leader and for letting this happen in the first place." He cracked an arrogant smile. "Ah, but I probably wouldn't be allowed to anyway."

Street knew that he couldn't reply the way he wanted. Stranahan was higher ranking, but, as important, and unfortunately for the general, the secretary of defense was right: all of this had happened under Street's command. That was a cold, hard fact that he wouldn't be able to talk his way out of. His only chance for redemption at this point was to resolve the situation.

General Street saw this as an opportunity to earn back some level of credibility, so he kept his emotions in check and chose to rejoin the conversation, all the while ignoring Stranahan's comments.

"So you're saying that by keeping their actions away from the press, and by trying to keep it out of public view, you actually enabled them, right?" The entire situation was beginning to come into view for General Street.

"That's right, Charlie. Big screw-up on our part, and we'll admit it."

General Street shook his head in disbelief. He also felt a certain amount of respect for the Black Heritage Army, their motivation, and their level of organization. Then, suddenly, his thoughts turned back to his personal situation. He became agitated and was terrified about the situation his kids might be faced with.

"Wait a minute! My kids are still at Benning! Someone get to a source on the inside. I've got to know what their status is—and I mean right now!"

In reaction to General Street's order, Stranahan looked to his left and gave a nod to a staffer who was waiting for instructions. The staffer immediately but quietly acknowledged the order with a nod of her head before she bolted to one of the computer stations.

"We'll get details right away, General. I guess I didn't know that you still had family back at Benning. I was under the impression that you were all on vacation together." Stranahan gave Street a slight nod with an interesting stare in his eyes. He looked almost sorry for the general. That was the most emotion that anyone was ever going to get out of Stranahan.

"In the meantime, I need you to tell me everything you know about this Ron Ballard—every damn detail. I want to know how he thinks and how he reacts to stress. I want to know about his wife, kids, family, background—anything that will tell me how to kill this son of a bitch and save this country." Stranahan began to work himself into a frenzy.

"What brand of scotch does he drink, how many cups of coffee does he have in the morning, how does he raise his kids? Most of all, I want to know how we straighten this nigger out so we can get our country back under control!"

Stranahan's last comment caught General Street off guard. After all, Stranahan himself was an African American.

Trying not to show his confusion, Street gathered himself. "Get Ballard on the phone and let me get into his head. I can figure out what's going on in a matter of minutes. Bottom line, sir, is that Ballard is weak. I've known that bastard for most of my life, and he'll cower down to whatever I tell him."

"Based on his responses to us so far, I'm not so convinced, General. But if you think you can do better, well then, have at it!" He turned around and yelled, "Lieutenant! Get that Ballard asshole on the line for General Street here!"

Within minutes, General Street was handed a phone with Ballard on the line.

"Hey, Ron, is that you?"

"I don't go by that name anymore, Charlie. I'm back to using my given name, LaRon."

Street rolled his eyes showing an absolute disrespect for Ballard. "Right, Ron—er, *La*Ron, sorry—what the hell are you doing, my friend?"

"First of all, I don't see us as friends anymore, Charlie. I've had a lot of time to think about this, and for the first time—possibly for the first time in my entire life—I am able to see things more clearly."

"Like what, Ballard? What are you talking about?"

"Like the fact that you're a damn racist, Charlie! Your daughter called mine a nigger on the playground the other day, for God's sake. When I first heard it, I was in denial, but then I started to look back and reflect on our friendship over the years. Now looking back, it's pretty clear what your true feelings toward me have always been, Charlie."

"LaRon, what are you talking about? We've been friends since our early days at West Point. Hell, I bailed you out of so many scruffs with the other guys, and you know it!" General Street held eye contact with Stranahan while he was talking to Ballard on the phone, making sarcastic facial gestures to imply that he was in control of the conversation.

"Do I, Charlie? You might be able to say that out loud and even give that impression to the people around you based on some of your actions, but deep down, I can see the *real* you now. You're the one man who has held me back as I've tried to move forward in my career, however subtle your actions.

"Charlie, you're one who has glad-handed me and pretended to be a friend, but all the while you were using me to get ahead; stealing my ideas and using them as if they were your own; taking my thoughts and direction on challenges we were facing and then presenting them to the brass as if they were your ideas."

The phone went silent for a few seconds, but it seemed like minutes as both men reflected on what was being said and contemplated their next action.

"All the while, you were intentionally keeping me down by making others think that I was weak or was in over my head."

"Ballard, that simply ain't true, and you know it." General Street's voice had the faint hint of doubt that is detectable when a person is lying. "I've always been here for you, LaRon—always will be."

"Bullshit, Charlie, and you know it!"

"Listen, Ballard, let's get to the matter at hand. You and your men have stolen government assets and have executed war crimes on innocent people. You've captured and detained civilians and military personnel, and you've broken damn near every law on the books—"

"Damn it, Charlie, that's not true and you know it! We haven't hurt anyone, and we don't intend to! We're simply taking back what is rightfully ours and you better get used to it. That's what you can't deal with, Charlie, plain and simple—"

"What about my kids then, Ballard!? What about them!? You say you're not hurting anyone, but you've got my kids hostage! No matter what I am to you—racist, friend, demon—I don't give a shit! But I can tell you that you crossed the line when you put my kids in harm's way!"

Both men stood silently in their respective war rooms, each holding an uncomfortable handset to his ear while trying to make sense of what he was hearing, what he was saying, and what he should say next.

"Tell you what, Charlie," General Ballard said, breaking the silence, "I'll let you come down here and get Jacob and Meagan yourself. They're just fine, by the way. I've got them right here with me."

"What about Kristy, their nanny?"

"You just come down here and talk with me in person."

Ballard intentionally avoided General Street's question about Kristy. "There's no way that we are going to resolve this over the phone. You come get your kids. And plan to spend a few hours with me working this out."

"Sounds good, LaRon, but I can't say that I'm the decision maker here. I can't negotiate with you 'cause I'm simply not authorized—"

"Bullshit, Charlie! I know that they've called you in to deal with me because of the friendship they thought we had. Besides, I don't give a shit what the president or that traitor secretary of state says. You're the only person that I'll negotiate with."

General Street looked over to Shanahan, who also had a receiver to his ear and had been listening to every word. Shanahan, holding his hand over the microphone at the bottom of the handset, nodded his head in the affirmative.

"All right, Ballard, I'm on my way. You know that others are listening, so I want your guarantee that no harm will come to me or my kids. I'm going to be in enemy territory as far as I'm concerned, and I want a guarantee that the kids and I will get out safe."

"Of course, Charlie, of course."

"All right then, I'll make arrangements to get down there as soon as I can. Oh, by the way, I'll be bringing a small contingent along with me, just to make sure that I can keep you at your word."

"That's understood too, Charlie. Believe me—and you can tell the others this—we don't want bloodshed or war. We would prefer to settle this peacefully, and we're pretty confident we can do it in a way that benefits both sides."

"I'm not sure about all that, LaRon. I just want to grab my kids, hear what you have to say, and then get the hell out. As far as I'm concerned, the rest will work itself out."

"Fine, Charlie." Colonel Ballard hung up and walked over to the window.

The midday sun was beaming over the trimmed green grass and freshly manicured flower beds at Fort Benning. He could see the humidity beginning to rise from the ground. The familiarity of his surroundings was comforting to him, which helped him to relax and remain calm in the storm of chaos that surrounded him.

He took a deep breath and turned back to look at Reggie Henderson, who had been sitting in a nearby chair and listening to every word. "What have we gotten ourselves into, Reggie?"

Both men just looked at each other, neither truly knowing the answer.

CHAPTER 12
Child's Play

Still reeling from the events that took place overnight and from his conversation with LaRon, Major Henderson nevertheless felt a sense of relief. Having General Ballard on the team took some of the pressure off and allowed him to focus on the aspects of managing a team that he enjoyed most.

Although he was the founder and original leader of the Black Heritage Army, that was never a role that suited him well, and he knew it. He enjoyed the one-on-one coaching sessions the most, as they were opportunities for him to develop young men and women into people of strong character. Although Reggie knew that he could never have a lasting impact on one hundred percent of the people whose lives he tried to turn around, he certainly enjoyed trying.

He had become known as a father figure for more than just a few soldiers. Those who knew him best described Major Henderson as a deep thinker who had an old soul, and as someone who truly cared for the people around him—not selectively, as he genuinely cared for everyone. They knew that Reggie would fall on his sword for them if needed, which was yet another character trait that caused his staff to remain very dedicated to him and his leadership.

He certainly enjoyed the day-to-day activities of managing a team more than he did building strategy and discussing politics. This was one of the reasons that he had been so eager to turn over the highest leadership position to General Ballard. While many people who didn't know him thought it strange that he might turn over leadership of the

Black Heritage Army with so little resistance, Major Henderson didn't think it strange at all, as now he could focus more on things like troop assignment, coaching, and morale and less on battle tactics and the consequences of winning or losing.

"Miss Adams?" he called out the office door to his assistant.

"Yes, sir." Having made her way over to his office to respond, she slid her head through the crack in the door. She had a big smile on her face as usual. Indeed, she was always positive no matter the circumstances, which was why Major Henderson had hired her in the first place.

"Please locate Sergeant Daemon Johnson, would you, and have him report to me as soon as possible."

"And is there anything I should tell him, other than that? Is there anything that he might need to be prepared for?"

"No, that's it, but I do need him here right away. Let's not waste any time."

"Of course, sir. I'll make sure that he's here in short order." She scurried out of the major's office and immediately got to work locating Daemon Johnson.

★ ★ ★

So far, Daemon had felt like the odd man out. His best friends, Anthony Rockson and Michael Masters, had specific roles that they were carrying out, reporting directly to the top brass. But so far, he hadn't been called upon. It had gotten into his head a little bit.

Daemon was the type of person who preferred to be alone if he wasn't with his closest friends. Never the kind of person to bond with new friends quickly, he struggled with the concept of making new friends in general. This was a direct result of his upbringing, to be sure; he never knew in whom he could truly put his faith and trust.

Back in South Central, Daemon had been misled and taken advantage of a few more times than his good friends had been, and this led to his immediate distrust of others. Not only had his own father left the family at an early age, but also a revolving door of men who pretended to be interested in his mother appeared thereafter. Each one of those men played the role of "good guy" for Daemon and made promises that they couldn't possibly keep.

As a child, he was let down time and time again, which was at the root of his inability to make quick friends. This was also the reason that he preferred to be alone, especially at times like this. He felt let down that he hadn't been called upon yet. But being alone with no one around him allowed him to search his thoughts, analyze whether he may have done something wrong, and sort through his feelings.

This was the way that Daemon was ultimately able to turn his life around: he escaped from the chaotic world and phony people around him and became lost in his own thoughts.

Each of the barracks on base had a great room on one end of the building. There were pool tables, Ping-Pong tables, video games, satellite television—everything a soldier needed to keep busy and entertain him or herself. Daemon still lived in the barracks in order to save even more money for the day when he and his friends planned to retire, and in the great room was exactly where he was on this day, trying to sort through several issues that were weighing heavily on his mind.

He was at the pool table, knocking in one ball after the other. Alone in the great room, he continued to rack one set after the other, working on his game by always forcing himself to take the more difficult shot rather than the simple ones.

"Are you Sergeant Daemon Johnson?" The young lieutenant's voice broke Daemon's inner thoughts.

"Yes, sir." Daemon turned, noticed the lieutenant's rank, and then stood at attention and saluted.

"At ease, Sergeant. I'm glad I found you so soon. Major Henderson wants to see you in his office right away."

"Sure. Do you know what he needs? I mean, is there anything I need to bring in order to be prepared, sir?"

"He didn't say, Sergeant, just that he needs you to report immediately for some sort of special assignment."

"Thank you, sir!" Daemon stood at attention and saluted the lieutenant once again.

The instant his salute was returned, Daemon bolted back to his space in the barracks. He quickly put on a clean shirt and grabbed his ready gear.

His barrack wasn't that far away from Major Henderson's office. Since Daemon didn't have his own transportation, he started walking. His walk soon turned into a trot as he began to contemplate the possibilities. *I'm finally being called to the major's office!* he thought. *What could my new assignment possibly be?*

Whatever it was, it had to be high profile and important, because his presence was requested by Major Henderson himself—exactly what Daemon was hoping for! Now he avoided the sidewalks altogether and began to jog in order to save more time as he headed straight toward the officers' building.

* * *

"Sergeant Johnson just arrived, sir. Shall I send him in?" Miss Adams had poked her head through Major Henderson's office door again.

"Yes, please, and thank you."

Reggie set his reading glasses on the paperwork he was reviewing, leaving everything as it was so that he could remember where he had left off. Paperwork: yet another task that he absolutely despised.

"Reporting for duty, sir!" Daemon said after swiftly entering the office and snapping to attention, waiting for the major to return his salute.

"At ease, Sergeant. First, how are you holding up, son?"

"Fine, sir, just fine. I am eager to get my assignment and am ready to serve."

"I'm sure you are. Please sit down." Major Henderson smiled, pleased with Daemon's eagerness to serve. He motioned toward one of the chairs on the other side of his desk and then sat back down in his own chair.

"Just relax, son. How are you doing—I mean, really?"

"Fine, sir. I've been a little bored waiting for an assignment. You know what I mean. It's been even more challenging since both Michael and Rockson have their orders. There's no one left for me to hang out with right now."

"I understand, I know how close you guys are." Henderson paused to let his next point have a greater impact. "You know, I've grown to love and respect you three boys as if you were my own sons. Watching the three of you grow up and develop into fine young men has been such a pleasure to me. Bottom line is that I didn't want any of you to be too far out of my reach. Do you know what I mean by that?"

"Of course, sir, and thank you. I think you know that we appreciate everything you have done for us."

"I do, Daemon, I know you do." He looked at Daemon and smiled. "Here's the thing, son. As you can imagine with an operation such as this, we've got a lot of moving parts to deal with. Some things I can tell you about; others have to remain out of view. Understood?"

"Of course, Major. You know I'll be the good soldier—I'm ready to do whatever it takes to help our cause, no questions asked."

"Great!" With the level of excitement that Daemon was showing, Major Henderson was almost embarrassed to give the sergeant his assignment. He stood and turned to look outside his window so that he didn't have to face him.

"We've uncovered an interesting situation, Sergeant, one that we couldn't have planned for even if we'd tried. Turns out that General Street left his kids behind."

"Sir?"

"Well," he said, turning around now to face Daemon, "part of the reason for the timing of Operation Freedom Reign and launching the initiative when we did was because General Street had just left for a vacation.

"We knew it would be a lot easier to secure assets without him around, but we also thought he took his entire family with him. As I said, it turns out that he left his two kids behind, his daughter and son."

"I still don't follow, sir. How does that affect me?"

"I need you to take care of General Street's kids until he arrives and we've had time to negotiate with him."

"Babysit? Are you kidding me?" Daemon, just now realizing the way he had reacted, corrected himself by lowering his voice and changing his tone. "I'm sorry, sir, but do you really mean for me to babysit the general's kids?"

"It may not sound like much of an assignment, Sergeant, but I can assure you that this is a very big deal. If we don't handle this correctly, we will look like criminals. The union political machine could easily make it look like we are holding two children as hostages, and that's the last thing we need right now. Understand?"

"Yes, sir." Daemon, ever the good soldier, stood at attention and saluted the major. "Ready, willing, and able, sir. Just let me know where to begin."

Major Henderson returned the salute. "I've got a private waiting for you downstairs. He'll take you over to the Street residence, where the kids are. He'll also remain on guard outside the residence while you make sure they remain safe.

"Keep your radio on so that I can tell you guys when to bring them over here for the exchange back to Charlie Street."

"Yes, sir."

"Oh, and one more thing you should be aware of, Sergeant. Street had left his kids with a nanny, someone who was a family friend of theirs. Last night she tried to escape with the kids in tow."

"No problem, sir. Is she in custody now?"

"Well," Henderson said before hesitating, "we experienced an unfortunate mishap last night. The nanny has been shot. She didn't make it."

Daemon stood quietly, an empty feeling having come over him. He looked Major Henderson in the eyes and could tell that he was hurting. Reggie was nearly in tears when he said, "No one wanted to have this turn into loss of life, and especially not innocent life, such as a nanny who was here to protect a couple of kids."

"I understand, sir."

"I'm not sure you do, but it's important for you to know this, because the kids could be pretty distraught. From what I'm told, they didn't see the action take place, but they may have seen her body at some point.

"The bottom line is that I want you to contact base services immediately if it looks like Charlie Street's kids are under emotional duress. As I've said, though, we don't think they saw enough, or understood the situation enough, to be in that state of mind. I think you'll be fine just taking care of them and helping them by offering a few distractions."

"Okay, Major, I'll certainly do the best I can."

"I know you will, Daemon—and believe me, your best is far better than most, which is why I called on you for this assignment."

"Yes, sir."

Daemon left the office a bit sluggishly. This wasn't exactly the type of assignment he was hoping for. More important, though, was his wondering how in the world he was supposed to entertain and take care of two kids. This was something that he had absolutely no experience with. If he were to be honest with himself, then he would admit that it scared him a little bit.

There was no time to doubt his abilities, though. If this was his assignment, then he would do it as best as he could. He made his way down to the parking lot and jumped up into the jeep that was idling in a stall, waiting for him. "Let's go, Private."

The jeep's suspension squeaked and bounced as Daemon and his driver passed the drainage curb at the end of Charlie Street's driveway. The private stopped just short of the garage door and let the small engine gurgle to a stop.

Daemon took in a deep breath. Taking care of two young kids seemed more intimidating to him than going out and fighting in the field. *How in the heck did I get myself into this one?* he thought to himself one last time.

"This man is here to take care of the Street kids—direct orders from Major Henderson." The private who had escorted Daemon quickly briefed the soldier standing guard at the front door.

"Good enough for me." The guard turned to open the door, and then let Daemon pass.

Daemon was taken aback. To him, the Street's home might as well have been a museum of American history. It was finely appointed with rich hardwood floors, a few plush carpets strewn about, and furniture that appeared to be more for show than for actual use.

Expensive, very ornate lamps and other items were located throughout the great room, which had twelve-foot-high ceilings. The room opened up to an even higher ceiling as it met the west wall, which featured floor-to-ceiling windows. The daylight entered the room—and the entire house, it seemed to him—almost as if he were standing in a holy place.

To Daemon, and compared to the residences of his upbringing, this home seemed like a palace. "So this is how the other half lives," he said out loud, unable to hide his stunned amazement.

"Who are you?" The high-pitched voice came from behind him. Little Meagan Street had entered the room and was standing there, holding a stuffed animal by the arm. She was escorted by a female private that had been watching the kids until someone else was permanently assigned.

Daemon straightened up, not knowing exactly how to reply in this situation. "Uh, I'm Sergeant Johnson." He then looked to the private for an affirmation that he was doing the right thing. She smiled and nodded approvingly.

"Do you have a first name?" Meagan continued.

"Uh, Daemon."

"Oh, hi, Daemon. I'm Meagan!" She smiled and walked closer to him. "Do you like dogs?"

"Dogs? I guess so—"

"I like dogs too! This one's name is Ralphie." She extended her arm, which was still holding the stuffed animal. "Want to see him?"

Daemon, still a bit intimidated by and frightened of the situation, sheepishly reached out to take the stuffed dog. "Ralphie, huh? Sounds like a good name."

"I know, silly. All of my animals have fun names! After all, that's what animals are for, right?" Her smile was addictive.

"I guess so, Meagan."

"Do you have any animals, Daemon?"

"No, ma'am."

"You should. They make you feel better when you're scared."

Daemon was starting to relax. It was becoming obvious that this was not going to be as difficult as he had thought. Meagan's comments and smile were helping him to drop the formal army persona, and it actually felt good! Maybe a mental escape such as babysitting two kids was exactly what he needed at this point in his life.

"Can you show me your other animals?" Having bent down to her level by this time, he leaned forward with his hands on his knees.

"Of course! Come on. They're in here." Meagan turned and bolted toward the more casual family room on the other side of the kitchen.

Daemon walked behind her in close pursuit, followed by the private.

"Who are you?" Another small voice and smiling face popped up from behind the sofa. Five-year-old Jacob Street had been sitting there, playing with his toy race cars.

"This is Daemon! He's really nice!" Meagan interjected before Sergeant Johnson had a chance to respond for himself.

"Oh, hello, Mister Daemon! Want to play with cars?"

"No, he's going to play with me and my stuffed animals."

"Wait a minute, guys, wait just a minute. I'm here to watch you and make sure that you are taken care of. I'm not here to play with your toys." Daemon was softening up more with every interaction, but was still reluctant and not sure what his boundaries were.

"Well, you can play with toys, too, as long as you're here, right?" Meagan's enthusiasm never left her.

"I guess so."

"Good! Then let's play with cars!" Jacob's response made it obvious to Daemon that both of these two kids needed some attention.

Daemon, letting his guard down because he knew that he could, relaxed his shoulders and took a seat on the sofa right between the two Street kids. "All right, show me."

The private jumped into the conversation. "Well it looks like you've got this under control, Sergeant. If it's okay with you, I'll get moving along."

"Absolutely. Thanks Private. I can handle it from here."

She exited the room while Daemon returned his full focus back to the children.

Both Jacob and Meagan started talking at the same time, each fighting for Daemon's attention. He was trying to acknowledge at least one comment from each of them. The level of noise in the room was rising when Meagan's comment caught his attention.

"What's it like to be black?" Both Jacob and Meagan were quiet because they wanted to hear the answer.

Daemon looked at her in disbelief. Did she really just ask him that? "Well, I guess it's—"

"'Cause Daddy always says that it wouldn't be good to be black. Why is that?"

Daemon was stunned. Not really sure how to respond, he could nevertheless tell that her question was intended to be innocent. Clearly she meant no harm. Instead, she was genuinely interested in learning more. He decided to engage with her line of questioning just to see where it ended up, if nothing else.

"Well. Maybe your daddy said that because when you're black, you're treated a lot differently than if you are white."

"Why?"

"That's a good question. I'm not sure if I can answer that one, but I can tell you that when I was your age, my life was a lot different than yours."

"What do you mean?" Meagan was interested now. Jacob stopped playing with his cars. He was also interested in what Daemon had to say.

"How old are you now, Meagan?" Daemon chose to divert the conversation.

"I'm eight years old."

"Eight is a great age to be. I remember when I was eight, but that was a long time ago. So have you enjoyed having your parents be on vacation?"

"Not really. I wish they were still here."

"You miss them, huh?"

"Well, kind of. The thing is that we don't have anyone to make us our breakfast, clean things up, and take care of us. I don't like it when I have to do things."

Daemon could see the spoiled side of Meagan coming to the forefront. "That's not so bad, though, is it?"

"I think so! I can't go out and play—oh, and we haven't gotten any new toys in almost a week! I don't like being here when it's this way."

"You know, you might like to hear what it was like for me when I was your age." Daemon could see that Meagan's comments were innocent enough. In truth, he had already decided that he really liked both Meagan and Jacob. They seemed to be pretty good kids, and he could tell that their hearts were in the right place, even if they were a little spoiled. So he decided to give them a different point of view.

"When I was eight, I wasn't able to go to school every day because sometimes it was too dangerous. My mom would keep me at home whenever the older kids in our neighborhood were causing trouble. Problem was that I really wanted to go to school! I liked it because it was a safe place where I enjoyed learning new things."

"I like school too," Meagan interjected, wanting to respond. Jacob was now also paying full attention.

"That was also the year that my little sister died. She was shot by someone who didn't even know her. We know it was an accident, but I really miss her."

Meagan and Jacob went from interested to shocked as Daemon continued.

Daemon noticed the change in their expressions, and he realized that the terminology that he used might have been a bit too strong. Still, he didn't really know how to act in a situation like this, so he decided to continue, doing the best he could.

"Then, when I was only twelve, my mom died. So that meant that I couldn't go to school at all anymore, and I really missed it. Some bad people came to our house and tried to make me live in some home with other kids, but I was scared and didn't want to. So I ran away. I found a friend of mine, and his family let me live with them from then on.

"I never had anyone to clean or cook for me, never. I can't even remember my birthdays because we couldn't afford to celebrate them. And after my sister died, I was all alone anyway.

"If it wasn't for my good friend Anthony Rockson, I might not be alive today either."

Daemon still sitting on the sofa, both kids were standing in front of him now, staring at him. This was the first time they had even considered that someone else might have a different life than they had.

Meagan was bright enough, and mature enough emotionally, to completely comprehend what Daemon had told her. And it upset her.

"Mister Daemon, I'm so sorry that your little sister died." She took a step forward and gave him a hug while he continued to sit on the sofa.

Daemon didn't know how to respond at first, but he slowly put his arms around her to return the hug. "Thank you, Meagan."

She leaned away from the hug, her hands still resting on his shoulders. "Maybe I can be your little sister? I really like you, Daemon, 'cause you're a good person."

He was taken aback and didn't have any idea how to respond. His eye shed a tear as he tried to deal with the emotion he was feeling. No one had ever touched him this way and this immediately, and yet here she was, little eight-year-old Meagan, causing him to get all emotional.

He looked over to Jacob, who had already returned to playing with his cars, and thought how ironic it was that General Street's kids would be the ones to touch him in this way and to uncover deep emotions that had been bottled up for so long.

Daemon turned back to Meagan, smiled, chuckled a little bit, looked down, and shook his head. He couldn't even imagine how her father would react if he found out that she had just consoled a black man—and even gave him a hug.

"So is your friend Mister Anthony still your friend?"

"He sure is. In fact, we work together right here on the base. He and I—oh, and our other good friend, Michael—have all stayed together and are still best friends."

Another new emotion played with his heartstrings. As he heard himself talking about his two best friends in this way, he realized how much they meant to him. He depended on them emotionally. They had truly become his family, his brothers.

Daemon looked back up and smiled at her. "Tell me more about your animals, Meagan."

CHAPTER 13
Love Sees No Color

Sergeant Michael Masters left the rest of his unit behind temporarily and took Jennie with him to see Major Henderson. In Masters' mind, Reggie Henderson, not the newly appointed General Ballard, was the guiding force behind the Black Heritage Army, so to him it made sense to start with the major.

And because Major Henderson had taken Michael and his two best friends, Rockson and Daemon, under his wing over the years, he knew that Henderson would be his best chance for getting an exception for Heather, if that were even possible. As a result of his feelings for her, he really wanted Heather to avoid lockdown. It would be even better if Michael could remain at her side.

Masters and Jennie walked straight to Major Henderson's assistant, who sat at her desk in the small greeting area.

"We're here to see Major Henderson. Can you tell him that Sergeant Masters is here?"

"He's at General Ballard's office for a meeting right now and probably shouldn't be disturbed." She replied as kindly as she could under the circumstances.

"I can appreciate what you're saying, but this is important; it's mission critical in fact. Listen, he and I are very close; can you at least just go tell him that I'm here? We'll wait as long as we have to, but we absolutely have to speak with him."

She stared at Michael, then shrugged her shoulders. "I guess so.

Why don't the two of you go wait in his office? If he can't meet with you, I'll come back and get you."

"Great, thank you—oh, and be sure to tell him that I've got a guest with me, if you don't mind."

Major Henderson had made his way down the hall to General Ballard's office, where they continued their discussion about what Julius Jackson had done to the Hoch family. Both men knew that they had to rein in that type of activity or else the Black Heritage Army would certainly lose the battle of public opinion.

The men were interrupted by Major Henderson's assistant. "There's a Sergeant Masters here to see you, Major." She stood in the doorway of General Ballard's office, her back leaning against the door to hold it open. "Shall I have him come back at another time?"

"No, that's fine. Take him to my office and tell him I'll be there in a few minutes."

Major Henderson looked at Ballard; the latter's jaw muscles flexed with frustration as he looked down and away. "There's no turning back now, LaRon. You know that, right?"

"Of course, Reggie, but that's not what I'm thinking. I'm more concerned with where we go from here and how we go about this the right way. You of all people should understand me on this one."

"I do, sir, I do. I just want to make sure that you don't have any lingering doubt with regard to the cause and that you're still squarely focused on our ultimate goal."

"Of course I am, Reggie. I've made up my mind and I'm fully committed. I'd appreciate it if you never bring that up again, by the way. Once I've made a decision, I don't look back. You know that about me."

The two men looked at each other, trying to read what the other had on his mind. The magnitude of their situation was beginning to wear on both of them. After a few moments, each could sense from the other that they were still on the same page.

Major Henderson stood, and looked at his friend with a soothing smile. "I better go see what Masters needs. He's the young man I have leading the local base sweep. And don't worry, General, everything will come together for us just fine. We're on the right path. With the two of us in this together, there's nothing we can't overcome. We'll be successful."

"I agree." Ballard's entire body relaxed as Reggie's comment began to sink in. "Let's catch up again later today at our daily debriefing."

"Sounds good, my friend."

As Major Henderson left the room, he could hear General Ballard's office chair let out a faint squeak. The general had spun his chair to gaze out his window. He wondered what he had gotten himself into.

* * *

They had waited for only a few minutes when Major Henderson walked into his office.

"Sir!" Both Sergeant Masters and Jennie snapped to attention to greet him.

He returned the salute. "At ease, Sergeant. Who's this with you, Masters?"

"This is Lieutenant Jennie Hamilton, sir."

"Hello, Lieutenant, nice to meet you." Major Henderson greeted Jennie politely and reached out his hand to shake hers. "What can I do for the two of you?"

Jennie didn't hesitate; she jumped right in before Sergeant Masters could say a thing. "Sir, Sergeant Masters has explained everything about the Black Heritage Army to me, but I have to say that I'm really concerned about your policy toward whites."

The major had already made his way through his office and was now sitting behind his desk, hardly paying attention to Lieutenant Hamilton. He was starting to shuffle papers on his desk. Having far too much on his plate, he took little notice of what Jennie was saying.

But suddenly what she had just said occurred to him and caught his attention. He looked up from his paperwork, leaned back in his chair, and slowly took off his reading glasses. "Go on."

"Well, my best friend is Heather Wilson. She is white, sir. To be honest, I have known her all my life and she is not racist, not the least little bit. I know for a fact that she would not be a threat to the Black

Heritage Army in any way. In fact, I'm confident that she would want to help our cause."

"And?"

"Well, sir, I'm asking that in this case we don't round her up with all of the other whites. I ask that we educate her on the Black Heritage Army, and then allow her to stay with me and to help our cause—"

"Stop right there, Lieutenant. I have experienced a lifetime of racism, both direct and indirect; I think I can safely say that each of us in this room has." He stood and walked around his desk toward her.

"I can tell that I'm old enough to be your father, and there is no way that you can possibly understand the underlying nature of most whites. I've got a lifetime of experience compared to your short time on this planet. And while you may *think* that this person is a friend, I can almost guarantee you that if she is white, she has had racist thoughts—even if they are buried in her subconscious. I can promise you that those thoughts exist."

"All due respect, sir, but that can't be true one hundred percent of the time, can it? I mean, especially with Heather. She—"

"Excuse me?"

"Sir, my apologies, but Heather and I are like sisters. We've lived our entire lives together, and I've seen her stand up and face difficult situations before. She has *always* been there for me, has defended me when others wouldn't, and honestly, she and I have never had an issue of any kind. I don't even think of us as being different. But all of that doesn't really get to the bottom of my point."

The room fell silent for just a moment. Jennie looked over to Sergeant Masters and raised her eyebrows as if asking for him to help her out. Then she turned her attention back to Major Henderson.

"Sir, do you really think that the Black Heritage Army can pull this off without *any* help from whites or people of other races?"

"Of course we can. Our people have a rich history—you should know that. We've accomplished so much over thousands of years. Before whites came to our native lands and overpowered us, enslaved us, and stole us away from our families, we were the people to be reckoned with on this planet. Going all the way back to the Moorish Empire, people of color have built entire societies and highly successful cultures all based on a true brotherhood. I'm surprised that you don't have a better appreciation for all of this. Didn't your parents teach you anything?"

"Of course they did! And I don't appreciate what you are implying, sir. Right now, I don't think that the ancient past has anything to do with what we are faced with today. The way I see it is that you're trying to use things that happened to our people in the past as an excuse for your own racist behavior."

"Jennie!" Sergeant Masters jumped in. He thought that she was going to get herself in more trouble than she could handle.

"No, it's okay, Sergeant. Let her go on. I'm curious to see where she's going with this." Henderson motioned to Jennie with a head nod. "Continue."

"You guys don't get it, do you? Can't you see that by excluding whites, and especially those that are lifelong friends of ours, you are being racist yourselves? That's my whole point.

"People—whether they be white, black, Hispanic—it doesn't matter—people are either good or bad. You can't judge that by the color of their skin. Yet that's exactly what you yourself are doing right now."

"But that's *exactly* what they have done to us for generations now, judge us by the color of our skin."

"Come on, sir, *everyone?* No way. That's just not possible, and I think that deep down you know it too. I guarantee you that Heather doesn't think that way. Not a chance." She paused to take a breath, hardly believing the courage she was displaying to support her friend.

"In fact, sir, I can promise you that she would embrace our cause and do everything possible to help the Black Heritage Army achieve our goals. She has always been there for me, and she's just that type of person."

"The point here is that we don't know who we can trust at this stage." The major was beginning to sound frustrated. Whether this was so because Jennie was standing up to him or because deep down he knew she was right, even he couldn't tell. "Our best strategy is to keep it simple—black is black, and white is white, at least in the near term."

"All due respect, sir, but it's just not that simple, is it? I mean, we're going to push away the very people that could be our allies. Don't you get it? By saying what you are, and acting the way you do, you are no better than any white racist out there. Just because your skin is black, it doesn't mean that you have the right to judge people of *any* color."

"I'm not saying that I have the right to judge others. I think you're missing the point."

"Oh, I can see the point. You think that the best way to get back at the individuals that have hurt you over the years is to put them all in one big bucket and punish them—all because of their skin color. Isn't that, by definition, racism?"

The room fell dead silent. Major Henderson turned to look out his window, still holding his reading glasses. He spun back to face his desk and started rifling through a stack of papers. "Ah, here it is."

"Not to change the subject, but, Michael, I've got a good relationship with you, Rockson, and Daemon, so I feel like you're someone I can trust."

Jennie and Michael glanced at each other, each raising an eyebrow at the oddity of their conversation's having come to a screeching halt.

"Sir, you've been like a father to all three of us," Michael said, wondering where the major was going. "Of course you can trust me. Jennie here too."

"Great. Do you know Sergeant Jackson?" Henderson glanced back down at the piece of paper he was holding in his hand. "A Sergeant *Julius* Jackson? If so, what can you tell me about him?"

"Yes, sir, I know of him. He came from the hood, just like me, T-Rock, and Dae. Louisiana though, as I recall. Difference is that shortly after joining our unit, he got caught up in the wrong crowd here on base. We tried to take him in and help him along, but then his mother died. That seemed to be his breaking point. And after that, he wouldn't talk to us anymore.

"We tried everything, just like we always have done in those situations, but it wasn't going to work for Julius. He was already too far gone, in my opinion. Does that help?"

"Yes, that helps quite a bit, Michael. While we were talking about who we can trust and who we can't, the situation with Sergeant Jackson just occurred to me." Major Henderson paused to think about how much detail he should share with Michael and Jennie. He saw no risk in continuing.

"We had a pretty bad situation with Julius. We assigned him to the field, perimeter patrol specifically, and put him in charge of a small unit. Unfortunately, it looks like he went too far and took things under his own advisement."

"I'm not following you, sir." Michael looked at Jennie and judged by the look on her face that she shared his confusion.

"We got a phone call from one of the members of his unit, and then later we also heard from a … Mrs. Hoch." Major Henderson had to glance at the paper in his hand one more time in order to find the detail he needed. "Apparently, Sergeant Jackson destroyed the Hochs' family home and killed the husband in the process. It looks like the wife survived along with her kids, but they were left in the field with absolutely nothing."

All three fell silent. Sergeant Jackson's actions were upsetting to each of them, but neither of them quite knew what to say next or how to respond.

Major Henderson broke the silence. "I've sent for Sergeant Jackson and removed him of his command. He should be here shortly so that I can get his side of the story and decide what to do with him."

Henderson shook his head slightly and then came back to the topic at hand. "Jennie, I'm glad that you came to my office today, but I've got a larger strategy that I have to keep in mind. It's my job to make sure that this conflict is successful and that the Black Heritage Army sees a victory—and quickly." He dropped the report file he had been holding and then pushed himself back from his desk so that he could stand again.

"This is the army, and I expect the two of you to follow orders. While I understand that you might think of Heather as a friend of yours, she's white—plain and simple. Right now, the Black Heritage Army is only interested in recruiting blacks."

"But, sir—"

"Let me finish. Even if what you say is true—and I'm not saying that you don't make a good point—but even if it is true, how could we possibly determine which whites are genuinely behind the effort? Do you see what I mean?

"Sure, you might be able to vouch for Heather, but what about the other whites that will claim that they are sympathetic only so that they can escape being in lockdown? Or worse yet, they might actually undermine our efforts intentionally, leak information to the enemy—things like that."

Major Henderson slipped his reading glasses back on and pulled the chair away from his desk so that he could sit back down. He seemed rattled, almost impatient.

"No, the right thing for us to do is to stick with our initial strategy. For the time being, I want to keep all whites secured until we can more accurately assess their intentions on an individual basis."

He gave the two junior officers a stern look over the top of his reading glasses. "Dismissed."

Jennie and Michael saluted and walked into the hallway. They stood for a moment, looking at each other. Neither was happy with the outcome, but both knew that the major had made up his mind. There was nothing more they could do.

They started to make their way back to Heather, who was still in lockdown back at their base apartment. They were both in deep thought about their conversation with Major Henderson and what had just taken place. Silent and a little bit somber, they climbed into the Humvee.

They were close to the apartment complex when Jennie was the one to break the silence.

"I thought that went pretty good. At least, the major seemed to soften his stance on the issue."

"What do you mean," Michael had a confused look on his face because he hadn't seen it the same way, "softened his stance?"

"I mean when the major said that whites should be held 'for the time being', and 'until they can be assessed'. I think both of those statements mean that we've got some flexibility with regard to Heather's situation. Don't you?"

"I'm sorry, Jennie, but I think that you're reaching a little bit with that assessment. I think he was pretty clear about what we're supposed to do with Heather."

"I disagree."

"Look, I know that you and I haven't known each other for very long, and I think you can see that I *totally* agree with everything that you said back there. But at the same time, I think the major might be right, at least as it relates to our strategy at this early stage. Besides, how could we possibly know who is on our side, or know who we could truly trust?"

"I know, Michael, but isn't that the point of what we just heard? I mean, you heard what the major said about that sergeant, Julius Jackson. He just murdered innocent whites from what I can tell—and *only* because they were white. Do you think that helps the Black Heritage Army or hurts their cause?"

"I don't know, Jennie. I guess the way I see it is that all of this is above our pay grade. Just like we've been taught, I think we have to trust our superiors and follow orders for the time being."

"I suppose so, but what do we do about Heather? She has the hots for you, by the way—you *did* see that, right?" Jennie had a sly smile on her face when she said this trying to lighten the mood and possibly manipulate the outcome. She looked across the vehicle to make eye contact with Michael.

Michael couldn't hide his excitement about Jennie's comment; it was the confirmation he was hoping for. "I thought I saw something there. She's definitely cute."

He paused and gazed out the driver's-side window to scan the base around him. "Honestly, I haven't had a feeling like this in a long, long time. You really think she's into me?"

"Oh, I know it for a fact! She's like my sister, and I can read her like a book."

Michael pulled into an open parking stall at the apartment building, turned off the ignition, and thought for a minute. "You know, the major didn't specifically say that Heather had to be in lockdown, did he?"

"Hmm, not that I remember." Jennie smiled as she caught on to where he was going with this, responding sarcastically.

"I've got an idea, Jennie."

Michael and Jennie walked back into the apartment and found Heather sitting in the living room, waiting. She was in her civilian clothes—civvies, as they are called in the military—clinging to the hope that Michael would be with Jennie when she returned. Heather beamed when he walked into the room again.

She had changed into a pair of shorts that revealed her curvy figure. She stood up with an excited little bounce in her step and flaunted a blouse that showed her tan skin. If Michael wasn't completely interested in her before, she made sure that he would be now!

"Where have you guys been?" The smile never left Heather's face.

Jennie gave Michael a strange look. "It's a long story, Heather. We'll bring you up to speed as we make our way over to the mess hall."

"Mess hall? I'm not even hungry." Heather was confused now, having no idea of what could be happening.

"Trust me, compared to other options the mess hall is exactly where you want to be." Jennie had a reassuring smile on her face. "Grab your things, and let's get out of here."

Both Jennie and Heather packed up a few things while Michael helped. Then they all made their way back outside.

Because he could be spotted taking a white person someplace other than where she was supposed to be, Michael looked around cautiously while leading the women outside. The three of them finally reached the Hummer and piled in as hastily as they could. The plan was to get Heather to the mess hall, even though it was controlled by the Black Heritage Army.

Every Black Heritage Army soldier who was off duty or had already completed his or her job had to have a place to go. Since most of the public areas, such as the gymnasium and civic center, were being used to house whites, they had decided to use the mess hall as a central meeting area where they could socialize and, of course, eat.

Being on the inside of the operation, Michael knew that the group of Black Heritage Army soldiers that typically hung out at the mess hall were moderate for the most part, serving in administrative roles as opposed to combat roles. This made him pretty confident that Heather would be accepted without issue. But if not, he knew that at least he would have enough support from the group to make sure that he and

Jennie could keep Heather safe without having to lock her up with the others. In the worst case, they could get her out of there without harm.

The feelings Michael had for Heather were so strong that he was willing to take the chance of putting himself at risk, even if only to win her over. There was no way he was going to let Heather get locked up.

More important, this gave him the opportunity to get to know her better, and that was something he was really looking forward to.

CHAPTER 14
Does Color Really Matter?

Captain Lancaster was confused and scared. Woken in the middle of the night by two soldiers who had somehow entered his home, he was still half asleep when he was bound and then thrown into the back of a Humvee.

He was groggy the entire time, but he was aware enough to see that the entire base was electrified with activity. Just during the walk from his front door to the end of the street where the Humvee was waiting, he spotted soldiers everywhere. They weren't running but were walking briskly and with a sense of purpose, some of them jogging as they went from door to door in his small section of Fort Benning.

When forced to enter the vehicle, Lancaster discovered that there were several other people already sitting in the back. Each of their faces held the look of fear—fear of the unknown. His mind racing, he scanned the vehicle to find an empty space to sit, but there was none. His hands bound in front of him at the wrist with zip ties, he was still able to raise them to the point of holding onto one of the cross members above his head.

"Anyone know what the hell is going on?"

The people around him said nothing. His question only broke the daze that each one of them seemed to be in, causing them to look up at him and shake their heads back and forth, not knowing how to answer. Each was afraid to speak.

The engine of the vehicle came to life. Lancaster, still standing with nowhere to sit, gripped the crossbar more tightly just in time to keep himself from falling over when the Hummer started moving forward with a jolt.

Now sitting in what appeared to be some type of holding cell no larger than his bedroom, he tried to calm down enough to gather his senses. He strained to remember any other details. He was confused since it had been dark and very early in the morning when he was abducted.

He recalled being separated from the rest of the group. One of the soldiers had mentioned him by name then segregated him from the others. While he was led down a dark hallway with small holding cells lining each side, he thought he heard the others all talking as if they were in one large room together. He wondered why he would be singled out from the rest.

Lancaster also remembered voices saying something about General Ballard and his orders to detain him. But how could that be? Ballard wasn't a general. The whole thing was confusing to the captain. Never having a high degree of confidence in himself, Lancaster was nervous— scared to death, in fact. What in the world could be going on?

He, alone with his thoughts and not knowing his own fate, sat in silence for a few hours.

"Hey." The hushed voice came from the cell next to him. "What the hell do ya think they're tryin' to do?"

"Excuse me?" It was beginning to get light outside, but inside it was still just dark enough that Captain Lancaster couldn't quite see the face belonging to the voice.

"It's me, Sergeant Peterson. Thanks again for covering for me yesterday—you made sure those niggers got what they deserved."

"What are you talking about?"

"You know damn well what I'm talking about! When you came out of the shop and told the major that those coloreds started the fight instead of me, you saved my ass. And you put those black bastards away at the same time. Great job, Captain."

"Wait a minute ... Peterson. *Peterson*. You're the one who started the fight?"

"Damn right, and you did a great job of making sure that it looked like it was their fault, not mine. Good job!"

"Just a second, Peterson, that's not what happened. I really did think that Rockson started the fight at the time, so what are you trying to tell me?"

"Man, are you really that frickin' naive? Are you telling me that you really had no idea what was going on?"

"I have no idea what the hell you're talking about, Peterson. Stop beating around the bush, and tell me what what's going on around here."

"Well, Captain, we all know that there're too many coloreds in this man's army, right?" Peterson sneered, using a term that had been commonly used by enlisted soldiers for decades. Originally uttered with a sense of pride for being a part of the army, "this man's army" referred to a fraternity of sorts, but in this case Peterson seemed to be using it to indicate a separation between whites and blacks.

"Damn assholes are given a get-out-of-jail-free card every time they mug somebody, steal something, or even commit murder." He used both his hands to rub his face up and down, partially because he was very tired, but also because he felt a great deal of frustration when thinking of how many African Americans there were in the army. He lowered his voice and was almost talking to himself. He moved his head from side to side, scanning the premises to see if there was anyone else around who might hear him.

"I guess they mostly kill each other off though, so it ain't all bad, now, is it?" He smiled wryly and chuckled at himself quietly.

Peterson's face was now visible to Captain Lancaster. It was a dead giveaway that something wasn't right with this kid. By his smile and the strain in his facial expression, it was obvious that he would be a perfect candidate to take on the role of trained killer—a sniper, for instance. It was a frightening thought, but Lancaster mustered the courage to keep the conversation alive.

"Peterson, you've got to be kidding me. Are you saying that there's a conscious effort to be racist toward African Americans around here, and an organized effort at the leadership level no less?"

"African Americans? African Americans? What the hell, Captain?

I'm so sick and tired of them being called the politically correct 'African Americans.' It's all a bunch of crap, if you ask me. You sound like one of them sympathetic muthas. I thought you were on our side!"

"Your side? I didn't even know that there were sides to all of this!" Lancaster shook his head in disbelief. "Peterson, I'm telling you that I just do my job around here—"

"Bullshit, Captain! No one just does their job in the army anymore. It's all politics now, and I think you know it. We found out about some underground nigger movement months ago, so we took it upon ourselves to start stamping it out, one *African American*," he sarcastically emphasized, "at a time."

"I have no idea what you're talking about, but I can tell you this: I'm not going to buy into your redneck paranoia. I guarantee you that there's no underground movement by African Americans or by anyone else, for that matter. Heck, I've got sixty percent of my own staff that's black." He shook his head again. "No, if there was some type of movement going on, I'd be aware of it."

"See, Captain, that's why we're gonna lose! Don't y'all get it? These guys is organized and unified while all us whiteys are still arguin' amongst ourselves."

"Just shut the hell up, Peterson." Captain Lancaster had had enough. He didn't like the direction this conversation was headed. Slipping back into his more nonconfrontational personality, he wanted to end the discussion before it escalated even more.

However, the more he thought about it, the more he realized that Peterson could be right. He considered the events of the previous day, the fight and its end result. He thought back to other, less obvious situations over the past few months, each of them involving a skirmish between blacks and whites. And that's when it hit him.

You're kidding me. No wonder. Now it's all so clear, Captain Lancaster thought as he leaned back against the cold, cinder-block wall and smiled. He shook his head, still smiling with amusement at himself for not seeing things more clearly, disappointed that it took a redneck like Peterson to help him see the light.

The men sat in their cells for one more day and night. Meals were brought in on regular intervals. the conditions weren't necessarily poor, but the detainees would go crazy if it lasted much longer.

As hard as he tried during that next day and the morning thereafter, he couldn't get any of the soldiers to talk to him; they refused to say a word. They only brought in meals and water, and escorted him and Peterson to the restroom from time to time. Other than that, they did nothing. They wouldn't respond to his questions. And with no one else coming or going, there was no way for him to know what had been going on outside of the holding area.

The lack of knowing, and the lack of quality conversation, was beginning to play with his emotions. Something needed to change or else he just might lose his mind.

It was early that second morning when Captain Lancaster's thoughts were interrupted by the overhead lights being snapped on, instantly flooding the once dark room with light.

"Hey, dumbass!" Peterson complained about the sudden brightness, raising his forearms and holding them in front of his eyes to fight the glare.

Staff Sergeant Rockson, with a few other soldiers at his side, charged into the room and directed his energy toward Peterson, who was sitting in the far corner of his cell.

"Shut up, whitey! We heard almost everything you've said over the past couple of days!"

"Screw you, nigger." Peterson never did have a shred of common sense, which seemed pretty obvious in this situation. He was the one locked in a holding cell and outnumbered by black soldiers five to one, yet he was still happy to shoot his mouth off.

"You dumbass son of a ..." Rockson was scrambling to find the right key to open the door to Peterson's cell. He was so fired up that he wanted to charge in there and beat the crap out of Peterson while he had the chance, but he fumbled with the keys clumsily, struggling to find the right one.

"Sergeant, that's not what we're here for. You know that!" Rockson wanted so badly to jump in there and teach Peterson a lesson, but one of his fellow soldiers had the good sense to hold him back.

Rockson stood back, gathered himself, and made one more comment to Peterson in an effort to have the last word. "Screw you, Peterson! I've got to remember that you're the one who's locked in that cage like a monkey and that I'm the one out here calling the shots."

Rockson had learned a lot about controlling his emotions—coaching he had gotten from Major Henderson. He stared at Peterson for moment, then took another deep breath and turned his attention to Captain Lancaster. "Hey, Lancaster, I've got orders to take you to Major Henderson."

Lancaster was visibly confused. "Sure, but can I ask what's going on?"

"No. Sorry, but right now you can't." He unlocked the door and let his soldiers walk into the holding area first. "Make sure that white idiot next door doesn't make a move," he said to them, motioning toward Peterson.

Rockson turned his attention back to Lancaster. "It's time to come with me, Captain."

Lancaster hesitated once again, more out of fear of the unknown than anything else, but he stood up, acknowledged Rockson with an affirmative head nod, and walked out of the cell, one of the soldiers holding his right arm and guiding him down the hall.

Just before Lancaster and the other soldiers exited the hallway, Rockson, who had held back so that he could be the last to leave, turned his attention back to Peterson and let the sarcasm roll. "You take care in there, sweetheart. I'll be back to check on you in a couple of days." He winked and smiled.

Rockson's comment caused Peterson to jump to his feet and punch the cinder-block wall out of rage, once again displaying his ignorance by nearly breaking his hand. He was a true racist by any measure, so the thought of his being taunted by a bunch of blacks was more than he could handle.

All of the Black Heritage Army soldiers chuckled at Peterson and shook their heads in amusement as they continued to escort Captain Lancaster down the hallway. They made their way to the parking lot and to the Humvee that was waiting outside, ready to take them to Major Henderson's office.

Along the way, Captain Lancaster continued to think about the conversation he had just had with Peterson, wondering if Peterson might have been right. All of the soldiers around him, and those walking around base, were black. "Hey, Rockson, can you please just give me a high-level idea of what's going on around here? At least tell me why I'm being detained?"

Rockson hesitated, knowing that his orders were to remain quiet, but he had worked for Lancaster for years and actually liked the guy. Lancaster had always run the motor pool operation fairly and had seemed to treat everyone, white or black, in the same way.

"I'll tell you what, Captain. I'm not supposed to say anything, but I think I can trust you after all these years." He turned sideways on the Hummer's rear bench seat next to Lancaster so that he could make eye contact.

"Years ago we created an organization now known as the Black Heritage Army." Rockson went on to tell Captain Lancaster about the effort, the reason that they founded the group, and the motivation behind their recent actions.

While he shared a few details about their organization, he didn't talk about Operation Freedom Reign specifically. He knew that it would be better for Major Henderson to present the magnitude of their operation to Lancaster in a way that would convince him to help their cause. They were going to need his help at this point; that was for certain.

Lancaster's fear was beginning to subside and his confidence beginning to increase thanks to a new understanding of what was going on around him.

In fact, Lancaster was motivated by his desire to help the African American effort; whatever they were up to, whatever they wanted to call themselves, he wanted to contribute. He was the furthest thing from a racist, and now he wanted to prove that to the men around him. More important, and now that he had the facts, he wanted to redeem himself for his actions the day before yesterday when he had unwittingly blamed the black soldiers for something that was clearly a racially motivated act of aggression by Peterson and his clan.

Major Henderson was sitting at his desk preparing for his meeting with Generals Ballard and Street scheduled for later that day. It was recently confirmed that General Street had agreed to return to base for a face-to-face meeting with his old friend, and new nemesis, LaRon Ballard. Of course, the General also wanted up pick up his kids and take them home with him.

"Sir, Captain Lancaster, as requested." Rockson stood at attention and gave a full salute.

"At ease, Sergeant. Thank you. Please sit down, Captain." Major Henderson made a sweeping motion toward an open chair, inviting Lancaster to join him. "Please excuse us for a while, Sergeant—oh, and be sure to close the door behind you."

Lancaster waited impatiently for the *click* of the door latch. Once he heard it, he immediately started talking. "Sir, can you please tell me what the hell is going on around here?"

"I'll get to that, Captain, but first I need answers to a couple of questions." Henderson could hear the nervousness in Lancaster's voice, so he lowered his tone and leaned back in his chair, all in an effort to put Lancaster more at ease. "How well do you know General Street?"

"Well, sir, it's more of a family relationship with General Street, not necessarily with me personally. We've represented him before, my family law firm, that is. Have you heard of the firm Lancaster, Kennedy, & Forbes?"

"Hell yes, I have! That's your family's law firm?"

"Afraid so. I'm not necessarily proud of it—"

"Your family has bailed more military officers out of trouble than any other firm out there. Everyone knows about that firm! The saying is that no matter what you've done, or what you've been caught doing, Lancaster, Kennedy, & Forbes will get you a get-out-of-jail-free card. Son of a bitch, I never would've thought that was you."

"Well, that's the point, I guess. It's *not* me, sir; it's my family. I got my law degree and was supposed to work at the firm, but I just couldn't do it. For generations, my family has used the firm to make friends with top leaders in Washington and in the military. Once they have represented you, or bailed you out of trouble, they hold all the power. Yeah, my family certainly knows how to play the political game as much as anyone."

Captain Lancaster paused and shook his head in disappointment of his family's reputation. "But you want to know if I know General Street, right?"

"That's right, Captain. We've got a meeting with him this afternoon. Do you think you can help us out, maybe provide us with some insights before the meeting?"

"Well, I do know him; in fact, we had lunch together just the other day. But again, he's closer to my father than he is to me."

"That's okay. Any insight you can offer will help. General Ballard knows him at more of a personal level—or at least he thought he did. Anyway, they've been friends for many years, but your perspective can also help us."

"I think I know enough about his tendencies to help you guys out, Major. I have been around him enough to know that he's a pretty rough customer, though, if you know my meaning."

"I think so, but please go on."

"Well, first, he is a dyed-in-the-wool racist with no question. I've heard him make remarks about how he feels that there are too many blacks in the army and how he thinks that African Americans are screwing things up around here. Remember, these are his thoughts and his words, not mine."

"Of course, Captain. You might want to know that I've already done my research on you and your background. Remember that you've got a lot of black soldiers reporting to you. I had a talk with many of them before deciding whether to let you out of that cell at all. I needed to make sure that you had a clean history as it relates to blacks and how you deal with our people.

"The feedback was really good, by the way. You've earned the respect of a lot of people, and everyone close to you says great things about the type of person that you are."

"That's great to hear, Major. I can assure you that I'm not a racist in any way, and I intend to prove that to you guys by helping you out."

Captain Lancaster paused briefly to contemplate Major Henderson's confirmation that he had met two of his life goals. First, the major had no idea that Lancaster was associated with his family's law firm. And second, the captain had managed to build a sound reputation for himself among the men and women in his unit. This affirmation made him feel better about himself as his confidence increased even more.

Lancaster continued. "The last thing I'll say about Street at this time, and what I was referring to when I said that he's a rough customer, is that he's got one hell of a temper. I've seen him snap and go off in a way that would intimidate even the strongest, most hardened man out there. He's got a short fuse. When he does let his anger out, you don't want to be around him."

"Interesting. I haven't seen that side of him at all, and I haven't even heard that about him."

"Of course not—and Colonel Ballard probably isn't aware of this either. That's because he doesn't *want* you to see that side of his personality. Remember, he's also one hell of a politician and he has the ability to control his actions when needed, which is motivated by his desire to keep moving up the chain of command. You'll want to be careful when you meet with him, because he won't hold back in this situation. You'll want to be ready for General Street to snap at any moment."

"That's great feedback, Captain, fantastic in fact." Major Henderson's feeling toward Captain Lancaster had changed dramatically in the short time they were together. He had a good ability to read people, and he could tell that Lancaster was someone they could trust.

"Listen, I plan to speak with General Ballard about this first, but I'd like you to plan on joining us when we meet with General Street. I think it would help our cause to have you in the room."

"Understood, sir. I'm happy to help in any way that I can, but can you tell more about what's going on around here? For example, you just referred to Ballard as a general, but he's only a colonel. What am I missing here?"

It had already become apparent to Major Henderson that Captain Lancaster was no threat at all and that, in fact, he was probably more of an ally than anyone could have expected. More important, the situation made him realize that that Sergeant Masters and his friend Jennie were right. The Black Heritage Army *would* need help from white people and other races. As long as it could be proven that they truly supported the cause, and as long as the Black Heritage Army had one hundred percent confidence in their intentions, a white person could join. It all made much more sense to him now.

"Sure, Captain, I owe you at least that much. I think you'll see, after what I'm about to tell you, why I had to try to figure out what kind of person you were and discover how well you knew Charlie Street before I shared the details." Henderson stopped to consider how much detail he should share with Lancaster at this early stage.

"Well, Captain, some years ago I formed an underground organization with a few others that has become known as the Black Heritage Army. While it started as a way for my people to support each other in the face of discrimination, it quickly evolved into a full-blown army of African Americans who wanted to change the very way that our people are treated in this country.

"In the past couple of days, we've managed to take over a handful of Southern states. Our effort is known as Operation Freedom Reign, and our goal is to build a culture of true brotherhood within the new Ubuntu territory."

"Ubuntu? What does that mean, Major?" Lancaster, while partially in shock over what he was hearing, was also beginning to get excited about what had happened; the possibilities were unparalleled. He felt energized about how he might be able to help the cause.

"*Ubuntu* is an African term that the great Desmond Tutu has used in his writings. It describes a culture where everyone is always available to others, where no one feels threatened, and where people know that they belong to a greater whole. In short, that's the kind of culture that we intend to build among our people and within the territory we have taken over."

"Wow. That's unreal," Captain Lancaster mumbled under his breath as he sat with a dazed look, truly in disbelief that any of this could have happened. He was struggling to comprehend the sheer magnitude of the events that had taken place. Never in his wildest thoughts could he have imagined something like this happening, yet the Black Heritage Army had done it!

"Sir," Lancaster said loud enough for Major Henderson to hear him, "how can I help?"

"Good question. To be honest, we didn't have any intention of allowing anyone other than African Americans into the cause, but now even that's being brought into question. If you think about the entire purpose of the Black Heritage Army and what we stand for, you can see why we are skeptical about allowing whites—or any other race, for that matter—into our organization."

"Candidly, sir, I want to make up for my actions toward those fine young men who were involved in the fight two days ago. More important, I genuinely agree with *everything* that you have shared with me, all of the goals of the Black Heritage Army, and especially Ubuntu. To be perfectly honest, this may be the first time in my life that I can see things clearly."

"I'm not sure if you fully understand, Captain, but this is a big undertaking. It would be a huge commitment on your part, possibly even a life-threatening endeavor. We're asking you to participate in our inner circle, to help our cause. In the end, if we aren't successful, you're going to be the target of the union leadership.

"I'm willing to bet that they would treat you like a traitor—especially with you being white and all. All of this is a pretty serious risk to you. Again, I only want to make sure that all of the risks are clear and that you completely understand what you'd be getting into."

"I do understand, Major. You see, this is it—this is the motivation that I have been waiting for. I feel like my life suddenly has more purpose, something more important than my family law firm, than the army itself. This is the type of challenge that I have been searching for and the type of opportunity I've been hoping to get out of life. And I have to tell you that something inside me tells me that this is fate. I am *supposed* to help the cause, I just know it. And I won't take no for an answer!"

Major Henderson paused in thought. He looked at Captain Lancaster and could see that his comments were genuine and that he was determined. Now he had to question a lifetime of his own thoughts about race, about men as individuals, about a man's inner being and not the color of his skin. *Ironic,* he thought to himself. *Now I'm thinking like a racist!*

Henderson turned his thoughts back to Captain Lancaster, who was frozen in his last position, waiting anxiously for an answer. "Okay. Here's what we're going to do. General Street is on his way to base for a meeting with General Ballard and us. Like I mentioned earlier, because you know Street as well as you do, I think you should join us. I'll talk to General Ballard and get his approval."

"Excellent! I'm looking forward to it, sir."

"Honestly, this meeting with Street is extremely important, and it would also help us to have a witness in the room. That's where you come in. For our own protection from the possible 'he said, she said' nature of a meeting like this, you can observe as a neutral party, which should be acceptable to Street—especially since you're white. Make sense?"

"Absolutely, it does, and even more so because he already knows me and my family. Either way, sir, I'm in!" He stood at attention and saluted Major Henderson.

Major Henderson returned the salute. "At ease, Captain. Wait outside my office for further instruction. I'll have to talk with Ballard, and General Street should be arriving any minute. Either way, I've got something else that I need to take care of first.

"Oh, and I'll also make sure that you have a chance to freshen up and get a good meal inside of you. Sound good?"

"Sounds great! I understand why you had me locked up, but it sure is good to be out of that cell!" He smiled back at Major Henderson.

Captain Lancaster walked out of the room with a newfound energy and a high level of excitement. He took a seat in the waiting area outside Major Henderson's office for the time being, took a deep breath, and smiled. His life suddenly felt full of purpose … finally.

CHAPTER 15
True Love Defends

Major Henderson sat in his office for a few minutes, reviewing in his mind the conversation he just had with Captain Lancaster. He knew that having Lancaster join him and General Ballard would help their position when talking to Charlie Street because of the history the two shared. More importantly, Lancaster's willingness to jump on board and help their cause led Major Henderson to rethink his position on whites and their role in the Black Heritage Army altogether.

Especially in the case of Lancaster, they would have a lot to gain. Lancaster's family was well networked in Washington, DC, and Lancaster himself had ties to people like General Street, so it was possible that the captain's involvement could help the Black Heritage Army develop more effective strategies. Lancaster might even be able to predict, or anticipate, actions and reactions by people like Charlie Street as the conflict continued to unfold. Helping them anticipate Union Army actions—to any degree—would greatly improve their chances of a victory.

General Ballard, and Major Henderson himself, could take an educated guess when it came to anticipating the union army's next move, but a guy like Lancaster could greatly improve the accuracy of their predictions. Being white, and coming from a more elitist family, Lancaster could potentially *think* like the union's army leadership and foretell what they might do next.

If they played their cards right with Lancaster, the Black Heritage Army could steer clear of costly mistakes, avoiding them altogether.

Lancaster could help them develop engagement strategies that would circumvent an effective retaliation by the union's army—*if* Lancaster truly was on their side, that is.

Can Lancaster really be trusted? Major Henderson asked himself. *And what about other whites?* How could he and the other members of his staff possibly determine whether a white person could be trusted, whether a white person was on their side or not?

He, still wrestling with years of believing things to be a certain way, began to doubt the conclusion he had made earlier while taking to Lancaster. These are white people after all, and in his experience whites were racist at the core—all of them, as far as he was concerned. His anger, rooted in years of being treated like a lesser human being, began to emerge once again.

One more time, he asked himself, *Am I acting racist toward whites?* He began to settle down. His thoughts turning to the conversation he had had earlier with Sergeant Masters and his friend Jennie, he began to feel a little guilty about the hard-line position that he had taken with them. It was obvious that Sergeant Masters had feelings for Jennie's friend Heather, and who was Henderson to get in the way of love?

Another great example, he thought. He shook his head ever so slightly as he contemplated the situation. In the case of Sergeant Masters, Jennie, and Heather, these were young people, representatives of the next generation. Maybe Henderson was simply too old in his way of thinking. Maybe his thoughts toward whites and his distrust of them—while he believed to be justified in this situation—didn't apply to the younger generations. After all, it is possible that racism of whites toward blacks was not as common in the younger generations.

No doubt racism still exists, but that's true of all races and cultures, isn't it? Any race or culture would have at least a few members who are racist toward other races or cultures, wouldn't they? Because the younger generations here in the United States have been exposed to a society that has gradually become more welcoming to blacks, maybe there are fewer instances of racism—and, in fact, fewer racists among whites in general.

Everything was beginning to cloud over in his mind. These were complex thoughts and emotions that he simply didn't have time for right now. Major Henderson was a bit confused for the first time, which shook his confidence to some degree, but he couldn't let that prevent him from doing his job and doing it well.

He reached up to rub his face with both hands, his elbows firmly planted on the top of his desk. Then he let out a sigh. No matter. Now wasn't the time to second-guess his decisions or actions; he had far too much on his plate, and very little time to waste on the emotions that were tugging at his conscience.

He had decided that he would definitely encourage General Ballard to allow Captain Lancaster to join them during their meeting with General Street. After wrestling with the pros and cons in his mind, Henderson finally realized that there was far more potential benefit, than there was risk, in having Lancaster in the room with them.

The issues of the conflict and the Black Heritage Army's takeover were overwhelming to him. The entire operation was far more challenging than he had ever thought it would be. Thank goodness that he had General Ballard helping him now, but there were some things that he had to deal with, situations he would have to take care of so that his longtime friend wouldn't have to, and so the general could focus on the larger goal.

The situation surrounding Sergeant Julius Jackson, and what he did out in the field, was a perfect example. When Major Henderson had gotten that call from a concerned soldier who was a part of Sergeant Jackson's unit, and after she relayed all of the details of what had happened at the Hoch farm in northern Alabama, Henderson was appalled.

So far, it seemed as though this was an isolated case of barbarism; at least he hadn't heard of any other cases yet, which is why it was so important for him to address the situation directly with Sergeant Jackson himself, and as soon as possible. He had summoned Julius to his office, removed him of his field command in fact, and demanded that he explain himself in person.

"Miss Adams," Henderson called to his assistant through the office door, which was left cracked open, "has Sergeant Julius Jackson arrived yet?"

"Yes, sir." There was a pause as she made her way into his office to respond more professionally. "He's waiting outside, sir. Is there anything else that you need before I send him in?"

"No, that's it. Just send him in."

She nodded and stepped back into the hallway. "Sergeant Jackson, the major will see you now."

Sergeant Jackson entered the major's office, his body language more casual than it should have been given the circumstances. Julius had reverted to having a lack of respect for authority, and he wasn't doing a very good job of covering it up. Still, he paused just before reaching Major Henderson's desk and raised his hand in a salute. "Sergeant Jackson reporting, sir."

"At ease, Sergeant."

Sergeant Jackson relaxed, lowered his salute, and casually stepped in front of one of the chairs, bending slightly as he started to sit down.

"I didn't say that you could sit down in my office, Sergeant!" Major Henderson's voice shook the room. "You're not here for a vacation. We have serious issues about your conduct that need to be addressed. Do you understand me?"

Sergeant Jackson slowly straightened himself back into a standing position, and faced the major from the opposite side of his desk. "Sir, all due respect, but what are we talking about here?"

For Major Henderson, it was all he could do to hold back his anger. He was frustrated with the reports he had heard about Jackson's actions in the field, but the sergeant's nonchalant attitude about the entire situation was flat-out disrespectful. Still, Henderson took a deep breath in order to calm himself. He wanted to straighten this young man out if he could, instead of simply punishing him.

"Look, Sergeant, I know that this is a challenging time for all of us. It's not easy to deal with any combat situation, let alone when it's your own countrymen that you're fighting against. But taking action like you did in northern Alabama is simply not acceptable."

"Sir," Jackson said, turning his head to the side slightly and rolling his eyes, "that white dude was a redneck piece of shit. Anyone could see that he was a white-trash mutha who'd been beatin' on his kids and wife—it was obvious! We did that dude and his family a huge favor by puttin' him down."

Henderson could hardly believe what he was hearing. The situation itself wasn't the issue anymore; it was Jackson's attitude about it all. The major searched his mind for the right words as he stared at the sergeant, trying to size him up even more. He took another deep breath, again falling back to his desire to save the young man if he could, and replied calmly.

"Son, I can appreciate that you *think* your actions are justified, but that's simply not what we want the Black Heritage Army to be all about. What you did is no different than what white people have been doing to our race for centuries. You made a snap decision about the man in front of you based primarily on his skin color, and then you took it upon yourself to be judge and jury.

"You can't go around killing people like that. I don't give a damn what you think the justification is; it's flat-out detrimental to our cause! More important, it's simply the wrong thing to do, son."

Julius had enough common sense to see that he wasn't going to win the argument, so he took the next best plan of attack and pretended to agree by remaining silent.

The men stared at each other, sizing one another up and trying to determine the best response. Major Henderson broke the silence first.

"Sergeant, we're here to change the world as you've known it. Our goal is to get our people to a position of leadership and authority that has never been seen before. We're talking about having a small country that is ours—and not just another underdeveloped country in some remote part of the world. We're talking about a highly developed country with a strong economy that will be under our control.

"Actions like the one you took out in the field could jeopardize our entire operation and destroy everything that we've built up to this point. Do you get what I'm saying here, Julius?"

"Yes, sir, I understand."

"Do you, Sergeant? Do you really?" Major Henderson had walked around his desk and was now standing right in front of Jackson. He stood staring at him—toe to toe, nose to nose, like a drill sergeant would a new recruit.

Julius took a deep breath and surrendered. "Yes, sir, I do under-stand. I can promise you that it won't happen again, sir."

"Damn right it won't, Sergeant. One more step out of line and I'll make sure that you won't see the light of day again—understand me?"

"Yes, sir, I do understand."

Major Henderson could sense that Sergeant Jackson had simply agreed with him just to get out of his office, but he had too many other things pressing right now. He would have to take Jackson at his word. Still, he would be watching this young man closely to make sure that he didn't step out of line again.

He continued to stare at Jackson, trying to intimidate him.

"You will remain on base with no specific orders until we have time to talk again. And let me be crystal clear with you: you will not cause any more trouble. You won't so much as walk on the grass without permission until I know that you understand the importance of what we're trying to accomplish."

"Yes, sir." Sergeant Jackson raised his hand to salute.

As a show of absolute authority over the young man, Major Henderson did not return the salute. He simply stared at Julius for what seemed to be a very long time.

"Just get out of my office."

He turned his back on Jackson and walked around to get back behind his desk. He had work to do.

Sergeant Jackson made his way out of Major Henderson's office, keeping a straight face until he reached the hallway. When he knew no one was looking, he let the cocky smile return to his face. He knew that he had just gotten away with murder, literally in fact, and he felt strangely good about it.

* * *

The brakes of the Humvee squeaked under the pressure of a quick stop as Michael, Jennie, and Heather came to rest in the first available parking stall at the mess hall.

Michael knew that this could be a challenge. Although he hadn't been given direct orders, he understood that Major Henderson wanted Heather to be in lockdown because she was white. He and Jennie had decided otherwise, however. They knew that Heather was no risk to them or to the Black Heritage Army, so they were going to let her hang out with them.

Problem is, they weren't sure if they could convince the other black soldiers at the mess hall that she wasn't a threat. Still, they wanted to try—and they were willing to put their own safety on the line if needed.

Both were determined to convince people that whites could in fact be a part of the effort. Michael and Jennie were also steadfast in their conviction that white people could be trusted, and they wanted to prove it—even if in a small way at this time. In their minds, the point had to be made. And they were out to make it. But this attitude could also place their careers at risk.

No matter, in their minds it was too late at this point; there was no turning back. They were committed to having Heather join them and to making their point with everyone else.

Still sitting in the Humvee, Michael looked over to Heather, who smiled back at him. Emotion overcame him when he saw her smile. There was no doubt now that he was in love. He had been interested in other women before, of course, but he had never felt like this. *Maybe there is such a thing as love at first sight,* he thought to himself.

"You understand that this may not be easy," he said to Heather, his million-dollar smile distracting her from caring about any possible risk that their current situation presented them with.

"I know. Don't worry, guys." She turned toward the backseat to look at her best friend, Jennie, as well. "We'll be fine!"

Michael and Jennie looked at each other with some trepidation, but Heather had already jumped out of the vehicle.

"Wait a minute, Heather! You're not going in there without us." Michael scampered out of the Humvee while Heather stood waiting near the front of the vehicle. He approached her, put a hand on each of her shoulders, and stood facing her.

"Look, this is serious, okay? I don't think you fully understand the nature of what is happening around you."

He looked over to Jennie, then back to Heather. "Just stay close to us and let us do the talking. I'm sure it'll be fine, but Jennie and I don't want anything to happen to you. Understand?"

"I've got it, guys. Don't worry! C'mon, let's get this over with."

Heather turned and walked toward the front door, her ever-present smile and positive attitude impressing Michael even more. He jumped in front of her to open the door, and to make sure that he was close when she walked into the mess hall. Jennie was right behind Heather, and Michael followed.

Black Heritage Army soldiers who were nearby ceased conversation almost immediately. The silence began to spread across the mess hall as they realized that a white person had just entered the room. All eyes were now on the three who had just appeared and were now standing just inside the doorway, unsure of what to do next.

Michael was not only handsome but also tall and visibly strong. He took in a breath and arched his back, making himself look even taller for a moment. He had a stern look on his face as he scanned the mess hall, looking into the eyes of each soldier who was brave enough to make eye contact with him. "C'mon, guys, let's go get in line. I'm hungry."

Michael's voice broke the daze that Heather and Jennie were in. While they knew there was a risk by entering the mess hall, they certainly hadn't expected such a cold greeting, which, in this case, was universal. As they looked around them, it seemed as though everyone was against them. Wasn't there any other black person who would support them?

Gradually, a few soldiers turned their attention back to their meals and to the conversations they were having with their friends. Both Heather and Jennie began to feel a bit more relaxed. Heather was re-lieved, in fact. What first had taken on the makings of a potential uproar now appeared to be a return to business as usual.

The two women looked at Michael, who was still waiting for them to acknowledge his recommendation to get in line. They nodded in approval. Slowly, Michael led them past the rows of tables to the end of the chow line. There they stood, remaining silent.

"What the hell is this?" One of the soldiers sitting nearby looked up at Michael with a confused look on his face. "There's no white people allowed in here."

"She's not just 'white people.'" He paused for a moment and looked into Heather's eyes. "She's my girlfriend."

"Man, I don't care what she is to you, she's white! You know that we don't allow whites in here. That comes directly from Major Henderson— and you know it!"

"Calm down, Corporal." Once again, Michael had the upper hand because he outranked the soldier. "This doesn't concern you. Besides, I'm good friends with Major Henderson. In fact, we just came from his office. If you have any issues with all of this, maybe you should try to talk to him directly."

Several of the Black Heritage Army soldiers nearby were listening in on this conversation. No one seemed willing to push Michael any further or to challenge what he was saying.

"Whatever you say, Sergeant," the soldier finally responded, although with a hint of frustration, or possibly sarcasm, in his voice. The soldier wasn't willing to push the issue because he was out ranked by Sergeant Masters and he certainly had no direct relationship with Major Henderson. Plus, he didn't know how to call Sergeant Masters' bluff, if he was bluffing, that is.

Michael let out a breath, but not in an obvious way. He was relieved that the situation hadn't escalated to more than a heated conversation. Still, he didn't want anyone around him to think he was weak. He looked at Jennie with a quick, reassuring nod and then put his arm around Heather. She melted into his embrace, leaned her head against his chest, and hugged him. His strength was yet one more appealing part of this man she was quickly developing feelings for.

Heather was still scared, as the situation around her was intimidating and she had no idea what the final outcome might possibly be. But now she knew that Michael was there to protect her. More important, it was pretty clear that he did have feelings for her too and that he was willing to stand up for her. She hadn't felt this good, emotionally speaking, for years.

The trio continued to slowly move forward in the line. Ahead of them, one soldier at a time gradually moved through the chow line, filling his or her tray with a main-course dish, then a side dish, and so on. The level of noise in the mess hall began to rise as more and more people returned to their own conversations. The seventy or more voices started quietly but gained momentum and volume once people raised their voices in an effort to overcome the echo of the other conversations around them, which was caused by the large expanse of the steel building they were in.

Michael, Jennie, and Heather looked around them and saw that people had returned to business as usual, which allowed them to relax even more. So far, it had gone better than expected, actually.

"What the hell is *she* doing in here!?" The yell came from across the room, near the front door, where Sergeant Julius Jackson had just entered the mess hall.

Julius, still reeling from his conversation with Major Henderson, was livid when he a saw a white person in their company. He charged through the mass of tables and across the room toward Michael, who still had his arm around Heather. Jennie moved over to separate them and then stepped in front of Heather, protecting her with her own body. She then slowly took a step back, moving both herself and her friend a few feet away from Sergeant Jackson and Michael.

"I asked you what the hell is going on here, Sergeant—and I expect an answer!" Julius was now toe to toe with Michael, his frustration visible in the veins bulging from his neck and the stare that showed an obvious desire to inflict harm, if given the chance.

Because the two men were equal in rank, all rules about showing respect for each other were null and void.

Michael now stood facing Julius directly. He chose to try to settle the situation with his ever-present calm demeanor, hoping to resolve the issue with words, not action.

"C'mon, man, you know that this is no big deal. No one else in here has an issue with her joining us for some chow."

"My ass, Sergeant! I can almost guarantee you that *everyone* in here has a problem with this! We are the *Black* Heritage Army, yo, and we don't want to include your white girlfriend or any other whites!"

"Listen, Sergeant Jackson, I can see that this is a real issue for you, so let us make it easy for you. We'll let you have your way by leaving. Just let us get out of here. We don't want any trouble."

"You already found yourself some trouble, bitch!" Julius was at the boiling point—more because of the frustration caused by being removed of his command, and his recent conversation with Major Henderson, than the issue at hand. Regardless, he needed to lash out at somebody.

"Whoa, whoa, just relax. We'll simply move on, Sergeant." Michael, both hands in the air as if he had a gun pointed at him, moved to stand directly in front of Jennie and Heather.

"Move on, my ass!" Sergeant Jackson shoved Michael with both hands, sending him back a step, nearly knocking over Jennie in the process.

The only thing keeping Michael on his feet was the soldier next to Jennie, who was behind him. He caught Michael and kept him from falling to the floor by grabbing him under the arms. The soldier pushed him back up and toward Julius.

Now Michael had had enough. He paused, only for a moment, and then lunged at Julius violently. The two men were immediately engaged in a brawl, their fists flying. Soon, they were rolling on the floor in an attempt to gain the upper hand.

The crowd around them began to spread so that there was more room for the scuffle itself to determine the outcome. The gathered soldiers began to cheer, not necessarily for one man or the other, but for the fight in general. This was more action than they had seen in quite some time. It created an adrenaline rush that many of them welcomed.

Heather was shocked and scared. Jennie was still holding onto her, trying to calm her down, but Heather would have none of it. She had very quickly developed a love for Michael Masters, so watching him risk injury was simply not an option for her.

Heather and Jennie, still in the front row of the crowd that had gathered, had an unencumbered view of what was going on. Suddenly and without warning, Heather broke Jennie's hold and dove into the skirmish, jumping onto Sergeant Jackson's back. She wrapped her left arm around his neck and tried to pull him off of Michael.

"Get off me, bitch!" Julius yelled. He grabbed Heather's arm and easily sent her flying to her back on the tile floor.

Heather's interruption freed up both men. As a result, they had gotten back to their feet. Michael looked over to Heather, who was obviously in pain. She seemed to be all right, but Michael was pissed.

The fight paused for a few more seconds while Julius and Michael each shuffled to their right, staring at each other, hands in front of them like two wrestlers about to engage.

Heather made her way back to her feet just in time to see Julius reach to the small of his back and remove a knife from its sheath. The blade flashed as it reflected the sunlight peering in from the large wall of windows on the south end of the mess hall. He was facing Michael, so there was no way that the latter could be aware of the weapon.

Now that she knew Julius had the knife, Heather scooted to her left, trying to get close enough to Michael that she could warn him. She was too afraid to say anything, and too focused on making sure that Michael wouldn't get hurt.

She made her way closer to Michael while the two men continued to move in a slow circle. Then, suddenly, Julius lunged toward Michael, his right hand holding the knife, his arm fully extended.

More quickly and swiftly than anyone could imagine, Heather jumped in front of Michael.

The blade made not a sound as it pierced her chest.

The room fell silent.

Heather collapsed into Michael's arms, her back to his chest. They slid down to a sitting position on the cold, hard tile floor, Heather on Michael's lap now. She strained to raise her head so that she could look at him. Blood began to seep from her mouth.

"What have you done?" Michael could not believe his eyes—everything had happened so fast. He felt anger toward Heather for jumping into the fray, but his sorrow overshadowed the anger.

"Please smile for me?" Heather's faint voice could be heard by nearly everyone because the room had become very quiet. She strained a faint smile herself, only wanting to see Michael's million-dollar smile one more time.

After forcing a strained smile as he looked into her eyes, he began to cry. Heather let out her last breath, her eyes still open and fixed on Michael's smile.

Julius Jackson was still on his feet, looking down at Michael, who was sitting on the floor with Heather's lifeless body on his lap. Julius looked up and scanned the room. All he could see were stunned faces all staring at him, and he knew that he wouldn't be able to get away with what he had just done. Not this time.

He leapt toward the door and broke into a sprint, jumping over tables and knocking people down along the way. Before anyone could think to react, he had made his way out the door and into the parking lot.

He ran as fast as he could. He had no idea where to go, but he knew he had to escape. He simply ran.

Jennie dropped to her knees next to Heather and Michael. She reached out and took Heather's hand in hers.

She wept.

CHAPTER 16
How Can You Tell Good from Bad?

General Street's plane arrived at Fort Benning early that afternoon. The Georgia humidity had already reached the point where even the slightest amount of physical exertion would cause a person to become drenched in sweat. The heat was stifling.

There was a full security escort of nearly twenty military police there to greet him, in position to ensure General Street's security. Stories about the general and his leanings toward white supremacy began to circulate immediately upon the launch of the Black Heritage Army's takeover, and both General Ballard and Major Henderson knew that protecting him would be paramount.

Street's recent actions also spread like wildfire among the troops—everything from his racist comments overheard in the mess hall to the way in which his record of granting promotions included only white officers.

The reality of General Street's being so openly and outwardly racist created a common enemy of sorts for the troops. His actions even helped some soldiers erase any doubt about their cause once and for all, and galvanized the Black Heritage Army around their mission.

Most important to General Street, however, was how his actions had put his own safety at great risk. Even in the union territory, an African American who might be sympathetic to the Black Heritage Army's cause could present a personal risk to Street. This was an added layer of complexity that had ongoing ramifications for both sides in the war.

Both the Black Heritage Army, with each of its branches in the Ubuntu territory, and what remained of the United States Armed Forces in the union territory had the enemy right within their ranks. Although the Black Heritage Army had done an excellent job of containing whites within the ranks of their military units, there were still plenty white people and people of other races running free within their territory. This presented a constant risk to the safety of African Americans.

Of course, on the union side of the equation no attempt had been made to contain African Americans; even the threat of such an action would have undermined their efforts to keep all races in the union territory—black, white, Hispanic, or otherwise—completely unified. African Americans were still the largest minority group within the union territory, and in some cases, such as Detroit, Philadelphia, Columbus, Indianapolis, and even Chicago, they were the majority race. Therefore, the risk of internal subterfuge was even greater for the union forces and members of their leadership, such as Charlie Street.

There was a sudden tap on General Ballard's door that broke him from his chain of thought.

"General," Major Henderson said as he walked in, "I'm told that General Street's plane has arrived, so he should be here within about twenty minutes."

"Thanks for the heads-up, Reggie. You and I both know it's imperative that General Street be able to arrive, and leave, the Ubuntu territory safely. Has everything been take care of for his arrival?"

"Absolutely, sir. Not only do I understand the importance of his safety, but I also appreciate that you'd have additional concern after what has happened with Sergeant Jackson in Alabama, for example."

At this point in time, neither man was aware of the additional violent actions that Sergeant Jackson had taken against Michael, Jennie, and Heather in the mess hall.

"You've got it. Jackson's situation causes me to think that we might be struggling to keep our own forces focused on the mission at hand. We've got to prevent our troops from crossing the line and descending into pure violence."

"I agree, LaRon, you know I do, but you don't have to worry about

Charlie Street. He's well protected, and the men I have assigned to him were hand-selected by me."

"Great. Once we get past this meeting, you and I should develop a specific plan to manage the troops better." General Ballard paused and turned to look out the window. "We've got to make sure that our men and women take the high road at all times. We can't have the Black Heritage Army associated with crimes against whites—or any other race, for that matter."

"I couldn't agree more, sir. By the way, do you feel prepared for this meeting with Street?"

General Ballard turned to face his friend again. He then moved to sit back down at his desk. "Thanks for asking, Reggie. I'd be lying if I said that I wasn't nervous about it, and not just about things like keeping General Street safe, but about the conversation itself. I'm not one hundred percent confident that I'll be able to keep my cool, let alone focus on the task at hand and our primary goal."

"I understand completely, but you were trained in negotiation for situations just like this as a part of your advancement, weren't you?"

"Interesting you'd say that, but the answer is no. I've been overlooked time and again for the more advanced leadership and negotiation courses." Ballard paused again, looked down at his desk, and shook his head. "Looking back it now, there's no doubt it was due to my race, since most of my peers were participating in that level of training.

"But, hey," he said, looking up at Reggie again and smiling, "that's why I'm in charge of the Black Heritage Army now, right?"

The longtime friends were able to take a break from the tension surrounding the task at hand by chuckling at Ballard's comment for a minute.

"I don't know, Reggie," Ballard said as he stood to pace the room again, "any number of things could go wrong. I know that Street is here to negotiate, but it's more important to him that he take his kids home with him, remember."

"Ah, that's right, LaRon." The light bulb turned on for Major Henderson. "Their *nanny* has been shot and killed."

"Exactly. If Charlie Street asks about her, we're going to have to tell him the truth—and in this case, the truth could blow up in our faces."

"Listen to me, LaRon, no distractions—understand? Our goal for this meeting is pretty clear: set the stage for a peace settlement that allows the Black Heritage Army to retain the territory we've already taken peacefully. Anything else that is dragged into the conversation will have to be addressed, but we can't let those topics distract us from the primary goal."

"Great advice, Reggie, great advice. I'm not sure what I'd do without you, my friend."

"Well, before you fall too deep in love with me, there's something I want you to consider for our meeting." He smiled at his own attempt to lighten the air and to get General Ballard's approval for the suggestion he was about to make.

"What do you have in mind, Reggie?"

"I want to have Captain Lancaster join us for the meeting with Charlie Street."

"Are you kidding me? That's the same son of a bitch who sent Rockson and the guys to the hole. Isn't he the very reason that we're all here in the first place?"

"I understand your emotion on this one, LaRon, but please hear me out. I've had a detailed conversation with the man, and I can personally guarantee you that he is not racist. More important, Lancaster had nothing to do with the situation surrounding Rockson and his friends, other than he was duped into believing that they were at fault. No different than you were. Just as important, Lancaster has a long-standing relationship with Charlie Street and knows him well."

"See, there you go! He's a friend of Charlie Street, which is exactly why we don't want him in the room with us."

"Wait a minute, LaRon, please stay with me on this. It's Lancaster's *family* that has the direct relationship with Charlie, not the captain himself. It's the very same family that Lancaster was trying to separate himself from when joining the army. He wants nothing to do with the politics and glad-handing that his family is known for.

"Candidly, I'm convinced that he's not racist. And after talking to him at length, I can honestly say that I truly believe that he's on our side." Major Henderson stopped for a moment, nearly unable to absorb what he had just said. He was actually placing his faith in a white man.

General Ballard, still pacing the room while rubbing the back of his neck, stopped and looked directly into Major Henderson's eyes. "Okay, Reggie, I trust you and I trust your judgment. If you say that having Lancaster participate will help our cause, then I've got to have faith in your decision. However, if this backfires on us, then you and I are gonna have to start all over. You get what I'm saying here?"

"I do. Trust me on this one."

"I will. Why don't you go get Captain Lancaster while we wait for General Street to show up? I'd like to make sure that all three of us are here in my office and are ready to go before Charlie walks into the room."

"Roger that, sir." Major Henderson hastily turned and left the room, knowing that he didn't have much time.

LaRon Ballard made his way back to the window in his office, and glanced at the horizon. He felt nervous, but he was confident about the task at hand, thanks in part to the great people he had around him. The conversation he had just had with Reggie was proof of that.

He wanted no more bloodshed, however, and no more stress on his sense of right and wrong. In addition, he wanted no more negative impact on truly innocent people. The actions of his own men, soldiers like Julius Jackson, tore apart his emotions. In his mind, LaRon felt that most whites were not racist, at least not to the point of inflicting physical harm on him or his men. Even if there were white racists who were more extreme in their thoughts and actions, he couldn't justify killing them in cold blood.

This was why, deep down, he was concerned about his ability to control some of the actions of the Black Heritage Army—not necessarily the group as a whole, but the actions of a few individuals within the group. It was his undying belief in the good nature of humankind, and his faith in God, that caused him to question his own involvement at times. But he was committed, fully on board—and it was too late anyway, as there was no turning back now.

LaRon had an entire community of African Americans looking to him for leadership and direction. He had made the commitment to lead his people. If certain individuals acted against his own beliefs, he would have to deal with them one by one from an emotional standpoint, and charge on. Victory for the larger cause was simply too important.

Ballard shook his head slightly to shake himself from his thoughts and to resume his focus on the task at hand. He had taken over General Street's former office, which suited him very well. In fact, Ballard's own animosity toward Street made it easy for him to purge the office of Street's belongings without regret. During a moment of frustration, he had swept all of Street's desktop memories into a trash can and ripped his certificates, photos, and medals of honor from the walls.

Although there hadn't been a lot of extra time after the initial take-over, Ballard had managed to replace all of Street's personal items with a few of his own. The office certainly seemed sparse compared to the fully decorated version of it just days before, but it clearly belonged to General Ballard now. Photos of Katherine and the kids, and a few cer-tificates—just to fill in a few of the many gaps on the walls—hung spo-radically around the office. It wasn't necessarily the warm and homey feel he wanted quite yet, but it was enough to make Ballard feel comfortable and as if his office had never belonged to Charlie Street in the first place.

"Sir," Major Henderson said as he reentered Ballard's office, Captain Lancaster in tow. "This is Captain Lancaster, although I think the two of you have met already."

General Ballard, antagonized because of his own internal frustra-tions with the entire situation and his recent conflicting thoughts about race, directed a resentful stare at the white captain. But to Lancaster it felt as if Ballard were sizing him up by looking into his very soul. The room was silent.

Captain Lancaster continued to stand at attention. He held his right index finger at his forehead, a position of full salute. He waited awk-wardly for any type of acknowledgement from General Ballard.

"Sir." The telephone speaker had broken the silence in the room. "The escort team has arrived with General Street."

"Very good, have them wait outside for a few more minutes." He never took his eyes off of Lancaster.

Then, General Ballard relaxed his face. The other two men could see the tension leaving his body as he pulled his stare away from Lancaster with a slight nod of his head. He looked at Major Henderson approv-ingly. "At ease, Captain."

Like any good leader, Ballard was skeptical of his direct reports when he needed to be. He wanted them to be able to convince him of their actions or ideas. With Reggie, however, he had a level of trust that went much deeper, as he valued the major's ideas and strategies without test. He could find no reason to doubt or question Henderson's plan in this case, either.

"Captain, let's get one thing straight: you are here only because of my trust in Major Henderson. At this point, I have no faith in you myself. You will follow my lead in this situation and nothing more. If you step out of line at *any* point, not only will I have you removed immediately, but also there will be severe consequences, understand?"

"Yes, sir, absolutely. I can assure you that I am here to help. I will do everything I can to promote the goals of the Black Heritage Army. Major Henderson has told me what I need to know; candidly speaking, I'm behind the cause one hundred percent."

"Right. Well, we're about to find out just how dedicated you are, aren't we?" He didn't expect an answer, and none came.

General Ballard pushed the speaker button on his phone. "Send in General Street." He stood tall in his full dress uniform, took a deep breath, looked at his friend Reggie one more time, then turned his attention to the door of his office.

General Street burst into the room, his face red with anger, his lungs panting. He was only able to take in short breaths, anticipating the conflict in front of him. It was obvious that he was here for business and business only. Charging straight to the middle of the large office that had so recently belonged to him, he stopped and looked around.

As he locked eyes with each of his adversaries one by one, his gaze was strong and confident. He had the demeanor of a professional boxer standing in the ring seconds before a fight.

"What the hell are *you* doing here?" Street barked while motioning to Captain Lancaster. He instinctually directed his first comment to the only other white man in the room.

"Good to see you too, Charlie." Ballard's voice was calm as he intercepted Street's question and brought his attention back to the person in charge.

"It's 'General Street' to you, Ballard."

"And it's 'General Ballard' to *you*, Charlie."

The two men stopped and stared at each other for a moment, realizing that directing their energy toward small issues like how to address each other was going to be a waste of time.

"I asked Captain Lancaster to join us as an independent third party. Since I've learned that I can't trust you, I want him in the room to make sure that the truth of our conversation comes out, given that he's white and all." He grinned.

"Look, Ballard, let's get down to business so that I can take my kids and get back to the real world." General Street's voice was more controlled this time, slightly less emotional.

"Sure, Charlie, it's really pretty simple. The Black Heritage Army wants Washington to recognize our efforts and the need for us to have a separate union, and then to endorse our actions. In return, we promise the continued safety of anyone—regardless of race or color—who doesn't want to stay here. We'll make sure that they are allowed free access to leave, and we'll provide them with enough resources to rebuild their lives elsewhere."

"That's ridiculous! What the hell do you think you're doing here, Ballard? You think this is a damn video game or something? You act as though you've won the war after only a few days—"

"We have won the war, Charlie! There is no way that the US government can oppose us now. We have too much control of these territories, and we've gained support from all corners of the United States. Any action against us by Washington would look far worse than what we have done, and you know it!"

"Bullshit! We can easily come in here and eliminate the two of you assholes, and the rest of your organization would fall apart. It's a simple war strategy, Ballard, and you know that it would work."

"You're overlooking the politics here, Charlie. We already have far too much support—and not just with our own people. You've seen the demonstrations in the streets, and so have we. It doesn't matter what part of the country they are in; there are millions of people who support what we are doing." Ballard paused to take in a deep breath. "No,

Charlie, I don't believe that killing us would be a good strategy on your part, and I know you won't do it anyway."

"Ballard, not only would I be willing to call the order, but I would do it myself if given the chance!" General Street's body was tense and his face was once again red with emotion. He had always had a short fuse.

"Just a minute, guys," Captain Lancaster's voice chimed in, temporarily breaking the tension, "let's get this conversation back to the issue at hand." Even he was surprised by the confidence that he showed by interrupting the two generals.

"Screw off, Lancaster—and by the way, your ol' man is going to be very disappointed when he hears about this crap." Street turned his full attention to Lancaster in an effort to further intimidate the young man. "Your granddad would turn over in his grave if he knew you'd become a nigger lover."

His last comment silenced the room, almost leaving an echo behind. No one had expected the conversation to turn in that direction.

Major Henderson was still standing back, a bit farther away from the others, observing body language and dissecting the nuances behind the comments being made.

It had been military custom for decades that when senior officers from opposing sides met to negotiate, they would be allowed to holster their side arms. This, while a show of respect for the others' rank, also set the stage for the ceremonial surrender of arms that had often occurred in world history. However it was only at this moment when it occurred to Major Henderson that both General Ballard and General Street were holstering their army-issue pistols.

Captain Lancaster was standing next to General Ballard, and both were behind Ballard's desk. General Street was on the opposite side of the desk, closer to Major Henderson but with his back toward the major.

"Damn it, Charlie! Are you really going to jump in here and use terms like that!? *Nigger lover?* Just who the hell do you think you are? This is my office now, these are my men, and you are in Black Heritage Army territory. You really don't get it, do you?" Ballard, clearly becoming more agitated, moved to his right, closer to Lancaster, trying to make his way around the desk to get closer to Street.

"There's nothin' for me to get, Ballard. I don't give a God damn what you and the other jungle bunnies think you can get away with. This is my world—a white man's world, you dipshit."

"Charlie! What the hell are you talking about? Look around you, man. Can't you see the reality of this? It's your childish, racist attitude that has caused this, and now that we're in control, you still can't wrap your mind around—"

"Screw you, Ballard!" General Street reached for his pistol and, with one smooth motion, pointed it directly at General Ballard. His movement was so quick that it caught everyone else in the room off guard.

Silence hit the room. Ballard raised his hands, palms facing outward, just to the level of his ears, letting Street know that he meant no physical harm. Major Henderson was frozen with fear and disbelief; he didn't have a weapon, and he was too far away from General Street to make any kind of a move. He wasn't sure what to do.

Meanwhile, LaRon Ballard slowly walked backward and slid back to the corner of his desk, instinctually looking for something to put between him and the short-tempered general who was now pointing a gun at him.

As he tried to make his way around the corner, he stepped right in front of Captain Lancaster. Suddenly—faster than anyone could have imagined—a single gunshot rang out. Ballard's body was spun to the left as his right hand instinctually grabbed his left bicep, which had taken the bullet fired from General Street's pistol.

Still standing right next to Ballard, Captain Lancaster sprang into action. Without conscious thought, he used his left hand to push General Ballard down and farther to the side. At the same time, his right hand reached forward and deftly gripped the handle of Ballard's pistol, which was still on his hip and in its holster.

As General Street stood in amazement and disbelief, Captain Lancaster instantaneously drew the pistol up to a firing position and squeezed off three shots with an amount of cunning agility that surprised everyone—even himself.

The consecutive rounds left a perfect triangle no bigger than the size of a quarter in General Street's chest. The general staggered back, fell to his knees, and tried to hold himself up by clutching an arm of the chair he had been standing next to.

His pistol having fallen out of his hand by this time, Charlie Street could do nothing but look at his shooter in disbelief. "This can't be," he mumbled through the blood that was working its way up to his mouth.

He stared at Lancaster as he fell to the floor, trying to understand how this could have happened. *Captain Lancaster is white. White! And he is the bastard that shot me?* he thought to himself as his last breath left his lungs.

His body collapsed to the floor. Lying on his back, his head turned to the side with his eyes frozen open and staring at Captain Lancaster, who was still pointing the gun in Street's direction.

Lancaster's face showed an obvious sense of power and confidence, a feeling that he had never experienced before. Like a prizefighter who had just knocked out his opponent, Captain Lancaster stepped forward and stood over General Street's body, almost with an air of arrogance.

He turned to look at General Ballard and then at Major Henderson. "Well, I guess that'll put an end to his bullshit." He smiled slyly and lowered the pistol, keeping it firmly in his grasp for an instant before finally resting it on General Ballard's desk.

Major Henderson didn't care about General Street's lifeless body at first. He was far more concerned about his friend. He raced around the desk to Ballard, who was now sitting on the floor, his back against the row of drawers on the steel filing cabinet behind his desk. He was writhing in pain, but it was pretty clear that his life wasn't in danger.

"What the hell just happened, Reggie?"

"Take it easy, General, you're going to be just fine." Major Henderson was down on one knee, next to Ballard, holding the general's arm to apply pressure to the wound. He turned his attention to the office door as several military police officers crashed into the room, responding to the sound of gunshots.

The MPs, all with weapons drawn, quickly spread across the room with the precision taught them in urban warfare school. "We heard shots, sir! What's the situation?" By this time, each of the five military police had their weapons pointed squarely at Captain Lancaster, who was within inches of the pistol still resting on Ballard's desk.

"It's not him!" Major Henderson could see what might happen next. "General Street fired upon General Ballard before Captain Lancaster returned fire and saved the general's life! Lower your weapons and get the medics in here right away! *Quickly!*"

The military police stood down immediately. Two of them ran out of the office to get medical attention, while the remaining men fanned out around the room. They continued to hold their weapons, just to ensure that no further harm would come to one of their leaders.

Reggie looked back to his friend LaRon, who was still grimacing in pain.

General Ballard looked up to Captain Lancaster, who was now standing right next to where the general was sitting on the floor. "Thank you, Captain, thank you."

Lancaster smiled. "Actually, it was my pleasure, sir. I'm glad that we were able to keep you safe from that asshole."

Ballard managed to let out a smile in response to Lancaster's comment. He then turned to face Major Henderson, looking him squarely in the eyes.

"We're in deep shit now, Reggie. We're in deep shit, aren't we?"

"I'm afraid so, LaRon, but let's not worry about that now. We've got to get you taken care of."

The medics entered the room and gently got General Ballard back to his feet. Refusing to lie on the stretcher, Ballard proudly walked out of his office, the medics in close pursuit.

Black Heritage Army soldiers had made their way to the doors that lined the hallway. A few of them had heard gunshots, and then the word had spread rapidly that the general may have been shot.

Seeing the hallway lined with soldiers caused the general to stand even taller. He was proud to have survived and was more motivated than ever.

A few soldiers started to applaud as he made his way to the exit doors. More and more soldiers began to join the applause for Ballard, which increased in volume as the men and women of the Black Heritage Army paid tribute to their newly anointed leader and displayed their unwavering respect for General LaRon Ballard.

CHAPTER 17
Where Do We Go from Here?

He walked into the war room, his uniform sleeve having been removed by the medics and his arm wrapped in bandages. Blood from the gunshot wound had seeped through the multiple layers of white cloth wrapped thickly around his left arm.

Major Henderson was the first to notice General Ballard entering the room. "A-ten-shun!" The room fell silent and everyone stood to salute their leader, General LaRon Ballard, who was now considered a hero for the cause, having been wounded while standing up to General Street and the union's army. Word of his actions had spread rapidly.

"At ease everyone." The pain from his injury caused General Ballard to wince as he spoke. The painkillers hadn't quite taken effect yet. "Major Henderson, how are we doing?"

"We appear to be in good shape, sir. We've got all outposts dialed in via video conference. We're getting their current status as we speak."

Are we still experiencing skirmishes along our borders or in the less populated areas?"

"It would appear not, sir. Things seem to have settled in, so to speak, and our field leadership hasn't reported any casualties—for either side—in more than twenty-four hours now. I think we're in good shape, sir."

"Very good." He scanned the room as he remained standing just inside the doorway. "Everyone, I want to thank you for your efforts and your dedication. I know that we've all put in some long hours. And although we've still got a lot of hard work ahead of us, I think we can all see a little light at the end of the tunnel. Keep up the great work."

"Reggie," he said, wincing again as he turned to face Major Henderson, "let's you and I go figure out the best approach for our latest situation."

"Understood, sir. My office or yours?"

"We better use yours. The military police haven't completed their investigation yet, and then there's the cleanup that my office needs." He turned toward the door.

His right hand swiftly rose to his face to wipe a single tear that had made its way down his left cheek. Just making reference to what had happened in his office caused his emotions to surface uncontrollably, as it led him to consider the fact that his friend of many years had been shot to death right in front of him.

He knew that he could mourn the loss later. There was no doubt that Street had intended to shoot him first, so it wasn't as though Charlie was innocent. But LaRon was still the emotional, caring type. As such, Charlie Street's death was not something he could easily push to the side, even though Charlie's true feelings had recently come to the surface.

The soldiers were still silent as the men exited the briefing room. LaRon was deep in thought while he and Major Henderson made their way down the hall to the major's office. Reggie entered the room first. Rather than sit behind his desk, he moved to stand in front of one of the visitor chairs while motioning LaRon to sit in the other, across from him.

"Is Charlie's death something you'd like to talk about, LaRon?"

General Ballard looked at Reggie with surprise, appreciating the fact that his friend could sense the emotional strain that he was feeling.

"No Reggie, not right now. There will be time for that once things settle down." He paused and used his right hand to rub his face, almost as if to erase what was on his mind.

"We've got a lot of work to do, not to mention the fact that we've got a pretty difficult conversation that needs to be had with Stranahan. I suppose there's no way to sugarcoat what happened."

"You're right, there isn't. We'll need to be direct and to the point, in my opinion."

"Reggie, what's the current status of Charlie's kids, Meagan and Jacob?"

"They are still at their house and being watched by Sergeant Johnson. Daemon's one hell of a good kid, LaRon, and I'm sure that Street's kids are well taken care of with him in charge.

"With regard to what happened to their father, our counselors have recommended that we not let the kids know at this time. They suggest that we let the kids get reunited with their mother in union territory, and then let her tell them what has happened. It's best if they are in a comfortable environment, and with people they know around them, when they hear the news."

"Roger that, Reggie. I agree with that approach wholeheartedly. What arrangements are being made for them to get reunited with their mother?"

"Well, we've got General Street's escort staff that's still here, of course. We'll simply get the kids packed up and then send them back with his staff. The challenge for us is timing.

"We'll want to notify Stranahan ourselves, of course, so we should do that before we approach General Street's staff. If they were to learn what's happened, I'm confident that they would communicate back to the union and to Stranahan—and we want him to hear it from us before anyone else."

"I agree completely. I've already instructed our coroner to prepare Charlie's body for the flight back to Washington, DC. We can have his body placed on the aircraft right after our conversation with Stranahan, and then have his kids board for the flight after that. We wouldn't want them to see anything that might suggest what has happened, so we need to get them on the plane without incident."

"Yes, sir, great point. The kids aren't aware that their father was on base, so they shouldn't suspect anything when we tell them that we're putting them on the plane to go see their mother." Major Henderson stood up from his chair. "I'll get a few staffers to work on this right away. As soon as I get back, let's get Washington on the phone."

"Agreed. I think we're as ready as we'll ever be." LaRon winced from the pain in his arm one more time.

* * *

By the time that Major Henderson returned to his office, the recording devices had been set up and a couple of witnesses had entered the room. The Black Heritage Army had been recording most conversations that had taken place since the effort began, all in an effort to capture the details of this historical event accurately.

Phone conversations, group discussions, war room activities, and even some radio communications were all being recorded by both video and audio. In the field, each unit had a videographer assigned to them, who captured in detail the strategies being employed, the spirit of the troops, and the essence of Operation Freedom Reign in general.

Everywhere around them, whether out in the field or within the walls of one of their many military bases, writers were also working diligently to capture events as they happened. Regardless of outcome, Major Henderson had known that this event and their actions would be like no other in history, and therefore everything had to be painstakingly recorded.

"Welcome back, Major Henderson. Are you ready to go?" General Ballard's voice silenced the hum of activity caused by the staff setting up the devices to document the phone call.

"Absolutely, sir. Let's do this."

The double ring broke the silence in Robert Stranahan's office. He was back at the Pentagon, sitting there with several other military advisors to the union forces and patiently waiting for the call from General Street.

Their plan had been for the general to walk into Ballard's office and put an end to the uprising. Neither Stranahan nor Street had any patience or tolerance for what the Black Heritage Army was up to, and although the highest levels of leadership in the United States wanted a peaceful end to the conflict, these men had other plans—if the opportunity presented itself.

They had conspired to stage an argument that would result in General Street shooting Ballard. In their minds, the plan was foolproof since both the president and Congress had authorized force—but only if negotiations broke down, and as a last resort.

However the politicians were more sensitive to the reaction that their constituents would have if force were to be used. They knew that managing public opinion was paramount, as perception was reality for the mass public.

No matter. All Stranahan and Street had to do was tell their leadership that Ballard had resisted and had physically threatened General Street. Everyone would believe it since the uprising itself was an act of aggression and since no one other than Street had a direct relationship with Ballard. This meant that no one else would know to question the story of the events they had planned to fabricate.

For all the president and Congress knew, and according to the picture that Stranahan and Street would paint for them, Ballard was a rogue soldier of less than stellar character, a man prone to violence and killing. Stranahan knew that if he could leverage this perception to his advantage and then build on it, his political leaders would never know the truth. Everything would play into their plan perfectly.

"Street, is that you?" Robert Stranahan, with a sly smile that hinted of overconfidence, put the phone on speaker, allowing other advisors to listen as well. He was assuming an early victory.

"Not exactly." The voice on the other end wasn't familiar to the secretary of defense. "This is General LaRon Ballard, leader of the Black Heritage Army. Is this the secretary of defense, Robert Stranahan?"

Stranahan nearly fell out of his chair. His cocky demeanor and arrogant smile quickly vanished, and his look became one of concern. He sat up straight and leaned forward to place his forearms on the table in front of him, moving his head closer to the speakerphone. His mind struggled to accept the reality that their plan must not have worked. His eyes were darting back and forth as he searched his mind to determine the next step he would have to take.

"Yes." He paused as he looked around the room at his advisory team. "This is Secretary of Defense Stranahan."

General Ballard's intelligence had told him that Robert Stranahan was both arrogant and overly confident, so part of his strategy was to aggravate him in the hopes that he might fly off the handle and do or say something that would turn the tide in their favor.

"Good. Mister Secretary, you and I have a lot to discuss, but I want to make sure that you are the right level of authority for me to negotiate with."

"What the hell do you mean, 'right level of authority'? Of course I am! And as far as negotiation, that's why Charlie Street is there with you. Is he also on the phone?"

"No, sir." The men in Stranahan's office could hear General Ballard take a deep breath on the other end of the phone line. "There's been an accident."

"An accident? Ballard, you had better put General Street on the phone right now or there'll be hell to pay!"

"I can't do that, sir. General Street is dead."

Stranahan's office immediately jumped into a state of frenzy; each advisor began scrambling, either to retrieve cell phones or to run out of the office to alert the leadership. Stranahan picked up the receiver, both to hear Ballard better and to mask the activities of his team behind him.

"Okay, Ballard. Let's just relax and talk about this."

Stranahan cupped his left hand over the receiver, raised his right hand, and snapped his fingers to get someone's attention. "Get the president—now!" he whispered to the staffer in an urgent tone. He then turned his attention back to his conversation with Ballard.

"I'm sure that there is a way for us to work this out. Now tell me exactly what happened."

General Ballard was noticeably perturbed at this point. "Like I said earlier, Stranahan, I need to know that you are the right person for me to talk with about this. I'm not going to waste my time with you if you're as powerless as I think you are."

"Powerless? You son of a bitch!" Stranahan, the handset still pressed against his ear, jumped out of his chair and started pacing with frustration. "I can tell you this, Ballard. We are going to come after you with full force now. There won't be any more bullshit from you or that 'Black Heritage' organization you started—"

"I didn't start it, Stranahan, but let me assure you that the Black Heritage Army is stronger, bigger, and more powerful than you—or anyone else in Washington—realizes."

"Screw you, Ballard! Now that you've killed a general, your days are numbered!" He slammed the receiver down. His rage had overcome him. Having been in similar situations before, Stranahan knew that the best plan of approach for him was to end the conversation, fall back, and regroup.

The resounding "click" of being hung up on caused General Ballard to snap his head away from the phone receiver. He was angry, like anyone would be after hearing that unmistakable sound. He held the receiver just an inch or two away from his ear for a few more seconds, turned his head toward Major Henderson, and then slowly lowered the phone back onto its cradle. He let out a sigh and took a moment to allow his anger to release its grasp on him.

"Well, Reggie, I guess that didn't go quite as planned. If that asshole Stranahan has any power at all, we could be in trouble. We have to hope that the president will get involved, at which time we can make our case to him directly."

Major Henderson didn't seem as concerned as Ballard was. He had more of a desire to fight, if necessary. After all, he was much closer to the organization, had been a member for far longer, and knew—without a doubt—how strong they were. There wasn't a shred of fear or concern in Reggie Henderson.

"You know, LaRon, we've got nothing to worry about. I think we have a lot more—"

"General Ballard?" Reggie was interrupted by LaRon's assistant, her voice shaky and broken. "The president of the United States is on line one."

The men looked at each other in amazement, and the room around them fell silent once again. No one could have expected the president of the United States to reach out to them as quickly as he had.

"Well, here we go …"

General Ballard placed his hand on the phone receiver, took a deep breath while keeping his eyes on his friend Reggie, and then lifted the handset to his ear. "This is General LaRon Ballard."

"Ballard? This is the president. How are you today?"

Stunned partly by the casual tone and partly by the small-talk question, LaRon stuttered his answer. "Uh, fine, I guess. And how are you, sir?"

"I've been better, as you can imagine, but that's exactly why it's time for us to have a talk. Are you in a place where we can have a meaningful conversation—man-to-man?"

"Yes, sir, go ahead."

"Well, General, let me start by saying this: I understand and appreciate your cause—I really do." Normally the President wouldn't acknowledge a promotion that wasn't officially recognized by the union army. In this case however, he wanted to resolve the matter peacefully, so he referred to LaRon Ballard as "general" as a show of respect. "If you know anything about me—whether it be from my numerous past campaigns, my business past, or my voting record in both Houses—you know that what I say is true, genuine, and from the heart. But here's the thing: there has to be a better way for us to go about this."

"I think it's a little too late for that, Mister President, wouldn't you agree?"

"Well, some might feel that way, but I don't think so. I think you can look at several times in our history—even at various historical accounts in other countries around the world—that when the country is torn apart, it has the ability to come back together. That's what I want our conversation to be about—a coming together."

"That all sounds well and good, but I don't think that we are as confident as you are—at least, not in our ability to come together, as you say."

"Listen, Ballard, you and I both know that you've already made a grave mistake in killing General Street, which we'll get to later. But right now let's talk about a few of the more simple items, things that we can both focus on to start bringing our two groups together."

"What do you have in mind, Mister President?"

"Listen, General, one of the first things we need to hash out is some sort of a trade agreement. So far you guys have choked trade routes in and out of the southern United States, and I'm sure you'll agree that's not good for either one of us. We need to make sure that all trade routes are one hundred percent open and accessible."

"I couldn't agree more, Mister President, and that's exactly why we haven't hindered any trade up to this point. I'm not sure where you're getting your information, but it's simply not accurate. We've left all interstate roadways wide open, the only exception being our checkpoints, which I'm sure you can understand.

"We stop all motorists to make sure that they are indeed civilian, because we know that the union, under your direction, could easily infiltrate our troops with spies or covert operations teams. As long as you don't try anything stupid, you've got nothing to worry about."

"Now listen here, Ballard," the president said, his temper starting to rise, "I don't appreciate what your insinuating. I can tell you that we have no such goal in mind, and I would not suggest such actions to my commanders. Last, I'll take this opportunity to remind you that I'm still your commander in chief."

It was at that very moment that the last, small amount of fog cleared for LaRon Ballard. With the president's last comment, he realized that he was more than just the leader of the Black Heritage Army as general. He was also the de facto political leader of the entire Ubuntu territory.

LaRon himself realized the he held as much power for his people as the president did for the rest of the union. This sudden epiphany instantly drove his confidence to an all-time high. His subsequent awakening unleashed an even stronger leader, a leader who was more capable of negotiation, knowing that he was on level ground with any of his adversaries, A leader who could move forward and act with a level of certainty, determination, tenacity, and poise that he hadn't necessarily had up to this point.

"Ballard! Are you there?" There had been just enough silence on the line that the president felt compelled to break it.

General Ballard, without saying a word, lowered the receiver from his ear and turned to look directly at Major Henderson. He gave a reassuring wink and smiled at Reggie. Then he pressed the speakerphone button on the phone base and gently placed the handset back in its cradle. All at once, he appreciated the need to record this conversation even more and he understood the benefits of allowing everyone else in the room to hear how he would deal with the president of the United States.

LaRon sat taller in his chair and leaned forward slightly so that his voice could be heard clearly through the speaker system.

"Mister President, the current state of trade between our two parties is just fine given the current circumstances. I have no intention of making any alteration to our existing strategies. Was there something else you wanted to discuss?"

The president was dumbfounded. He had come into this call thinking that he would simply flex the muscle that his political office projected and that Ballard would cave to his demands easily. The sudden change in tone from General Ballard caused the president to realize that he too had to change course. He calmed himself and decided to take a more diplomatic approach.

"What about civilian travel, General? You guys have tightened the noose around the airlines, railways, and boat lines as these relate to allowing civilians to travel in and out of the South. That's another thing that I'd ask you to loosen up, if you would."

"While I can appreciate your request, I'm not willing to do that just yet. Again, and as before, we feel it is imperative that we maintain control of who leaves and enters our territory.

"Once we have a written agreement in place and you—along with the rest of the union—acknowledge that we are an independent nation, we'll open everything back up one hundred percent under new trade agreements."

"Damn it, Ballard, you're crippling both of our economies with your short-sighted actions on this—"

"Our economies will rebound just fine, Mister President; the key is for you and the rest of the nation to move quickly in ratifying our desire to be independent, plain and simple."

"Okay, listen to me on this: let's at least loosen some of the restrictions that are in place while we sort this out. If you can agree to that, I can assure you that there will be no punishment for you, your staff, or any of your people when this is all over. Agreed?"

"I can't do that and I won't do that, sir."

"Why not, Ballard? I mean, let's face it—you guys decided to draw a line in the sand and actually declared war on the United States of

America. Even with that show of disrespect, and the enormous disregard of the people of this great nation, I'm saying that I'd be willing to let you and your leadership off the hook, with no punishment. Then, we can legislate your grievances into a series of bills that will give your people what they want, but without all the bloodshed and divisiveness."

LaRon Ballard's head turned back to Reggie with a look of disbelief. He paused for a moment before addressing the president with a firm tone.

"Did I just hear you say 'your people'? Excuse me, sir, but what exactly do you mean by 'your people'?"

"Now, Ballard, hold on just a minute. You know that I didn't mean that for anything more than it is. I mean 'your people,' gosh darn it! You know, *all* of the people in your span of control—and everyone that resides within the southern states that supports your cause. Are you going to try and turn my comments into a race thing too?"

"You see, Mister President, that's just it. I don't have to turn this into a race thing, because you already have. Don't you get it? This is exactly the reason that the Black Heritage Army and 'my people' had to take this course of action to begin with—why the Black Heritage Army exists at all. You, and the rest of the people in this country, will always, always be racist toward 'my people.' That's just the nature of things—and I honestly don't see any way that we can legislate proper virtue, values, and the right way of thinking. It just doesn't work that way. Never has, and you know it."

"Well, Ballard, don't say that I didn't give it a try. I am trying like hell to avoid an all-out war here, and you simply can't demonstrate the basic level of common sense to see that. I am trying to save you from the rabid dogs like Stranahan here, but I'm not sure what else I can do or offer."

"Nothing, Mister President. Nothing."

Both sides of the phone were silent for a few seconds. The men on each end of the line were looking at their respective support staff. It was evident on their faces that they were searching for a peaceful solution and were fearful of the alternative. Unfortunately, nothing was coming to mind.

"Well then, Ballard, it appears that you have made your decision."

"I suppose so, Mister President. It looks like this means that the war will continue—but understand this: any future bloodshed is on *your* hands now."

Epilogue

The ring of the telephone startled Don and Paula Wilson, who were sitting in their living room watching the news. Like nearly everyone else in the part of the country still controlled by the union, they tuned into the national news every day in the hopes of getting more details on the civil war and learning more about the intentions of the Black Heritage Army.

The war had been raging on for nearly a week now. Just like so many other parents, Don and Paula strained to focus on the background camera footage of every news report in the hopes of seeing their daughter. For those people who had a family member in the military, anything to let them know that their loved one was alive and in good health was enough to prevent them from lying awake in bed all night.

This was especially true in the case of Don and Paula Wilson. Their daughter, Heather, had been stationed at Fort Benning, Georgia, in the heart of Ubuntu territory, when the Black Heritage Army took over military assets and then declared war on the rest of the union.

For parents and family members in this situation, it was a very difficult time, because all communication in and out of the Ubuntu territory had been eliminated. There was no way for them to check in with their loved ones, no way to know whether they were safe or even still alive.

Don slowly made his way to the kitchen to answer the phone, which rang for at least the tenth time. Still not making much money from the furniture store, he hadn't been able to replace the outdated, corded telephone hanging on the kitchen wall.

He picked up the receiver, finally eliminating what had become an annoying, relentless ring that echoed through the house. "Hello?"

"Is this Mister Wilson, Mister Don Wilson?" The voice on the other end of the line sounded very businesslike, so much so that Don could tell that something was wrong.

"Yes, it is; can I help you?"

"Sir, this is Sergeant Trevor Johnson of the Black Heritage Army. It is with regret that I have to inform you about this, but your daughter has died."

Silence.

Still holding the receiver to his ear, Don turned his shoulders and face toward Paula, his left hand on the countertop to prevent him from falling to the floor. The look in his eyes was enough. She broke into tears, knowing that Heather was no longer with them on this earth.

"Mister Wilson?" Surprisingly, the voice on the other end of the line sounded impatient.

"Yes, I'm here, damn it!" Don was angered by the lack of respect that Sergeant Johnson displayed with his impatience, but it made no difference to the sergeant.

"Good. Well, we are willing to make arrangements for you to pick up the remains, if you like. Of course, these are difficult times, but we have opened two areas of our border to allow families to gather remains. Is this something you would like to do?"

Don was appalled. There was not a hint of care or concern in the voice of this young man who called the Wilsons to tell them that their daughter was dead. At the same time, Don knew that he was at the mercy of the Black Heritage Army. Don and Paula *absolutely* wanted their daughter to be buried nearby, so he held back his anger.

"Yes. Her mother and I would certainly like to pick up Heather and bring her home. What do you need from me?"

"There are six points of entry to our territory. You are to report to Gate 4, which is just south of Memphis, so you can grab a hotel room and stay there if you like. From Memphis, you'll take Interstate 55 south to the Mississippi border, to the town of Southaven." Sergeant Johnson finished very drily and businesslike.

Always being a caring individual, Don realized that the sergeant must have a number of calls like this that he had to make. This helped the grieving father to understand the impersonal nature of Johnson's tone. "What should we bring, and how does this work?"

"Sir, we recommend that you bring a pickup truck or a vehicle large enough to carry the casket. Also, I have your name listed as Don Wilson. Is that right?"

"Yes—but no, wait. It won't be me coming to get her. We are going to send our son, Paul, so his identification will be the one you're looking for."

"Understood. I'll let the gate personnel know that a Paul Wilson will be receiving. That's where her remains are being stored, and it's only a temporary facility, so he needs to get there as soon as he can. This is the last communication you will receive." Sergeant Johnson hung up the phone suddenly, before Don could respond.

Don slowly placed the receiver back on its cradle. He walked over to Paula, who was hardly able to hold herself up after the news of her daughter's death. He held her, and they wept together.

* * *

Paul Wilson was a tall, handsome, and strong young man, just three years younger than his sister, Heather. Although he was three grades behind her in school, the two siblings were close enough in age to develop a very strong relationship. They had become very close before she left for college and then went on to the army, and their bond had tightened even more in recent years.

They spoke to each other often, sharing details of their lives with each other and confiding issues that they couldn't discuss with their parents. Paul remembered each of Heather's friends, but especially Jennie.

Jennie had become a sister to Heather. More important to Paul was that she was beautiful. Paul had had a crush on Jennie since middle school, and now, even eight years after they had both left home, he still harbored feelings for her.

He was devastated when he heard the news from his parents. But right now, he couldn't let it become an issue. There was no time for him to drown his sorrows, no time to truly deal with the emotions that were triggered by the news of his sister's death. He had to get on the road to Mississippi right away, and pick up the older sister whom he had always looked up to.

* * *

It was hot and humid in Southaven, Mississippi, but that wouldn't stop Michael and Jennie from staying there until Heather's family arrived to pick her up. They had petitioned to be the personal escort of her body, which was granted, and they were also given permission to stay with her as long as needed to ensure that her body was safely transferred to Heather's family.

Michael was still reeling from the loss of such a deep, albeit short-lived, love.

Jennie was devastated by the loss of her longtime friend and sister. Jennie had no other family; she was an only child, so Heather truly had become a sister to her over the years.

Both Michael and Jennie felt the deep, painful emotion of sorrow at Heather's death.

Standing outside, melting in the heat and humidity, Michael and Jennie were on their third day in Southaven. With no specific orders other than to see to the security of Heather's remains, they were left to stand outside the storage facility.

"You know what, Jennie?" Michael broke the silence. "I just don't know about all this."

"What do you mean?"

"I mean in the beginning—and up to the point of Heather's death, actually—I was just charging forward, blindly following the rest of our people. Do you know what I mean?"

Michael paused. He and Jennie looked at each other for a moment. He didn't expect a response to the question; he was more just thinking out loud at this point.

"I mean that it all seemed like such a good idea, you know? I had definitely experienced racism in the army—throughout my entire life, for that matter—and the Black Heritage Army meetings were such a great outlet for me." He paused, took a deep breath, and looked toward the western sky. A single tear streaked down his right cheek.

"We used to talk about the issues we faced, and we supported each other in a *positive* way at those meetings. Then, they just kind of changed. They moved away from a positive, supportive environment to more of an anger-fueled session about how to 'get back' at whites and how to 'take over' what was rightfully ours."

Jennie remained quiet. She was a great listener in the true sense of the word, which was partly the reason that she had become such a good friend to so many people. She knew that Michael was trying to work through his emotions, so, in her opinion, now was not the time to interject her own thoughts or viewpoint. Besides, she didn't have the long history with the Black Heritage Army that Michael did, so she couldn't possibly understand the thoughts he was wrestling with.

"I don't know," Michael continued, "it's just that none of this feels right to me anymore. Here we are, killing each other over differences that are sometimes real, but just as often they aren't. Sometimes they're just *perceived* differences from what I can tell. Do you see what I'm saying? Please say something."

"I do see what you mean, Michael. But I wasn't at the Black Heritage meetings. I haven't had the amount of time in the organization that you have had. Remember that you told me about the cause on the day we met, so I think my perspective is much different."

Their conversation was interrupted by a small military jeep approaching fast, dust billowing behind it. The brakes squealed as the vehicle came to a stop in front of them.

"I've got someone named Paul Wilson here to pick up the remains of Heather Wilson." The private looked at Michael, then at Jennie. "Can you get her ready for transport?"

"We'll take care of it. Send him over." Michael quickly responded.

The private spun the jeep around, back to the direction he had just come from, so that he could escort Paul and his truck back to the storage facility.

Michael and Jennie made their way inside. They each placed a hand on Heather's casket, both wanting, and wishing, to feel the emotion of love and friendship one last time before she left them forever.

Paul was escorted through the security gate. He pulled up to the storage facility in his old, beat-up 1982 Chevy pickup. There was a jeep on either side of his truck directing him to the proper location, each with two Black Heritage Army soldiers, guns in hand, ready to take action if he were to do something wrong. A small cloud of dust wafted around him and into the open driver's-side window once he finally came to a stop. It had been a very long drive; he was exhausted.

He climbed out of the truck and stood there, waiting for instruction. He was a bit confused, because the "storage facility" in front of him was really nothing more than a large tent. For a moment, he thought that maybe he had been duped, which heightened his suspicion toward the escorts. His heart raced for a just a moment as he thought that maybe *he* was being captured or that he had walked into a trap of some sort. But then he saw a familiar face.

Jennie emerged from the tent. "Wow, Paul, you have really grown up—you look great." Her voice somber.

"Jennie? What the heck are you doing here?" Paul relaxed a little bit now that he knew that he was in the right place and that no harm would likely come his way.

"I'm here to help you with Heather. Didn't they tell you?"

"They didn't tell us a damn thing! Dad said that the guy who called was totally rude and a complete jerk. Why are you here, Jennie?"

"I'm here because Heather was like a sister to me. You know that. We asked to be here so that we could say good-bye to her one more time." Jennie motioned toward Michael, who had just emerged from the tent.

Paul's emotion turned from fear of being captured to anger at the entire situation around him. He looked at Michael, who was now standing next to Jennie. "Who the hell are you?"

"I'm Michael Masters. I was, well, I was in love with your sister, Heather. Man, I'm so sorry that things turned out this—"

"Sorry? You're *sorry?* I don't know who you *think* you are, and, to be honest, I don't give a shit!"

He turned his gaze back to Jennie. "How could you let this happen to Heather?

"She trusted you—*we* trusted you—to be there for her and take care of her. You claim you were like sisters, but if that was the case, you would have done something to protect her and my sister would still be alive, here with us today."

Jennie understood why Paul might be angry, but she couldn't think of anything she could say to convince him of the truth. It was all she could do to hold back the tears caused by the possibility that she would lose another good friend in Paul.

All three were silent for a moment. While they stood in the sweltering heat, four soldiers were moving Heather's casket from the temporary rolling rack to the back of Paul's pickup. It was late in the day now. The setting sun created a glare that seemed to sparkle when it met the lingering dust at the rear of the truck just as Heather's body came to rest. It was almost as if she knew that she would be back in the right place now, back at home in Omaha with her brother and parents.

Michael, always one with a big heart, looked at Paul and reached his arm out, placing his hand on Paul's shoulder. "Look, Paul. We're real sorry about all of this—"

"Get your damn hands off me!" He slapped Michael's arm off of his shoulder, stepped forward, gritted his teeth, and pointed his finger right at Michael's nose. "I don't know who you are, or who you *think* you are, but I can tell you this: I am going to spend the rest of my days hunting you down. I will not stop until you are dead—as justice for Heather. You feel me?"

He turned his attention back to Jennie. "And that goes for you, too! I joined the union's army last week right when news of that stupid damn Black Heritage Army crap made the news. We all know what you've done, so don't try to play the game of friendship with me.

"Just so you know, I start my military training next week. That means that I'll be in the field in about two more months. And, just like I said, I plan to hunt you guys down and get revenge for what you've done to Heather!"

Paul was walking away from Jennie and Michael as he was talking.

He opened the driver's-side door of his truck while staring at them the entire time. He stood there for a moment, then slipped on his sunglasses and turned to face Jennie one last time. "Sorry that it has to end this way. I actually liked you a lot, Jennie."

Before anyone could say another word, he quickly jumped into his truck, fired the engine, and tore off toward the exit gate, spraying dust and gravel everywhere.

Both Michael and Jennie raised an arm to shield their faces from the dust caused by Paul's rapid exit and spinning tires. As the dust finally settled, they looked at each other in disbelief of what had just happened. That was not the outcome that they had expected.

"Like I said earlier, I don't know about all of this, Jennie." Michael looked down in disappointment and shook his head. "I'm beginning to think that maybe it *wasn't* all that bad before Operation Freedom Reign. Now it seems like we're the ones who have caused more divisiveness and that we have actually motivated more people toward racism.

"I don't know: I guess I can't be the only having these thoughts of regret. But I also know that we have to live up to our commitment to the Black Heritage Army at this point."

"I know, Michael, I know." Jennie looked up at him and tried to smile. "Problem is that the battles are escalating now. That means that whether we like it or not, you know we're going to get assigned combat duty when we get back."

"I know. I've heard that the union is sending more and more troops—especially out in the more remote areas like the outskirts of Tennessee. It scares me, Jennie. I really don't want to kill other Americans, but at the same time I have to think back to how it was before we took over.

"Somehow, I've got to convince myself—once again—that all of this is worth it."

She was finally able to force a crooked half smile. "I guess it's like any other war in history; our personal beliefs don't matter at this point. We are soldiers, and soldiers have to follow orders, right?"

"Yeah, I guess that's right." Michael put his arm around his friend and looked at her reassuringly. "I just hope we don't run into Paul when we're out there. He sounds pretty determined."

Book Review Request

Thank you for purchasing my book! I certainly hope that you enjoyed reading it as much as I enjoyed writing it. I would truly appreciate your feedback on the book itself, whether you discuss the premise or your thoughts on the concept in general. Please take a few minutes to write a positive review or post your thoughts about it at Amazon.com. In addition, I can be reached in a number of ways by using the contact information I've inserted below.

I look forward to reviewing your opinions and suggestions. In return, I will do my best to respond to your comments as soon as I can.

Sincerely,

Randy Arellano
Author of *The Next Civil War*

Website: www.rgarellano.com
Facebook: www.facebook.com/NextCivilWarBook
LinkedIn: www.linkedin.com/in/randyarellano

The term "Black Heritage Army" is copyrighted by the author and cannot be used in any manner without express written consent.